NO GOOD DEED
Grave Diggers Series
- Book 5 -

by
Chris Fritschi

DISCLAIMER

This is a work of fiction. Names, characters, businesses, places, events and incidents are either the products of the author's imagination or used in a fictitious manner. Any resemblance to actual persons, living or dead, or actual events is purely coincidental.

No Good Deed
by
Chris Fritschi

V1

ISBN:
ISBN-13:

Click or visit
chrisfritschi.com

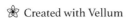 Created with Vellum

CONTENTS

To Karen. Your encouragement, honesty and belief in me fuel my spirit.

ACKNOWLEDGMENTS

The pages of his book are the result of all the people who gave their input, guidance, and knowledge. Thank you all.

A special thanks to all of you, you know who you are, for the encouragement and finger wagging that kept me on my toes through the development of this book. The critical, but honest, input from my beta-readers Cinnamon, Becka, Samantha, Lauren. You guys make me look good.

Enough can't be said for my wife who spent endless hours listening to me brain-dump over this book. Her patience and support never flagged.

1

FIRST IMPRESSIONS

The crescent moon hung in the night sky like a cold, mottled scythe. Its silver light frosted the edges of the jungle foliage and turned the rough, gravel road nearly white.

For the drunk soldiers returning home, the well lit path wasn't enough to keep them walking straight. Before they could stop him, Private Finegard veered off the road and tumbled down the overgrown embankment, into the brush below.

"I'm not getting him this time," said Durst.

Weaver and Stanley rambled up next to Durst and looked down at the mumbling heap in the bushes.

"You guys," called Finegard. "Come on."

The three looked at each other, seeing who would cave first until Durst and Stanley stared down Weaver.

"Okay," grumbled Weaver, and trudged down to get him.

Durst could see the distant floodlights of Fort Hickok and felt home sickness well up inside him. He kept it from his friends, rather than risking being teased or questioned about it, but Fort Hickok was more home to him than anywhere he'd ever lived.

He came out of his daze, feeling like he'd been standing there a long time.

"What's taking so long?" he asked.

Stanley flinched at the sound of his voice, snapping out of his own haze. They both looked down the embankment, but neither of their friends were there.

"Weren't you watching?" said Stanley.

"Weren't you?" asked Durst.

"Why should I?" asked Stanley. "Not supposed to be any Vix around here."

"That's what they say until one of them's ripping you open."

Stanley looked at the surrounding jungle with new eyes. The tangled wilderness was alive with the murmur of unseen things hidden behind the inky darkness. The sense of eyes watching him sent a trickle of cold fear up his spine.

"I don't like this," he said. "We should go."

"What are you talking about?" asked Durst. "They're probably taking a leak. Hey guys, where are you?"

They listened but only heard the sounds of insects and wildlife.

"See?" said Stanley, taking the silence as a sure sign of danger.

"Yeah, I see they're drunk and stupid," scoffed Durst. "They're lost. Come on. We gotta find them."

"Not me," said Stanley. "It's dark. Something could be down there waiting for us? We need reinforcements." He turned towards the lights of the fort and waved his arms over his head.

"Hey!"

"Dude, shut up," said Durst. "You're being an idiot. They can't hear you from here."

"Someone's coming," said Stanley.

Durst didn't see anyone coming from the fort, then saw Stanley was looking the other way.

Headlights were quickly approaching and Stanley lurched into the road to flag them down.

Three vehicles came to a stop, washing Stanley in their high beams.

"Get outta the road, you moron," barked someone from the lead truck.

Stanley started to speak but choked on clouds of road dust.

"Sorry," said Durst, stepping into the headlights. He grabbed Stanley and pulled him out of the way.

Stanley feebly waved him off as he bent over, coughing.

The rumble of engines died and Durst heard footsteps approaching behind the glare of the headlights.

"Explain yourself, Private."

Durst squinted against the glare of lights but couldn't make out the speaker.

"My buddies went down the..." He stopped as a figure stepped from behind the lights and walked up to his face. The stranger leaned forward and Durst heard two quick sniffs.

"You've been drinking," said the stranger.

"You want to know what's going on or not?" said Durst.

The figure stepped to the side and the headlights caught his face in stark relief.

Durst instantly saw the distinctive camo pattern of the stranger's army combat uniform and his eyes automatically glanced at the rank insignia on the chest.

He saw the black embroidered eagle, the rank of a full colonel, and came to an unsteady attention. His hand flew to his forehead in salute, bumping his head.

The corner of the colonel's mouth curled in a smile, enjoying the private's scramble to show respect.

Shuffling up beside Durst, Stanley spotted the colonel's rank. "Oh crap," he said, coming to a sloppy attention.

"Sir," said Durst, trying hard to speak without slurring. "Two of our friends went down the embankment and we don't know where they are."

The colonel stared at the two privates, making them shift uncomfortably.

"I'm Colonel Wade," he announced. "I am the new base commander."

"Oh crap," said Stanley.

"Let me see if I understand the situation," said Wade. "I have four privates off base, after curfew, drunk, and two of you have gone missing. Have I missed anything?"

"Where'd you guys go?" yelled Weaver, scrambling to the road. "There's bodies in the trees."

"Sergeant Lewis," snapped Wade. "Secure these men."

"Yes, sir," growled a voice.

The drunk privates sobered up quickly as large, barrel-chested MPs rushed into view. Before they knew what was happening, the MPs had flex-cuffed them.

"What's going on?" said Finegard, as he crested the berm of the road. "Did ya tell'm about the dead guys?"

Lewis grabbed Finegard by the collar and lifted him to his feet. He walked the drunk over to Wade.

"Take me to these dead guys," said Wade.

"Yes, sir," said Finegard, pointing down the road. "They're right over there."

With an MP keeping him from falling, Finegard led them a short distance from where he'd fallen down the embankment.

"Up there," he said.

Wade's MPs turned their flashlights onto the trees, revealing three dead soldiers hanging by their necks.

One of the MPs stifled a gasp, but Wade stared at the dead men, unmoved.

"Sergeant Lewis," said Wade, "cut these bodies down and…"

"Don't do that," blurted Stanley. "… Sir. They're going to turn into Vix."

"Look at their faces," said Wade. "They've been dead for less than an hour. And besides, they're evidence in a criminal investigation. Sergeant, put the bodies in the truck."

"Yes, sir," said Lewis, pointing to the other MPs. "Swanson, bring the truck up here. Parks and Muni, help me cut them down."

Parks and Lewis, and Muni drew long knives and went down the embankment.

"He's right, sir," said Durst. "They could turn at any time."

"Are you inferring I'm stupid?" asked Wade. "That an officer knows less than a private?" His eyes narrowed and he stared darkly at the drunk soldiers. "Or maybe it's not about that. Maybe you four had something to do with this."

All four protested their innocence, alarmed at the accusation.

The canvas-covered truck squeaked to a stop and Swanson climbed out as the other MPs appeared, dragging the bodies behind them.

"We don't even know those guys," said Weaver.

The prisoners stared, unable to pry their eyes away from the gruesome bodies. The faces of the dead were contorted in pain, their eyes unnaturally bright in the glow of the moon. Deep gouges and tatters of flesh hung from their necks as the dying men had clawed at the strangling rope. Blood stained their hands; their rigid fingers looked like talons. Everything about them screamed they had suffered a terrifying and agonizing death.

The captive men trembled at the sight, but Wade was untouched, hardly sparing the dead a second look.

"The timing that the four of you would be out here at almost the same time these soldiers were hung if very curious," said Wade. "Sergeant, when we get to Fort Hickok put these men in the stockade for questioning."

"Yes, sir," said Lewis. "Want me to load them up in your vehicle?"

"And have them vomit in my car? Put them in the truck."

All of the drunks burst out in protest, refusing to get into the truck with the bodies.

"Quiet," snapped Wade, drawing his pistol and pointing it at them. "I'm ordering you into that truck. Sergeant Lewis, you are authorized to shoot any man who disobeys my order."

Lewis and the other MPs drew their guns and the cuffed soldiers went pale.

"With all respect, sir," Stanley pleaded, "those bodies could turn at any moment."

"I won't have you question my intelligence or authority," said Wade. He holstered his gun and headed back to his car. "Get those cowards in the truck," he shouted over his shoulder.

Lewis herded the frightened soldiers into the back of the truck at gun point.

"Quit your whining," he barked. "This bunch is yours, Muni."

"Got it," said Muni, climbing behind the wheel and starting up the truck.

Muni glowered over his shoulder at the prisoners, making sure they knew he was watching. They looked back, squirming under his stare. He turned back, grabbing the wheel and put the truck in gear.

Lewis trudged back to Wade's car and got in the driver's seat. Wade was frowning, deep in thought and Lewis started the engine in silence.

Muni had already started for the base and Lewis easily caught up and followed behind.

In the back of the truck, the four prisoners stared at the corpses with naked terror. A pothole rocked the truck, jostling the dead bodies.

Weaver yelped when a lifeless hand fell on his boot. He kicked it away, feeling bile crawl up his throat as he gut-clenched into a ball.

"Get us outta here," cried Weaver.

"Shut up," said Muni. "We're almost there."

The play of lights and shadows played tricks on their eyes, giving the bodies movement. The four captives squirmed, vainly trying to keep away from the dead bodies, jostling on the floor of the truck.

Muni steered for another pothole, chuckling as the tire hit, triggering gasps of fear from the prisoners.

The truck jolted, flinging the dead hand against Weaver's boot again.

He gasped, pulling his boot back, but the hand didn't fall away. Disgusted, he tried to shake the hand off his boot. To his horror the hand clamped down on his foot like a vice.

A wail of terror poured out of Weaver as the corpse turned its head and look up at him. The other men screamed and kicked as, one by one, the corpses began to rise.

Muni was chuckling at the cowards when the back of the truck erupted in shrieks and cries.

"Knock that off," he bellowed, "or I swear I'll beat you all to a pulp."

The rear of the truck instantly went quiet. A growing sense that something was wrong tickled at the back of Muni's neck, making his hair stand on end.

Over the rumble of the truck he heard a low growl and he glanced at the rearview mirror but couldn't see into the dark truck bed.

"That's it," said Muni, trying to sound angry, but the chill running up his spine made his voice crack. "I'm gonna beat the hell..."

A bloody hand reached out from the back of the truck and dug its fingers into his chest. His eyes bulging, he screamed, thrashing to break free, but the air was strangled in his throat as the bones in his chest cracked.

Agony bolted through him. Blood welled up around the fingers as they sunk in and pulled. Muni watched in horror as his ribcage was peeled open.

"What the...?" said Lewis.

Wade looked up, briefly confused as the lead truck sped up, pulling away from them.

Lewis grabbed his radio off the dashboard. "Muni, what are you doing?"

The truck was flying over the road, heading for the front gates of the base.

Spotlights blazed to life from the watch towers and their beams cut through the dark, washing the speeding truck in blinding light.

A loud speaker from the watch tower bellowed a command for the truck to stop. But the truck was eating up the distance with no signs of slowing.

Wade could hear the base alarms wailing and flashes of orange fire blinked from the top of the wall as tracer fire pumped out from a heavy machine gun.

The fifty caliber rained down fire as eleven tons of truck barreled towards the base. Muni's eviscerated body sagged against the wheel pulling the truck hard left. It veered sharply from the gate, but was moving too fast for the turn and rolled over and over, flinging debris, glass and dust into the air.

The gun kept shooting as the truck tittered then fell against the wall with a screech of metal.

Staring at the wreckage, Lewis' mouth sagged open.

"Wha..." he stammered.

"Sergeant," said Wade, hardly above a whisper, "gather my men and see if you can find any sur..."

The night lit up in a ball of fire as the truck exploded. The base wall disappeared into shards of twisted metal, flinging the guards into the air like rag dolls. A hail of flying gravel crashed against Wade's car shattering the windshield as a wave of heat blew over them.

The front gate opened and a disorganized knot of soldiers rushed towards the flaming truck that now lay in the breach of the wall. Shouting over each other, they staggered back from the intense heat, overwhelmed and confused.

"Get us inside the camp," said Wade.

Lewis sat in a daze, not hearing the order.

"Lewis!"

"Yes sir," said Lewis, and drove past the wreck, through the open gates.

Scattered wreckage burned and crackled everywhere. Small fingers of smoke began to rise ominously from a nearby building threating to catch fire.

Past the destruction, Lewis pulled over.

Wade got out of the car and, brushing the dust off the car window, checked his reflection and adjusted his cap and ACUs.

As a knot of soldiers ran past, he heard someone giving orders. Wade called out, telling them to stop.

Bewildered, all eyes were on Wade and his big MP as they stepped into the middle of the group. Lewis took up position behind Wade and fixed the others with a glare.

"I'm Colonel Wade," he said, clearing his throat. "Your new base commander. What's being done about this situation?"

The leader of the group glanced between Wade and his uniformed gorilla. "First Lieutenant Corbin, sir," he said, and started towards the glow of flames. "All I know is there was an explosion. I'm heading to the scene to get eyes on."

"What happened," said Wade, "was as I approached the base my truck was attacked by Vix."

Worry and fear rippled through the gathered soldiers as everyone looked towards the sounds of the roaring fire with alarm.

Corbin pulled his radio off his belt. "This is Corbin. There's possible Vix in the area. Everyone must be armed. Mazt," he said, pointing to one of his group. "Pass the word. Lock down the camp. Put together a fire team and sweep the base."

"Got it," said Mazt.

"No noobs," said Corbin. "Experienced people only."

Mazt nodded and took off at a run.

"Where did you see the Vix?" asked Corbin.

He started for the gate with the remaining few in tow. Coming around a building, the soldiers gasped in shock as the full scope of devastation came into view.

"About thirty yards outside the gate," said Wade, indifferent to the chaos.

Catching the lie, Lewis glanced at Wade, but said nothing.

"Leadership in this base is either criminally inept or nonexistent," continued Wade. "Whoever's responsible for the death of these soldiers will be punished. I want to see the roster of duty officers first thing..."

"Bodies," yelled a soldier, freezing the group in place.

Mingled among the scattered debris were three corpses. Two were badly burned and one a mangled mess, but all were unrecognizable. They could have been anyone from the truck or the guards on the wall.

Heading to the nearest body, Corbin drew his pistol.

"What are you doing?" said Wade. "I was telling you I want to see..."

Corbin's pistol cracked as he shot the corpse in the head.

"Stop that," ordered Wade, storming over to the first lieutenant. "That body is evidence."

"Sir?" faltered Corbin. "These could turn into Vix at any moment? They have to be shot."

"Are you disobeying my order?" said Wade, his face darkening.

"For the safety of everyone here," said Corbin, nervously, "these bodies must..."

"Sergeant," barked Wade. "Arrest this man."

Corbin couldn't believe what was happening.

"Under the Uniformed Code of Military Justice," recited Wade, "article 89, disrespect of a superior officer, and article 90, assault or willfully disobeying a superior officer, you are under arrest."

Lewis snatched Corbin's pistol from his hand and reached for a set of flex-cuffs.

The other soldiers stared in shock at the sudden and surreal twist of events. Distracted, nobody noticed the nearby body begin to twitch and climb to its feet.

"I am in command here," announced Wade. "My authority is law."

"Run," screamed a soldier, their eyes wide with terror.

Everyone looked to see a mangled Vix charging down on them. One of the soldiers fumbled with their gun and dropped it as everyone else scattered.

Lewis plowed over Corbin, running for all he was worth; the direction didn't matter.

The Vix flew at them, but one unlucky soldier caught its attention and it veered sharply away from the others, quickly closing the gap on its prey.

Wade stood alone, shaken and confused. He saw movement from the corner of his eye.

"Sergeant Lewis?"

The remaining cracked and blackened corpse picked itself off the ground. Its head slowly turned as pale eyes roved over its surroundings.

Wade's breath caught in his throat as he reached for his gun. His heart hammering in his chest, he couldn't take his eyes off the Vix. As he backed away, he stumbled and kicked a piece of wreckage.

The Vix's head snapped around, fixing Wade with a snarl. With unnatural speed, the thing bolted for him.

Wheeling backwards, Wade pointed his gun and fired, his shot going wide. Yanking the trigger, his gun cracked. Blood and pulp flew off the charging Vix but didn't slow it down as it rapidly ate the distance to Wade.

Whimpering, he kept shooting until his gun clicked and the Vix filled his vision. Smoking, talon like hands reached for him as its mouth snapped open and closed. Cracked and scorched teeth clashed, chips flying off, as the Vix's jaws opened.

Wade's head jolted back from a booming shockwave. He stumbled back as bone and charred gore splattered his face and chest. He screamed, raising his arms to fend off the Vix, as something heavy fell against his legs.

Gawking in shock, the Vix lay crumpled and unmoving at his feet, the top of its head a gory bowl of unrecognizable slop.

Wade looked up into a gaping black void. A wisp of grey smoke wafted up from the barrel of the big Colt .45. A pair of cool, grey blue eyes stared at him from behind the gun.

"Wha...?" sputtered Wade. "Who... who are you?"

"Sergeant Major Jack Tate," he said, lowering his gun. "Sorry about the uniform."

2

IT'S REAL

I t felt like Tate had just closed his eyes when someone started knocking on his door. He shambled out of bed and opened it, taking a the bright sun in the face.

"Is this a new look for you?" asked Kaiden

Tate's stubbled face creased into a smile but his red eyes looked weary and haggard.

He moved out of the way, letting her come inside.

Kaiden stepped in, wrinkling her nose. "Keep the door open."

"Sorry. It's been a long night."

"I'd like to say my eyes are watery because I feel bad for you," said Kaiden. "Do us both a favor and take a shower."

Tate nodded without enthusiasm and shuffled into the bathroom, while Kaiden opened a window.

A few minutes later she heard the shower come on and leaned against the wall by the bathroom door.

"I heard there was some excitement last night," she said.

"Yeah," said Tate. "Our new base commander made a surprise appearance."

"Very thoughtful of him," she said. "Is the new hole in the wall his stab at the re-beautification of Fort Hickok?"

"Long story."

"I'm all ears."

She had to wait as Tate soaped up his face and rinsed it under a rewarding stream of hot water.

There's the new CO's story," he said, wiping water off his face. "Some I believe and some I suspect is BS. Then there's the part where I came in and that's why I haven't slept. He found three soldiers executed outside the base. Truth. Then he said his truck was attacked by Vix. Bull."

"How do you know?" asked Kaiden.

"I overheard his personal MPs talking about it."

"I do love a good murder mystery," she said.

"This one may not have a happy ending," said Tate. "Rosse, Monkhouse and Fulton are missing. They went to town last night and haven't come back."

"Oh." Kaiden went quiet.

She heard the water turn off and the rattle of the shower door slide open.

"I wasn't allowed near any of the bodies," said Tate through the bathroom door.

"You told him your men are missing?" asked Kaiden, idly watching his shadow from under the door.

"Yes."

"Is this guy a total jackass to everyone, or just you?" she grinned.

"It wasn't my best first impression," said Tate. "We might have gotten off on the wrong foot." He paused but didn't elaborate. "Anyway, his excuse was the bodies were evidence."

"I know you don't want to hear it..." said Kaiden.

"Then don't say it," he grumbled.

He knew that wouldn't stop her, and he was right. "He's not wrong. Three people were murdered."

"Don't you think it's important to identify the victims?" asked Tate.

"You're not wrong either," said Kaiden.

"After I get dressed, I'm heading over to their quarters again," murmured Tate, swabbing his armpits with deodorant.

"Let me buy you breakfast first. It's the least I can do since I woke you up."

"I need to know where my men are," said Tate firmly.

"I know how thorough you are," said Kaiden. "If you didn't find anything last night, you're not going to find anything today. You wouldn't have let yourself miss anything. If they're okay, they're okay. If they're dead, starving yourself isn't going to bring them back."

The bathroom door opened with a billow of soap-scented steam.

Tate stepped out in a clean shirt and boxers. "You're all heart."

"Sorry," said Kaiden, unmoved. "I didn't realize going hungry made wishes come true."

She frowned as Tate began pulling on his pants.

"You're kidding, right?"

"What?" he said, then looked down at his pants. They were splattered with dried blood and dirt. "Oh..." He took them off and dropped them on the floor.

While he opened a drawer and pulled out a fresh pair, Kaiden kicked the dirty ones out the door.

"Hey," protested Tate.

"Relax," she grinned. "Nobody's going to steal those. They reek. Come on. Breakfast. I promise I'll help you look for your guys."

"They're yours, too," said Tate.

Kaiden may not have been part of the team in any official capacity, but the rest of the team, including Wesson, had come to accept her as one of their own... mostly. He knew Kaiden wasn't the touchy-feely type, but she did care about them, in her own way.

When things got dangerous, the team had looked out for her as much as they did for each other.

Sometimes it was hard to see Kaiden's softer side, if you could call it that. She had a strong independent streak, and the way it showed could get on his nerves. After he'd learned about her ties to a black ops intelligence division, he understood her secretive nature which helped make her slightly less annoying.

Tate checked himself in the mirror. He thought twice about shaving, but after last night, he just didn't care. He couldn't deny the old base commander was a waste of space, but the upside was he didn't live and die by regulations.

"Let's go," he said, gesturing to the door.

He and Kaiden stepped outside. He squinted under the bright sun, scooping up his filthy pants and tossed them back into his quarters.

"Don't blame me," said Kaiden, "when you come home and those things have crapped everywhere and chewed up the furniture."

He looked at her, unamused. Together they headed down the path towards the dining facility. Everything looked normal, but last night had rattled people and Tate could feel it in the air.

They were halfway across the courtyard when they heard a familiar angry voice, loudly complaining.

Relief and concern filled Tate as they saw three of Wade's MPs herding Rosse, Monkhouse and Fulton in the other direction.

By the time Tate reached them, Rosse was facing off the three MPs. His barrel chest was puffed out and his thick hands were clenching into fists the size of sledgehammers. The MPs towered over him, but the ex-prision guard was unintimidated and ready to take them all on.

"I swear, the next one of ya primates even touches me..." snarled Rosse.

"Sergeant Rosse," barked Tate.

Monkhouse and Fulton blanched and put distance between them and their friend. They knew that tone in Tate's voice and they didn't want anything to do with it.

Rosse's jaw was set as he mad-dogged the MPs until Tate put his hand on his shoulder.

Rosse broke eye contact and looked at him.

"Take a step back, sergeant," said Tate, firmly.

"Who're these bozos?" asked Rosse, still hot.

"What's happening here?" asked Tate, knowing if Wade's MPs were involved it wasn't good.

"He's resisting arrest," growled one of the MPs.

Tate focused on defusing the situation first. Explanations could wait for later.

"Sergeant Rosse," he said. "You'll follow the instructions of these MPs to the letter. Is that clear?"

"But..."

"Is that clear?" barked Tate.

The last thing Tate needed was for Wade to see his people as troublemakers. Last night's messy introduction was a bad way to start off with a new colonel, especially one with a god complex.

Rosse blinked in surprise. "Uh, yeah. Sure, Top."

"The same goes for the rest of you," said Tate.

"Is there a problem, Sergeant Lewis?" asked Colonel Wade. "Sergeant Major Tate. Why am I not surprised to find you in the middle of this?"

Tate closed his eyes for a moment, cursing his bad luck.

"Sir," he said. "These are the men I was looking for last night."

"Sergeant Lewis?" persisted the colonel, ignoring Tate.

"These three were caught trying to sneak onto the base..." began Lewis.

"That's crap and you know it," snapped Rosse. "Nobody was sneaking. We was..."

"Confine these men to their quarters," said Wade. "If they resist, use what necessary force you require to make them comply."

"Who's this ba...?" asked Rosse to Tate.

"This *officer*," cut in Tate, "is Colonel Wade. He's the new base commander."

"You men are to stay in your quarters until further notice," said Wade.

"What for?" said Rosse.

"Sergeant," seethed Tate, "one more word out of your mouth and you'll be humping a 60-pound ruck until you die from stupidity or old age."

Rosse's mouth flapped shut.

"Three soldiers were murdered last night," said Wade, "and I'm keenly interested to know if you had anything to do with it."

Rosse started to protest, but Tate's scowl cut him off before he spoke.

Tate didn't think the situation couldn't get any worse. He was wrong.

"Hi," said Kaiden, appearing behind Wade.

"Judas Priest!" said the colonel, nearly jumping out of his skin. "Who the hell are you? Do you think that's funny? Don't you ever do..."

"You must be the new colonel," said Kaiden, as if she'd done nothing wrong.

Tate wanted to explain she didn't do it on purpose; it's just what she did, but it wouldn't do any good. On the heels of that thought, he realized nothing he could say or do was going to help this situation. This dumpster fire was turning into a train wreck of dumpster fires.

"I can clear up any questions you have for these men," said Kaiden.

The colonel glanced at her fatigues for rank and name, neither of which she ever wore.

"You're out of uniform," he said. "Is she another one of your people, Sergeant Major?"

"Sir," began Tate.

"I work with Tate," said Kaiden, "but let's stay on track. These men were with me last night."

The colonel looked at his three prisoners, who tried to keep a poker face, but clearly had no idea what Kaiden was talking about.

"If that's the case," said Wade, "report to my office."

"I'm sorry, Colonel," said Kaiden. "I'm sure it's a nice office, but I'll have to decline the offer."

"What the...?" said the colonel, dumfounded at this open defiance. "Sergeant Lewis, take this soldier into custody."

The big MP moved towards Kaiden but stopped when she held up an ID card in his face.

Lewis read it, then looked at the colonel with a shrug.

"What's that?" said the colonel, taking it out of Kaiden's hand.

Tate was close enough to see the card. Printed across the top was, 'Defense Intelligence Agency', with the agency logo next to it. Tate had never seen a DIA ID card before, but knowing Kaiden, it was as good a forgery as you could get.

The DIA was a military intel agency that reported to the Department of Defense; their agents did not answer to anyone but their boss. In short, Kaiden was holding a *I can do anything I want* card.

Tate knew it was a complete fake, and hoped the cocky move didn't blow up in Kaiden's face.

It fooled the colonel, who flushed with frustration.

"What's the DIA doing on my base?" he demanded.

Tate remained stoned face but looked at Kaiden meaningfully, warning her off provoking the colonel further.

He watched, nervously, trying to will her to be polite as she weighed her response.

"Unfortunately," she said, "I'm not at liberty to discuss my activities. I'm sure you understand."

Tate quietly sighed with relief.

The colonel tapped her ID card on his fingers while he considered his options. He didn't like not getting his way.

"I see," he said, handing Kaiden her card. "You may not be under my authority, but these men are, and I have a murder investigation to conduct.

Sergeant Lewis," said the colonel. "Confine these men to their quarters."

"Yes, sir," said Lewis.

"Their activities are classified," said Kaiden, loud enough for Rosse, Monkhouse and Fulton to hear. "It will limit what they can tell you about last night."

Lewis paused, looking at the colonel for direction.

"Take them," said Wade.

Without another word, the colonel turned and walked away.

"See what I mean?" said Tate.

"I don't know," said Kaiden, watching the colonel. "He seems like a real charmer."

"DIA?" said Tate. "Really?"

"It comes in handy," said Kaiden, putting the card in her pocket. "Want one?"

"Seriously?" he said.

"No," smiled Kaiden. "I predict that guy's going to make your life a lot more difficult."

"I've had jerks like him before," said Tate. "Let's eat."

They turned and headed to the dining facility for a long overdue breakfast. They were glad to get inside and feel the relief of the cooled air.

Kaiden hadn't said anything since the courtyard. They found an empty table and sat down with their food. She frowned at the chili omelet on Tate's tray.

"No comments," warned Tate. "I'm down twenty pounds."

He looked at her tray for something to criticize, but it was fruit and oatmeal.

"I think that colonel is going to be a problem," said Kaiden.

Tate was surprised she was still on the subject, and it troubled him. She had an uncanny knack for reading people, and her comment reinforced his own anticipation of future run ins with Wade. An officer with an axe to grind made a bad enemy.

His appetite for the chili omelet disappeared and he dropped his fork on the tray.

"You're a lot of fun to be around," he grumbled, pushing away the tray.

"Maybe," said Kaiden, "but look at all the calories I just saved you from."

"I'm going to find out where my guys were last night," said Tate, getting up from the table.

"You're welcome," she said.

Tate looked at her, waiting for an explanation.

"I just covered for your people," she said. "Any questions the colonel asks them is a dead end. All they have to do is say they can't divulge their activities."

She was right, and it would have the added bonus of irritating the heck out of the colonel.

"Thanks, smiled Tate.

Kaiden smiled and turned back to her fruit as Tate walked out. She glanced up as the door closed behind him then reached across the table and took a fork full of his omelet.

It was late morning and Tate could feel the weight of the sun's heat beat down on him with an almost tangible weight. He pulled his weather-beaten boonie cap out of his back pocket and put it on. The faded and sweat-stained hat had been with him around the world; a page-less memento of life's experiences.

He crossed the courtyard and headed into a row of quarters where Fulton lived. As he rounded the corner and Fulton's front door came into view, Tate felt a wave of relief that one of Wade's MPs wasn't guarding the door.

He knocked and didn't have to wait long before Fulton answered.

"We didn't murder anyone," blurted Fulton, his young face lined with worry.

"Take it easy," said Tate. "I know that."

It was clear this had been weighting on Fulton and the worry drained away as he let Tate in.

He found a place to sit down and waited for Fulton to join him. Looking around, Tate felt a pang of guilt that Fulton's quarters were neat, everything put away and clean.

"What's going on?" asked Fulton. "Am I under arrest?"

"You're going to be fine," said Tate. "If anyone asks about what you did last night, the only thing you say is you're not at liberty to answer."

"But what if it's an officer, or..."

"It doesn't matter who," said Tate. "Kaiden's covering for you, but I have to ask." He paused, his expression solemn. "Did ...?"

Fulton guessed what he was about to say and came out of his chair. "No. We didn't have anything to do with that." Shaken, he started pacing the room. "I don't even know what happened. We hardly stepped foot on the base and those three big dudes grabbed us, saying we're murder suspects. Murder! Do I look like a murderer to you?"

"I know you're not," said Tate. "But I need to cover all the bases. Even if it means you know something about it."

"Nothing, I swear. I wouldn't do something like that."

"I've known good men who fell down the rabbit hole of bad choices. One thing led to another and until they didn't see anyway out, or maybe the bad inside them took hold. Whatever the reason they ended up doing terrible things," said Tate heavily. He shook it off and smiled. "All right, I believe you. Give me the short version of what happened last night."

"Rosse said he knew about a couple of new clubs in town that just opened, so we... you know," shrugged Fulton, "went."

"Went," smiled Tate, getting the implication. "Why didn't you come back last night?"

"We did," said Fulton, "or almost did. When we got close there were sirens and lights everywhere. Someone yelled Vix and we didn't have our weapons, so Monkhouse said we better get out of there. We stayed in town until things died down. I guess they didn't."

Fulton was in his mid-twenties and Tate appreciated what it must be like for someone his age to be stuck in a back water military base with little to do but listen to the radio. Rosse had taken Fulton under his wing, more like a big brother than a father figure. The one role Rosse was least adept at was a chaperone.

The conversation dried up, leaving the radio in the background to fill the empty space.

"Here's something they won't tell you in the news," said the DJ. *"My sources tell me that, quote, security breach in Kansas City, unquote, was a cover up. The official story is they don't know how Vix got inside, but we know better. What you can believe is Clay Rockport and his family were all killed. Was it tragic? Yes. Was it an accident? Maybe. Or maybe it was a planned assassination. Did you know Clay was investigating suspicious freight trucks? Unmarked, all white freight trucks that were..."*

"Conspiracies?" Tate scoffed.

"Conspiracies are made up stories," said Fulton. "Revolution Terry knows what's really going on."

"Revolutionary?" frowned Tate.

"No, the guy that runs the show," said Fulton. "Revolution Terry. It's a play on words."

"Yeah, I get it. That's the, uh, the pirate radio station," said Tate. "I thought you stopped listening to that."

"It's the only station I can get here," said Fulton.

"I knew a guy who listened to that stuff all the time," said Tate. The memory of his old teammate made him smile. "He started seeing conspiracies everywhere."

"Yeah," said Fulton uncomfortably.

"I'm not picking on you," said Tate. "Just think for yourself. Those things can be a slippery slope. Soon you'll see cover ups and underground states in everything."

"You mean deep state," said Fulton. He cleared his throat and changed the subject. "So, hey, what's going to happen with us?"

Tate explained about the arrival of the new colonel with a warning to keep a low profile. "Somebody hung those soldiers and I think whoever did it was sending a message."

"What kind of message is that?" asked Fulton.

"I don't know," said Tate, rubbing his jaw. "Or who, but the sooner we know the answers the better it'll be for all of us."

"Kaiden's good at stuff like that," said Fulton. "Profiling and all that voodoo stuff. You think maybe those dead guys were part of something secret going on with the base?"

"That's what I'm talking about," chuckled Tate, as he stood up to leave. "That White Hat crap is going to have you jumping at shadows. Honestly, the world's a pretty boring place."

"I guess," said Fulton.

"I'll check on you later. Remember what I said. You're not at liberty."

"Thanks, Top," said Fulton, following him to the door. "See you later."

Fulton closed the door behind Tate, feeling more confident knowing Kaiden was covering for him. He glanced at the radio, wondering if Tate was right about conspiracy theories. He picked up the radio to change the station.

"... One of our own in the White Hat community is telling me there's trouble down south. Three soldiers were killed. Hung in the middle of the night. I can't name names but sounds like the kind of place Wild Bill would hang out."

Fulton's hand froze on the radio dial and his mouth fell open. Wild Bill's last name was Hickok. The DJ all but said Fort Hickok.

He knows! It's all real.

He glanced at the door, thinking he would tell Tate what just happened, but realized that he wouldn't share in his excitement.

In fact, he was sure Tate would take a dim view of being in the spotlight attraction of a pirate radio station.

3
_____

BLACKMAIL

Leaving Fulton's quarters, Tate was feeling better after talking to the private. It had answered one question, but left another wide open. If not Fulton, who was feeding information to Revolution Terry.

Reaching the end of the building, felt something was out of place. Tate stopped to put on his boonie cap, using the opportunity to casually look around. His instincts were telling him there was something out of place amid the typical flow of routine commotion.

Then he saw it.

Standing in the shadow of another row of quarters, an MP was looking at his clipboard. There was nothing unusual about him until he glanced up and saw Tate looking at him. The MP quickly looked down, pretending to examine something on the clipboard before tucking it under his arm and walking away.

So, Wade wasn't done with Tate after all. He was having him watched. Tate made a mental note of him. He was smaller than the others; thin, and his uniform hung on him. Maybe he was Wade's B-team. He hadn't seen this one in the base commander's entourage before.

Tate was getting a clearer sense of Colonel Wade and it wasn't good. He didn't like being under a microscope and was convinced anything the MPs reported could be twisted and used against him.

It was a new problem and meant he'd have to keep his head on a swivel, but right now all he cared about was catching up on sleep. That wasn't going to be easy.

———

Tate's raw eyes pried themselves open as someone lightly knocked at Tate's door.

The knocking continued, persistently, annoyingly and...

He rolled over, blearily trying to see what time it was.

2:07 AM? What the...?

They knocked again, not loud, but insistent.

Throwing his legs over the edge of the mattress, he sat up, rubbing his eyes.

"Hang on," he croaked.

In the darkness he groped for his pants on the floor, but couldn't find them. Then he remembered he'd put them away. Tate silently cursed Fulton for his tidiness and guilting him into squaring away his own place.

He turned on the bedside lamp and, squinting from the light, got a pair of pants from the dresser.

The knock came again.

"I said hang on," snapped Tate, zipping up his pants.

Grabbing the doorknob, he pulled it open, ready to chew out the idiot on the other side, but the words stuck in his throat as he looked into the barrel of a gun.

Looking past the gun, Tate saw the face of the same thin MP that had been watching him.

"Don't do anything stupid," said the MP. "I'm not supposed to hurt you, but I will if you make trouble."

Everything Tate thought he knew about Colonel Wade had suddenly changed. He had hugely underestimated what lengths he would go to. He knew the colonel was on a power trip, but this was psychotic.

He put his hands out for the gunmen to cuff him, but the guy just smirked.

"Don't need them. I got this," he said, waving the gun in Tate's face.

The MP was smart enough to keep his distance, making any move to disarm him, foolish.

For the moment, Tate's only option was to pretend he wouldn't put up a fight and hope the MP dropped his guard.

"What happens now?" asked Tate, trying to sound as if having a gun in his face at 2AM happened all the time.

"You do what I tell you," said the MP, sounding equally casual. "Back inside and sit on the floor."

Tate backed into his quarters, facing the other man.

"Sit there," said the MP, gesturing to the floor. "Put your hands behind your head and interlock your fingers."

Tate followed his instructions, wondering what was going on until the MP tossed him a shirt and boots.

"Get dressed."

As Tate pulled on his boots, the MP sat on the bed, studying him.

"I heard you was some hardcore ex-Delta Force dude. I was expect'n you'd pull some ninja, black ops move; try to take my gun."

"You sound disappointed," said Tate. He laced his boot, wondering how learned about his old life in Delta. Finished, he stood up slowly.

"A little, yeah," said the MP, standing.

Tate tried to mask his surprise and confusion when the MP holstered his gun. He wondered if this guy was trying to bait Tate to take it from him.

"Don't do something stupid," said the MP. "I can't be going around the base with a gun on you."

"Risky," said Tate. "How do you know I won't pull a ninja move on you?"

"I got you covered, bro. I got your girl."

Tate's blood turned to ice as his mind raced to know who he meant. It was either Kaiden or Wesson. It was hard to imagine Kaiden being taken, not without her killing a couple of attackers. Wesson was a capable soldier, but she didn't have the training, or experience, like Kaiden.

"Sergeant Wesson?" asked Tate, struggling to keep his expression neutral.

"Yeah, the redhead," said the MP. "She's no hurt an' she'll stay that way as long as you do what I say. You copy Mr. Ninja?"

"I copy," said Tate. While outwardly placid, he was mentally swearing an oath to find everyone involved with Wesson's abduction. There would be a reckoning. "It's late and I'm tired. Can we get this over with."

To his surprise, the MP got up and walked out the door, obviously expecting Tate to follow. It wasn't lost on him that this stranger wouldn't have turned his back on Tate if he wasn't holding all the cards.

That didn't stop Tate of thinking how easy it would be to snap his neck.

The MP led him to an aging Humvee.

"Nothing but the best for the Army," smirked Tate.

The US Army had resented having the All Volunteer Expeditionary Force pushed on it and it showed. While *real troops* were outfitted with modern weapons, communications, vehicles and gear, the AVEF got obsolete junk.

The irony wasn't lost on Tate. He'd always thought it was a huge waste for the Army to scrap billions of dollars on equipment the moment something new and shiny came out. The old equipment was consigned to sit and rust in miles of open fields called bone yards.

Well, now he got his wish. The AVEF needed equipment and the Army needed a place for its junk, and they had a lot of junk. The only advantage was that spare parts were in good supply.

Fort Hickok had its own bone yard of obsolete equipment. The things that had been stripped to the frame were dumped in the Graveyard; a bulldozed field outside the base's security wall.

The base had established a half mile perimeter, called the Safe Zone, which was supposed to be clear of Vix. In spite of monthly patrols, it wasn't safe, or clear; South America was overrun with Vix.

Sooner or later they'd always straggle into the Safe Zone, which meant that every trip to the Graveyard was risky.

Tate climbed into the passenger side of the Humvee, its canvas door rattling as he shut it.

The old V8 diesel engine coughed to life as the MP started it up and put it in gear. Except for the nightly security patrols, there was nobody out.

Expecting to be taken to the stockade, or maybe Wade's office, Tate was puzzled when the MP turned in the opposite direction and headed towards the remote storage area.

They passed rows of storage structures into an area Tate wasn't familiar with. It was definitely in the sticks; the road wasn't maintained and the Humvee rocked and bounced over the worn potholes and washboards until they reached a cluster or aluminum shacks.

The MP pulled the wide vehicle next to one of the shacks and turned off the engine.

Tate followed him as he got out and led him to one of the shacks. The small building looked like it hadn't been used in years. Weeds hugged the sides of the walls and smears of corrosion ringed the riveted walls.

The MP knocked on the door before opening it.

"Inside," he said.

"Thanks," said Tate. "I never would've figured that one out."

Stepping inside, he saw four people sitting around a simple table near the back.

Deep shadows made their faces look cadaverous and sunken under sparse, neo-diode lighting.

Three men and a woman considered Tate with blank expressions. All of them were armed with guns except one woman who displayed a polished dagger, tapping the flat of the blade on her fingertips.

Another figure moved in the shadows, behind the group. Tate could hear muffled wheezing and the clink of chain. He thought they were holding someone prisoner, but as he got closer an unmistakable stench singed his nostrils and the shadowy figure lunged at him with a growl.

He leapt back, knowing it was a Vix before it broke into the light. His hand instinctively reached for the tomahawk he'd left in his quarters.

The group at the table laughed.

"How do you like our watch dog?" asked the woman.

It was chained by the neck to the wall, its arms shackled to its waist and a leather muzzle strapped to its face.

No matter how many chains it wore, Tate felt naked without a weapon as the Vix stared at him with milky, green eyes. Jagged, stained teeth clacked as it snapped its jaws at him.

"You're all going to die," said Tate in disbelief.

"Put it back," said the MP.

One of the other men picked up a chain on the floor and pulled. Tate could see the chain ran through steel rings, ending around the Vix's neck. The man pulled until the Vix was against the wall then wrapped the chain around a hook, locking the Vix in place.

The MP pulled a chair away from the table and gestured to Tate to sit.

"Get the boss," said the MP.

Another of the group took out a satellite phone and punched in a number. He listened for a moment, then handed the phone to Tate.

"I'm here," said Tate flatly. He guessed whoever was on the phone was running the show. "What do you want?"

Scratchy laughter came over the sat phone. "Oh man, you're grumpy when you don't get your beauty sleep, eh?"

Tate knew the voice but couldn't put a name to it. He didn't have to wait long to find out.

"It's me, San Roman."

Tate squeezed his eyes closed, wondering what contest in Hell he'd won to deserve this.

When the outbreak hit South America, the Vix ripped through the population like a fire through dry grass. Nobody was safe, including the drug cartel. High level members were lost, creating a power vacuum.

At the time, Nesto San Roman was a young, hungry and brutal nobody working for the overlord of the cartels. The overlord died during the outbreak and it wouldn't have surprised Tate if San Roman had used the outbreak as an opportunity to kill his boss and take over his operation.

The cartels fragmented into civil war, but with Roman running the biggest operation, he had the brute force to punish the smaller cartels who challenged him, which he did with vicious pleasure.

Tate didn't know how crazy he was until he'd made a deal with the drug lord in return for valuable intel. The deal had put him under the psycho's thumb. The amount of trouble that was causing Tate was becoming more and more apparent.

"I tell you, man, I'm a little hurt you didn't remember me."

The only time they met face to face was in a back room of Tate's favorite nightclub, the Blue Orchid. Roman put his chrome-plated hand cannon to Tate's forehead and threatened to splatter his brain over the wall.

"I remember," said Tate.

"You're damn right you do," said Roman, his mood taking an unpredictable turn. "I got a situation you're gonna take care of."

"What do I...?" started Tate.

"Hey, shut up," screamed Roman. "I'm the one talking. Not you."

The line went silent for a moment and Tate began to wonder if Roman had hung up.

"That's better," said Roman, his tone returning to normal. "There's a bunch of punks in town. The uh, the Brotherhood. Stupid name. These fools think they can take over my territory."

"Can they?" asked Tate.

"You are some kind of stupid," chuckled Roman. "Of course not. But I got a whole network going on and these pricks are messing with it. I need to send them a message and you're my delivery boy."

Tate bit back the words he ached to say and took a couple of deep breaths before speaking.

"What do you want me to say to them?" asked Tate.

"What?" asked Roman, surprised. "No stupid, not that kind of message. You're going to kill a couple of them. That's the message."

"Our deal was that I'd warn you if the army got near your territory," said Tate. "Nothing else."

"Don't tell me what the deal is," snapped Roman. "I make the deals. Give the phone back to my guy so I can tell him to smoke you. Give him the phone. I'll wait."

If the situation wasn't so serious, Tate could have laughed out loud at the idea that Roman honestly thought he would dutifully hand over the phone to be executed.

"I have another idea," said Tate.

"You have another idea when I say so," said Roman.

"I mean I have an idea that can help you," said Tate. "Years ago, I was in a town near the northern border of Congo. A group of rebels were making trouble for the local warlord. Nobody cared if they wiped each other out, but there was a village full of civilians caught in the middle of the fighting. I got a meeting with the warlord and negotiated a deal to put the rebels on his payroll. It took some working out, but he agreed to make them an offer. The rebels accepted. Crime went back to business as usual and the civilians were left alone."

"So you're saying you want me to hire these punks?" said Roman, incredulous.

"Think about it," said Tate. "Making them part of your operation expands your reach and strengthens your network. It's cheaper than losing people in a war with them."

The phone was quiet as Roman thought it through.

"Yeah, that makes sense," said Roman. "I like it. You see? I knew you were the right guy to take this to. After this I got a whole list of problems you're gonna help me with."

It was quickly dawning on Tate that Roman wasn't done changing their deal. He had long-term plans to use Tate and that was very bad. The longer this went on, the deeper he'd be digging his own grave.

"Okay, so instead of killing a couple of them," said Roman, "so they know to stop messing with my town, kill a couple of them so they know what happens if they don't work for me."

"Or," offered Tate, "nobody gets killed and you just talk to them to see what kind of deal they'd accept."

"Yeah, okay," said Roman. "I can do that. I'll set up the meet."

"Great," said Tate, glad to get this monkey off his back. "I hope it works out."

"Hold on, man. Ain't no hoping. You're gonna do the meet."

"I'm not getting tangled up in your turf war," said Tate.

"Let me lay it out for you," said Roman. "You do what I tell you, or I let your army boss know you've been trading military secrets with the leader of a drug cartel."

"I never gave you classified intel," said Tate. Roman was bluffing. Roman had let Tate interrogate a prisoner and in exchange he had agreed to warn Roman if the army was going to start patrols in his area. It was a necessary evil that helped expose The Ring, but Tate hated himself for making the deal.

The army was years away from expanding its operations in Roman's direction, so Tate had never given Roman a shred of information. But, that didn't stop Tate from feeling like a rope was closing around his neck.

"I got you on video, meeting me at that nightclub," said Roman. "I had to edit it some, but it looks real convincing. When your boss sees that he's gonna believe anything I tell him."

A minute before, Tate saw Roman's threat as a vague intimidation, but all of that had just changed. Roman had just bumped himself up to a real and immediate danger.

He was going to take down Roman. Before that could happen he had to know where, in the vastness of the jungle, he was running his drug operation.

He held the reigns on anger and said nothing. It was better to give Roman lots of room to run his mouth. Somewhere in all of his bragging could be important information Tate could use. The tape might not be the only thing Roman had. He needed to know what he was after and not leave anything behind that might come back to bite him.

"There's pictures of you and Dante," continued Roman as he chuckled.

"That's all?" asked Tate.

"I got enough,' said Roman. "You're gonna be a good dog and do what I tell you. Right?"

Tate remained silent, repeating in his mind, *be smart.*

"I'm talking to you!" screamed Roman.

Tate could hear the insanity in his voice.

"Right," he said.

And just like that, Roman was calm, as if the previous tantrum had never happened.

"Cool," he said. "I'll set up the meet. My people will tell you when and where."

"I'm stationed on a military base," said Tate. "I can't come and go as I please. Try to set it up for a time when..."

"Shut up," snapped Roman. "I know all that. I'll make it so you can leave the base, no problem."

Tate looked around the room at Roman's henchmen. They seemed uninterested in the conversation, but he knew they were listening and watching everything he did. He'd be shot or stabbed before he tried any of his 'ninja' moves.

"I underestimated you," said Tate. "Smart move, running your smuggling through the base."

"That's why you're the dog and I'm holding the leash," said Roman. "I got my direct line to the city. Nothing happens in that base or town I don't know about."

A piece of puzzle fell into place. "Why did you hang those soldiers outside the camp?"

"That was another message," said Roman. "I didn't feel like talking that time."

"I have a new base commander," said Tate. "He thinks I'm involved. I'm taking a lot of heat because of what you did."

"That's even better," said Roman. "As long as they're looking at you, I don't have to worry about them tripping over my shipments."

Roman wasn't giving specifics, but Tate's time in Delta had taught him how important small scraps of information could be.

Roman had power, but like so many, he made the mistake of equating power with safety. He was free to threaten, beat and even kill people without consequence. Tate couldn't wait to show him how wrong he was.

Getting at Roman wouldn't be easy.

In the old days he had the best gear, intel and people in the military. Even then, with all those resources, missions were difficult and risky. He didn't have any of those things now. But he did have years of experience and the skills as a Delta operator, even if they were rusty.

"Put me back on with my guy," said Roman.

Tate handed back the sat phone.

The MP took it and listened as Tate watched, wondering what Roman was telling his man.

He hung up and motioned to Tate. "Let's go."

They left the shed and climbed back into the Humvee.

"I don't remember seeing you on the base before," said Tate.

The driver didn't respond. He kept his eyes ahead until they pulled up to the path leading back to Tate's quarters.

"Get out, Mr. Ninja."

"What about my sergeant?" said Tate

"Get out," said the MP, putting his hand on the grip of his gun.

"Not until I know Wesson's safe," said Tate.

The MP drew his gun, but Tate acted first. He grabbed the back of the MP's head by the hair and roughly yanked back. Tate's free hand latched onto his trachea like a bear trap and squeezed until the MP gagged for air.

"Roman needs me a lot more than you," seethed Tate. "I'm going to rip out your throat right now if you don't do what I tell you." He eased his grip just enough for the MP to breathe. The steel grip on his throat and the fire in Tate's eyes was all the convincing he needed.

"Okay," the MP gurgled.

"You're taking me to where you're holding Wesson and we're leaving with her," growled Tate.

He let go of the MP's throat and shoved his head against the driver's door. The MP clutched his throat, wheezing for breath as Tate grabbed his pistol and pushed the barrel into the gasping man's crotch.

"I'm telling you, she's fine," said the MP, desperately trying to shrink away from the gun. "We never touched her, man. I just that so you wouldn't put up a fight."

Tate pulled back the hammer on the pistol.

"You feel that sensation?" asked Tate. "That at any moment you'll hear a bang and you'll see your own blood spill out? Let that burn into your brain. Because if you, or your crew, ever threaten me and my people, I'm going to make this nightmare a reality."

"You can't touch us," said the MP, failing to keep the quiver out of his voice. "Roman'll smoke you."

"Let me connect the dots for you," said Tate. "Who do you think was doing your job before he got strung up from a tree?" He gave it a moment for that to sink in.

"Okay, okay," said the MP. "We're cool."

"No, we're not," said Tate. "I can see it in your eyes. As soon as I let you go, you're planning to get your crew and jump me. I'll kill you now."

"Wait!" pleaded the MP, almost in tears. "I could work for you. Like, Roman'll think I'm working for him, but I'll be your inside guy."

"How much is he paying you?" asked Tate.

The MP sneered like something left a bad taste in his mouth. "He doesn't pay me spit."

"What's he got on you?" asked Tate.

"My family," said the MP. "They work his fields."

"You step out of line and he kills one of them," said Tate. "Sounds like Roman."

"He shot my mother," said the MP. Tears welled up in his eyes and Tate saw the raw grief in them. "He made me watch."

"What's your name?"

"Cruz."

Tate let go of Cruz's hair and moved the gun away from his groin.

"Looks like both of us need Roman out of the way," said Tate. "I think I can help your family."

It was a lie and Tate knew it. He didn't have the first clue where Roman called home, or any idea how he would find out. But he had to start somewhere and getting Cruz on his side was more than he had a minute ago.

Tate eased his conscience by telling himself that if some nebulous opportunity presented itself, he really would help Cruz's family.

Cruz rubbed the back of his head, easing the pain.

"You can't touch him," said Cruz. "You're just one guy."

"Now we're two," said Tate, handing back the gun.

Cruz looked at the gun for a moment before taking it.

Tate thought that if the fates decided he was a horrible person and deserved to die for lying to Cruz, then this was their chance to pass judgment.

Tate inwardly sighed with relief as Cruz holstered the gun.

"Keep your head down and don't do anything that would make your crew think you've switched sides."

"Yeah," said Cruz. "I got your word about my family, right?"

"Yes," said Tate, getting out of the Humvee.

Cruz held him in his stare. "Your word."

"If I can get at Roman, I'll help them get away."

"I hope you know what you're going," said Cruz.

Tate watched him drive off.

"Me too," he said, before heading back to his quarters.

4

THE BROTHERHOOD

I'm *being followed.*

Tate noticed the headlights behind him a few minutes after he drove into the city. The left headlight was dimmer than the right.

When it was still behind him after the third turn it got Tate's attention. He went down a couple of streets that weren't on his way but wanted to confirm he wasn't getting paranoid.

He wasn't.

Earlier in the day, Cruz had appeared at his door with short instructions from Roman.

The Blue Orchid. 11:30 PM. The meeting with the Brotherhood was on.

From everything he'd heard, the Brotherhood sounded like a young organization. Reckless and erratic. Older, more seasoned, groups knew the routine. Nobody went cowboy and started shooting. He wouldn't have expected the meeting to be at the Orchid. Tate wasn't complaining. It was a big step up from meeting in a run down warehouse, or back alley that stank of urine.

Tate made another right turn and the car with the dim headlight appeared behind him.

They were keeping their distance, trying not to arouse suspicion.

It wasn't working, but the extra breathing room give Tate the opportunity he was looking for.

At the next light, he turned and floored it. The engine whined in protest, but picked up speed. The beat-up car wasn't going to win any street races but sped up enough to reach an alley before the following car turned the corner.

He swung into the first alley, praying it wasn't blocked or a dead end. The narrow beam of his headlights showed a clear path.

"Here we go," he said, switching off the headlights as he picked up speed.

Except for the occasional weak light over a shop's backdoor, there was nothing but black. Tate quickly lost his orientation and gripped the steering wheel like a vice, keeping the car from drifting into a wall.

A streak of light flashed in his rearview mirror as the following car raced past his alley, thinking they had lost him down a different street.

He switched on his headlights in time to see a brick wall racing at him. He slammed on the brakes, pitching the nose of the car down, sending the back-end fishtailing. The brakes locked, and the worn tires only slid on the greasy asphalt.

Ahead, the alley hooked right and Tate yanked the wheel over, throwing the car into the turn. It looked like he was going to make it as the car veered into the turn, then the tires screeched and the car went into a slide.

"Son of a ...," he blurted as he zoomed, sideways, at the wall. Tate stomped the gas pedal, smoking the tires, hoping to pull out of the slide. No good.

He braced for the hit, scrunching his eyes against flying glass. The car hit with a crunch of metal. The spinning tires grabbed hold and the car took off.

There was no time to check for damage. The people following him would have realized by now what he had done and were doubling back. Any second now, their headlights would appear at the mouth of the alley.

Steel screeched against brick as Tate pulled away from the wall.

Now passed the turn, he noticed a new wobble, but the car still moved and that's all he needed from it.

He entered a new street, then made a few more random turns, always checking for that dim left headlight, but it never appeared. He'd lost them.

By the time he pulled up outside the Orchid, Tate was convinced he'd been followed by Colonel Wade's goons.

That guy's beginning to get on my nerves.

Between Wade and Roman, his troubles were stacking up. He was on the bottom of the food chain and it sucked.

"Good evening, mister Tate," said Rocko, as Tate came up the short steps outside the Orchid's double doors.

"You too, Rocko," said Tate.

Teddy Moon, the owner of the Blue Orchid, had poured his heart into making people feel welcomed to his club. He'd hired Rocko as a bouncer for the decidedly unwelcomed.

Tate couldn't imagine anyone could be drunk enough to pick a fight with the bouncer. Rocko was six-foot-five and solid as cement. His doorman's coat strained at the buttons across his broad chest. Tate couldn't decide if the tailor ran out of material, or Teddy had specifically ordered it one size too small, but either way it gave the illusion that Rocko was a giant.

In Tate's opinion, no illusion was necessary. The bouncer could snap someone in half like a dried twig.

"How are you...?" Tate stammered, doing a double take as Rocko stepped into the light of the streetlamp above. His face was battered with a long cut running down the side of his jaw.

Rocko saw Tate's surprise and flushed with embarrassment. Tate tried to save the man a little dignity and pass off the awkward exchange with humor.

"What happened?" he asked. "Get into a scrap with the wife?"

"No sir. She hits too hard," chuckled Rocko. "Just a little trouble with some unwanted visitors."

"Take care," said Tate, leaving it at that.

Maybe it was possible to get that drunk.

He handed Rocko a tip as the giant opened the door for him.

"Have a pleasant evening, mister Tate," said Rocko.

Tate checked his watch as he entered, among the low din of the crowded club. He was a couple of minutes early and glanced at the bar for an empty seat, thinking he might have time for a whisky.

"Jaaaaack!" called a familiar voice from across the room.

"Hi Teddy," said Tate, smiling in spite of himself.

He told himself it would be nice to come to the club and not be fussed over for once, but that wasn't Teddy Moon's style. Just like the club, Teddy was warm and welcoming and a little over the top.

"Jack," said Teddy, with slight reproach. "I thought we were friends."

"Commodore," corrected Tate.

Teddy had told Tate that all his friends called him Commodore. He never said why, and Tate hated to admit to himself that he was burning with curiosity to know how he got that nickname but took it as a point of personal pride and willpower not to succumb. In his heart of hearts, he knew that Teddy had a fantastic story to go with the name, but Tate refused himself the initiation rite of being the select few that knew the story.

"So good to see you," said Teddy.

"You too?" said Tate falteringly.

Always groomed and polished, underneath it all Teddy looked haggard and worn. Tate wouldn't say Teddy was his friend, but he liked the guy and it troubled him to see the club owner in this condition.

"You look terrible," said Tate.

Teddy blinked and Tate wished he'd been more tactful, but tact wasn't a skill he got to practice often.

"I'm fine," said Teddy with a dismissive wave. "There's someone waiting for you in one of the private rooms."

Tate could have thought of a lot of places to met up with a street gang but his favorite spot wasn't one of them. Roman didn't pass up a chance to add insult to injury.

"That can wait," said Tate. "I saw Rocko's messed up and you don't look much better. What's going on?"

Teddy looked around the bustling club as if someone was watching. Tate didn't know if there was a real threat or if it was Teddy's sense of the dramatic.

Teddy ushered Tate to an empty space near the bar and looked around again. Satisfied nobody was listening, he explained.

"There's a new gang toughs in town," confided Teddy. "They're looking to take over, including the Orchid. My place has always been hands off. Everyone knows that."

As soon as Teddy said 'gang', Tate was sure it had to be the Brotherhood, the same gang Roman was having trouble with.

Tate was hardly street wise, but he knew there were all kinds of things that happened in the city, and there was an unwritten rule that the Blue Orchid was off limits. The new gang were making up their own rules and beating the hell out of anyone who didn't go along with them. Suddenly, the chances of the Brotherhood accepting Roman's offer didn't look good.

"I heard about them," said Tate. "If there was something I could do about it, I would."

Teddy's face broke into a smile and he shook Tate's hand. "You're a good joe," he said. He had a love for the era of the 40s and stars of the silver screen and it was reflected in everything from the decor of the club and Teddy's style of suits, to the way he slicked back his hair and his pencil mustache.

"Don't worry about me. These tough guys are all the same. They think they're in the big leagues, but they'll bite off more than they can chew. Then they'll get what's coming to them."

Teddy glanced at the clock over the bar and took Tate by the elbow. "Your appointment's waiting," he said. He guided Tate across the club floor to the door leading to the Orchid's private rooms.

Standing next to the door was a smartly dressed bouncer who unlocked and opened the door when he saw Teddy approaching.

"It's the Moroccan room," said Teddy. "Always good to see you, Jack."

"You too, Commodore," said Tate, putting a smile on Teddy's face.

The bouncer held the door open for Tate as he watched Teddy disappear into the crowd.

The bouncer nodded to Tate as he walked into the hallway and closed the door behind him.

The sounds of the busy club disappeared, leaving Tate alone at the end of a long hallway. Thick carpet sank under his shoes and the warm glow of the art deco sconces had the desired effect of making him feel like he was back in the 40s.

He stopped at the door with the brass plate engraved with Morocco.

Before going in, Tate took a breath, mentally preparing himself for the role of negotiator. He knew it wouldn't be easy. This gang was young, cocky and on a confidence high from all their wins.

The more he thought about it, the more convinced he became that they'd laugh him out of the room. They'd taken over a lot of the city, spitting in Roman's face and getting away with it. Now he was about to ask them to work for the losing team.

And I'm the lucky messenger, smirked Tate. *And we know what happens to the messenger.*

He prepared for a room full of gang members, with Samuel making a show of strength. He entered, finding the room empty except for one person and it wasn't Samuel.

"It's pleasant to see you again, Sergeant Major," said Dante Barrios.

"I wasn't expecting you," said Tate.

Dante was the right-hand man and advisor to Roman and the two of them couldn't be more different. Dante was polished, educated and thoughtful; a professional. But his well-groomed features and custom-made suits didn't change the fact that he worked for a ruthless, violent psychotic.

His knowledge of business and law had benefited the growth of some major criminal enterprises and put his skills in high demand. After the Vix, employers became scarce and with them, employment opportunities. Which is how Dante ended up working for Roman.

"Roman requested I accompany you to the negotiations," said Dante politely.

Tate couldn't imagine Roman *requesting* anything but kept that thought to himself.

"Providing they're willing to listen, I can provide the terms of the agreement."

"It's a safe bet to say this isn't your first rodeo," said Tate.

Dante chuckled, flashing his brilliant-white teeth. "Yes, a very safe bet."

"All right," said Tate. "Let's get this done."

Tate breathed deeply, feeling the fresh air on his face as they stepped out of the club. He nodded goodbye to Rocko who returned the gesture.

"My car's around the side," said Tate. "It recently had a little body work, so I have to get in on your side."

Just then a silver, metallic BMW pulled up in front of them. The valet got out of the car and handed the keys to Dante.

"Or we can take yours," said Tate.

"You don't mind?" said Dante, smiling.

Tate couldn't remember the last time he'd been in a car that wasn't military grade, or a battered rust bucket.

"No, no," he said. "I'm good."

"Would you like to drive it?"

"Uh," stumbled Tate.

The last time they'd met, which was also the first time, Tate had stuck a gun in Dante's face, stolen his prisoner, and forced him to lie to Roman, which, if Roman ever learned the truth, would be Dante's death sentence. Dante had every reason to resent and distrust Tate. His offer completely threw him.

Dante read the confusion in Tate's expression and smiled.

"Ah, our last encounter," he said. "In my profession, holding a grudge is counterproductive. Being smart is much better than being emotional."

Tate didn't regret anything he'd done. He'd saved the life of that prisoner who turned out to be an invaluable asset.

Dante, on the other hand, made a living working for criminals, weapons dealers and drug lords. Yet, Tate hated to admit it was hard not to like the guy. Apparently, civility and charm had its uses. Tate pondered if these were skills he should work on.

Getting in, he took a moment to enjoy the rich leather seat and clean lines of the dashboard. So much had changed after the Vix and in a way the car was a bitter reminder of what was lost.

"We should be going," said Dante, pulling Tate out of his thoughts.

With the push of the starter button, the M5's powerful V8 engine rumbled to life.

"A gas engine?" asked Tate in surprise.

"Some would say it's primitive," said Dante. "But power cells lack soul."

Yeah, he's getting on my good side.

It wasn't long before they were in the industrial area of the city. They turned down a long road with potholed streets branching off to drab warehouses and equipment yards. They drove to the end of the road where a single street wound behind an old, brick shell of a building. Tate guessed it had been a factory back in the day.

The BMW's headlights panned across piles of junk and the rusted hulks of work trucks sitting on bricks, their carcasses picked clean long ago.

Suddenly headlights lit up across from them, making Tate squint as they caught him in the face.

"Every single time," he said, shielding his eyes. "Do they all watch the same movies?"

A skinny guy in a tank top waved Tate towards a large roll-up freight door, which opened into the building.

Tate's gut clenched at the idea of driving into a concrete box with a steel door between him and the only way out.

Lambs to the slaughter.

He stopped next to the skinny guy and rolled down the window.

"We can talk out here," said Tate.

"You ain't talk'n to nobody if you don't do what you're told," he sneered.

"Rather sets the tone, doesn't it?" said Dante.

44

Now that he was closer, Tate could see the guy couldn't have been more than twenty.

"Kids," said Tate, as he rolled up the window. "That's just perfect."

"You were a kid once," said Dante.

"Yeah," said Tate. "And I was a dick too, but I was taught to respect my, uh, people older than me."

Reluctantly, Tate steered the car through the large door. He nodded grimly as he saw the steel, roll-up door closing behind them.

"This just keeps getting better," he grumbled.

The open factory floor was littered with the bones of long-dead machinery, their steel frames picked clean by scavengers years ago. Puddles of oily water reflected the moonlight from the broken windows high above.

Fires burned from steel drums revealing several figures standing around them. They watched, expressionless, as the car passed by.

"None of this feels right," said Tate.

"Like you said," smiled Dante, "it's not your first rodeo."

They were shown where to park. Tate was tempted to arm the car's alarm just to see the gang's reaction, but quickly put the idea out of his mind.

They walked across the gritty, cracked concrete floor to the clustered gang members. Tate glanced up seeing catwalks above them, but it was too dark to tell if anyone was up there. He had enough experience to know they were without seeing them.

As they got closer, Tate could see they were all young and hard looking. Some of them were mad dogging and glaring; others sticking their chins out and frowning down their noses. None of them would have lasted ten seconds against him in a one on one fight, but that wasn't how gangs worked.

Tate singled out the only one who didn't look like he had something to prove.

"Nesto San Roman sent us," said Tate. "Are you the leader?"

"Ain't no leader here, man," said the kid. "We're a brotherhood."

"Right," said Tate.

They weren't wasting any time trying to make this more difficult than it needed to be, but Tate would play along if it helped grease the wheels.

"Even a brotherhood has a big brother. I'm thinking that's you."

"Big brother," said the kid, breaking into a smile. "I like that. Okay, yeah, that's me."

Tate held out his hand. "I'm Jack."

The kid looked confused for a moment, looking at Tate's hand. Then took it, shaking hands.

"Samuel," said the kid, momentarily dropping his attitude.

Tate knew that before they showed up, Samuel had already played out this meeting and how he would control it. By doing small, unexpected things, Tate was taking Samuel off script, which allowed for other possibilities.

"You wanted to talk," said Samuel, his attitude snapping back in place. "So, talk."

"Roman wants to work a deal with the Brotherhood," said Tate.

"A deal? That's why you're here?" said Samuel. "Why do we need a deal from some punk? We're doing pretty good just taking what we want, right?"

The other kids murmured in agreement.

"We already got half the city," said Samuel. "What's he gonna do about it? Nothing!"

"I know that's what it looks like," said Tate, "and I know you guys haven't been here very long, but in case nobody else has told you, Roman is not your typical bad guy."

"Same with us, and there's more of us," said Samuel.

"I can tell you guys are close," said Tate. "Like you said, a brotherhood. You guys look out for each other, I respect that. If one of you gets killed, you all feel it. But Roman, he doesn't know what brotherhood is. He's like a king. A crazy, vicious, murdering king."

Dante quietly coughed in disapproval.

"What I'm saying is," continued Tate, "if you kill one of his, Roman doesn't feel a thing."

"He comes into our territory and we'll kill more than one," said one of the gang.

The others laughed in agreement.

"You could kill twenty of his guys," said Tate. "He won't feel a thing."

"He sent you two," said Samuel. "Looks like he's feeling something."

"You have, what, thirty?" said Tate. "He's got a couple of hundred."

"This is just the start," said Samuel. "We got bothers and sisters from all over coming here, and when they do, we ain't stopping with the city. You can tell that punk we're coming to his front door. His whole operation is gonna be ours."

Tate tried to keep the exasperation out of his voice. This meeting was going south fast.

"Samuel," said Dante, stepping in. "Nesto San Roman is making you an offer to work for him. If you do, he'll pay you well, take care of your needs, and best of all nobody in your brotherhood gets hurt."

Tate looked wondering at Dante, confused why he was getting involved.

"That sounds like a threat," said Samuel.

5

FROM BAD TO WORSE

And that's the end of the game, thought Tate. Samuel wasn't going to back down and all his chest beating was winding up the others.

"I think it's time for the messengers to leave," Tate said to Dante. "We're sorry for taking up your time," he said to Samuel.

"It's not a threat," said Dante, persisting to Tate's surprise. "But you should understand that Roman won't give up the city without a war. He's willing to sacrifice as many lives as it takes to destroy you. Are you willing to say the same?"

The mood of the gang was darkening and Tate could feel the hostility radiating off of them.

"Just think it over," said Tate, taking Dante by the arm as he walked for the car.

"He don't know what war is until he messes with us," shouted Samuel.

"Get in the car. Get in the car. Get in the car," urged Tate, as he heard the stamp of feet on the rattling metal catwalk above.

The thump of the M5's doors gave Tate little comfort. He looked over his shoulder at the big, freight door behind them. It wasn't opening. The gang member standing next the chain which opened it crossed his arms and grinned.

"What were you thinking?" snapped Tate. "You don't threaten someone with war. Especially when there's a bunch of them and two of us. Even I know that."

"I was being realistic," said Dante, undisturbed.

"You heard the part about more of them coming here," said Tate, starting the car.

"Yes," said Dante. "I did."

Tate looked out to see the gang was standing next to the car, scowling down at him. He cracked the window just enough to speak through.

"Let's take some time to cool off," he said, slowly shifting the car into reverse without drawing any attention. "We can come back and work this out."

Samuel and his brotherhood stared at Tate as if they hadn't heard him.

"Open the door and we'll leave," said Tate. "Roman can wait for a little longer for your answer."

"Yeah, I got your answer right here," said Samuel, shoving a pistol against the crack in the window.

Tate floored the gas and the M5 jumped back, its wheels blowing up white smoke as they spun on the concrete.

Samuel's shot missed, hitting the hood of the car with a dull thud.

In an instant the M5 was flying, in reverse, towards the steel door. Tate slammed the brakes, throwing him and Dante against their seats.

With the steel door closed, they weren't going anywhere and the gang knew it.

The gang was walking towards the car. He was boxed in and the Brotherhood didn't have to rush.

"You'll have better luck if you hit the door head on," said Dante.

Tate looked at him questioningly.

"Speaking from experience," he said, "I'll beat this car into scrap before it'll get through that door."

"This car has a kinetic energy bumper," said Dante. "Whatever it impacts it multiplies the force in return."

The gang spread out like a row of executioners and opened fire.

Tate ducked below the dash as bullets slapped into the windshield but didn't penetrate.

"Bullet proof?" he asked, sitting up.

"Bullet resistant," said Dante. "But let's not test how long it'll hold up."

"Right," said Tate, shifting into drive and hammering the gas pedal.

Gang members dove out of the way as Tate sped through them. The M5 ate up the distance to the opposite wall and he twisted the steering wheel as he hit the brakes. The back end whipped around, pointing the front of the car at the steel door.

"Just hit it?" asked Tate, looking for assurance they weren't about to get their necks snapped. "Like a battering ram?"

"Close enough."

Bullets thudded into the M5's glass and body as Tate mashed the gas pedal to the floor. The car shot forward in a cloud of burnt rubber. The steel door filled the windscreen and Tate braced for the impact.

Metal screamed and twisted as the M5 plowed into the door, tearing part of it away from the rollover tracks on one side. But it wasn't enough. The door still held.

Flecks of shattered brick and dust sprinkled over the car as Tate threw it into reverse and gunned it. Burnt rubber billowed around them, but the car wasn't moving. The bumper was snagged on the door.

Tate looked to his left, seeing Samuel holding the barrel of his gun inches from the glass.

Flame and strobing light flashed as Samuel fired repeatedly into the same spot on the window. Pulverized dust began breaking off on the inside of the glass.

Tate knew, at any moment, one of those bullets was coming through.

He floored the gas and the M5's tires wailed as they spun, pulling against the door.

"You better hurry," said Dante, gesturing to Samuel.

Tate's window was beginning to deform as Samuel loaded another magazine and began drilling at the weak spot he'd created.

Tate shifted gears back and forth, flinging the car against the door and back as Samuel loaded another magazine.

Suddenly the M5 broke free and they were hurtling at the opposite wall. Tate struggled against the panic clawing to taking over as adrenaline pumped through his body.

Something fell from the catwalk above them. Glass shattered on the hood of the car and it disappeared in a ball of fire. Both men inside flinched, feeling the heat pulse into the car.

"Fireproof?" asked Tate.

"I'm afraid not," said Dante.

Unable to see through the flames, Tate shifted into drive and accelerated. He didn't care what the bumper was made of; if they missed the door, this car would not survive a brick wall.

"Hang on," he said.

The car hit but didn't stop.

The door's steel panels exploded into the parking lot as the M5 punched through like a fiery cannonball.

The tires screeched in protest as Tate turned hard, narrowly missing the scrapped trucks, and headed for the street.

The flames died down as the wind whipped them away. Smoke and steam bled out of the hood, streaming along the sides.

Tate could hear metal grinding from the engine as he gripped the wheel to keep his hands from shaking. They were free, but not out of the woods.

"We're in trouble if they chase us," said Tate. "Can you call for reinforce..."

Tate's body was slammed into the door as a freight truck plowed into the side of the M5. The car was flung into the air and came down with a teeth-jarring crunch, rolling over and over, throwing the two men inside like rag dolls.

It was the last thing Tate remembered before the world went dark.

Coughing, Tate's body spasmed as consciousness painfully returned. He opened his eyes, confused and disoriented. It didn't make sense why the seats of the car were above him.

A splinter of memory; the grill of a truck filling his window and it all came back to him.

Harsh sunlight bounced off the street and he blinked the grit and dust from his eyes. Slowly the pieces of last night began to connect until, in a rush, he remembered.

He tensed with a gasp, looking for the faces of the Brotherhood about to execute him, but he was alone.

He relaxed, becoming aware that part of him protested in pain.

Dante.

Tate couldn't see him. He wasn't in the car and the passenger door was open. Tate crawled out and pulled himself to his feet with a groan.

On the other side of the street was the freight truck, the front end a smashed wreck. The gang must have had planned ahead and had the truck ready.

The driver's side of the M5 was caved in and the impact should have killed Tate, but the hardened armor of the car had absorbed the crash.

"Good boy," said Tate, patting the BMW.

He scanned the area, but Dante was nowhere to be seen.

His head was beginning to pound as he worked out the most likely sequence of events after he blacked out. The gang must have taken Dante, which was good news because it meant he was alive at the time.

Another thought flashed in Tate's mind, a nightmare that sent tendrils of ice down his spine.

He imagined the Brotherhood had left them in the wreckage of the M5 with him unconscious and Dante dead. He would have woken up as Dante, now a Vix, ripped into his flesh.

Tate shook his head, pushing the thought away.

"Not helpful," he said out loud and started limping to the nearest busy street.

Hours later, Tate drove through the front gates of the base and parked outside the infirmary.

During the grueling drive home, he discovered his left arm was dislocated and the pinching sensation on the back of his head was from a ragged cut.

"I slipped," said Tate, as the nurse filled out the admittance form.

He didn't have to wait long before he was called into the examination room where the doctor took inventory of his injuries.

"Slipped, huh?" said the doctor, firmly probing his cuts.

"Hey!" snapped Tate in pain. "Can you take it a little easy?"

The doctor looked at him unsympathetically before returning to his task.

"Last time I slipped like that, I woke up without my wallet, my date and my car," he said.

Tate checked his back pocket, relieved that he still had his wallet.

"Well, two out of three," said Tate. "Except it wasn't a date, or my car."

The nurse came in, looking uncomfortable with Lewis, one of Wade's MPs, right behind.

"The colonel wants to see you," growled Lewis.

"I'm in the middle of something," said Tate.

"This man has multiple injuries that require treatment," said the doctor.

"I got my orders," said Lewis. He brushed past the doctor and put his hand on Tate's shoulder.

"If you take that man out of here," said the doctor, "I can guarantee that the next time you come in here for so much as a scratch, you'll leave minus a testicle and spend the rest of your days with a colostomy bag strapped to your waist."

The big MP's hand recoiled as if he'd touched hot metal.

"Relax, meatball," said Tate. "I'll go with you after the doctor's finished with me."

"Wait outside," said the doctor, turning his back on Lewis.

Lewis scowled at Tate, before disappearing through the door.

An hour later, with a bottle of pain killers and his arm in a sling, Lewis walked Tate into Wade's office.

"You requested to see me, Colonel?" said Tate.

Colonel Wade looked at Tate with open surprise. Tate's clothes were torn and wrinkled. Spatters of dried blood stained his shirt and bandages covered several cuts on his face and arm.

Wade shuffled a file, buying a moment to collect himself.

"Explain yourself, Sergeant Major," he said.

"I was mugged last night," said Tate.

Wade fixed him with a hard stare.

"Sir," added Tate.

"What were you doing off base?" asked Wade.

"I heard there was a new taco stand in town," said Tate. "I must have gone down the wrong street."

"You got mugged looking for a taco stand?" pressed Wade.

"It might have been the guys that were following me," said Tate.

Tate caught Wade's glance at Lewis, who shook his head in denial.

Tate's suspicions the colonel was having him followed were confirmed.

"Why would someone follow you?" asked Wade, returning to his poker face.

"You're guess is as good as mine, sir," said Tate. "If you want to open an investigation, I can provide you with a good description of their car."

"Put it in a report," said Wade dismissively. "I called you here to inform you that I'm releasing your men from confinement."

Tate was pleased to hear it, but knew it was just a matter of time; Wade didn't have anything on them and they both knew it. Wade wanted to make a point of who was in authority and it didn't help that Tate was the only one who questioned it.

"I've been going through the camp's personnel records," said Wade.

It suddenly became clear that Wade wasn't going to leave this alone and the satisfied tone in his voice began raising those familiar red flags in Tate's mind.

"You and your people had your designation changed a while back," said Wade. "Previously, you were tasked with search and destroy of the Vix population. One of the primary roles of this base and its soldiers. Now it appears..." He paused while flipping through the pages of an open folder. "Well, I'm at a loss know what you do. There's nothing in here. No mention of your commanding officer, or your MOS. How is that possible?"

The Military Occupational Specialty code was the Army's system of identifying the specific jobs of every member of the military. When Tate formed the Grave Diggers, he never thought to check their files.

After Colonel Hewett had recruited Tate and his team to work for The Ring, Hewett had pulled some impressive strings to bump Tate's rank from sergeant to sergeant major. A ridiculous leap that should have raised an investigation, but Hewett was a quiet but powerful player in the pentagon.

The change in rank was the most Hewett could do to give Tate and his team the considerable autonomy needed in order to run missions for The Ring.

That autonomy was beginning to feel paper thin.

"I can't explain the condition of my file, sir," said Tate. "I believe you'd have to speak with the previous base commander."

He doubted Wade would even bother. Pink elephants could have paraded through the base and the previous commander wouldn't have raised an eyebrow. He took the meaning of 'hands off' to a whole new level when it came to anything to do with the running of the base.

Wade was turning out to be his complete opposite.

"Let's fill in the blanks," he grinned. "We can start with who you report to."

Tate straightened up, bracing for the storm he was about to ignite.

"With respect, sir," he said formally, "I'm not at liberty to speak on the matter."

Wade blinked a moment, not sure what he'd just heard.

"Would you like to repeat that?" he said, slightly flushing.

"Sir, my team and I are tasked with responsibilities above your clearance level."

"That's crap and you know it," snapped Wade. "I'm ordering you to tell me the name of your superior officer. I'll take up my issues with them."

"I can contact my commanding officer with your request to speak to them," said Tate, wondering how he was going to make this go away.

The closest he could come to an explanation was saying he was involved with black ops, but that would create more questions than answers.

The truth would go over even worse. *The Grave Diggers run covert missions for an underground cabal, The Ring, whose long game is to destabilize the United States government in order to take over the nation in a bloodless coup.*

Except even that wasn't true anymore; after Tate discovered the true goal of The Ring, he and the Grave Diggers began running their own counterintelligence to sabotage and undermine them.

Tate didn't have an official commanding officer. He was working with Colonel Earl Hewett, a mole inside The Ring, who provided Tate with targets of opportunity to disrupt their agenda.

"The duties of my team and I are classified, sir," said Tate formally. "As I said, Colonel, I can notify my commanding officer that you wish to speak to them."

Wade was fuming, but he could not order someone to reveal classified information.

He made Tate stand for a long time as he puzzled out his next move. He wouldn't let this go and Tate rightly suspected that this conversation would be the start of a crusade Wade would pursue until the truth came out.

Then again, if he shook the wrong bush and The Ring took notice of him snooping into their business it was very likely he'd end up dead.

"I want to hear from your CO immediately," said Wade.

"I'm unable to dictate my CO's priorities," said Tate. "Sir."

He could have left it alone, but Tate couldn't resist a final dig. It was a bad habit he should have learned to drop a long time ago.

"Dismissed," barked Wade.

Stone-faced, Tate saluted and left the office, wondering how he was going to produce an imaginary officer.

As the front door of his quarters came into view, Tate couldn't remember the last time he was so glad to be home, but his sense of sanctuary wasn't going to last long.

Hot air closed around him as he walked inside. The timer on his air conditioner was broken, again. He didn't think it was possible, but it was hotter inside than it was outside.

He jabbed the on switch. While the AC feebly tried to cool the air, he stripped down for a shower.

His damaged shoulder, bruised muscles and cuts punished him for taking off his shirt, but the pain meds bought him enough mobility to function.

After the initial sting on his cuts, the soothing water had a renewing effect. For the first time since he couldn't remember when, he took a deep breath and felt himself relax.

The moment was abruptly derailed as he heard the sound of someone rapping on his door.

Swearing, Tate dropped his head, resigned to the surety that he wasn't going to catch a break today.

"Hang on," he said, toweling off.

The person knocked again and again. If they were trying to piss him off, mission accomplished.

They can wait.

He took his time getting dressed, but mostly because the pain slowed him down.

He opened the door and was met by a wave of heat and bad temper.

It was the girl from Cruz's group of smugglers he'd seen in the storage shack.

He was taller than her by several inches and wordlessly stared down on her.

"I was in the shower," he grumbled.

"Come on," she said, her brown eyes looking at him with bored distain.

"Private Torres," said Tate, seeing her rank and name on her fatigues.

"Yeah, you know my name," she said. "So what?"

"Nothing," said Tate. "It's better than 'hey you'."

She drove them to the shack without another word. Except for the Vix, it was only Tate and Torres. The Vix were secured to the wall, but he still didn't like it.

"Seriously," he said. "What is that about? Some twisted status symbol?"

"Better than a guard dog," said Torres. "Sit down."

Tate sat down at the table as she opened one of the dusty crates and took out a sat phone. After keying in a number, she listened until it connected.

"I got him," said Torres, then handed Tate the phone. She sat down across the table from him and crossed her arms.

"Yeah," sighed Tate, prepared for another of Roman's tantrums. He wasn't disappointed.

"They wrecked my car," screamed Roman. "And they took Dante. You let it happen."

"The Brotherhood had it set up from the beginning," explained Tate.

"This is on you," raged Roman. "I should have your legs chopped off and make you watch my people feed them to that stinking Vix. You said you could handle it."

"I said I'd try."

"You know how much trouble you cause me?" yelled Roman. "I'm gonna kill you. First, I'm going to find everyone you know. I'm going to kill them. I'm going to deliver their heads at your front door, every night until I run out of heads and *then* I'm going to kill you."

Tate hung up.

It wasn't that he didn't believe Roman would follow through on his threat. He knew Roman meant it, but he had to break him out of his murderous rage and get him to listen.

The sat phone buzzed and Tate answered.

"Tate, you mother fu ..."

Tate hung up.

Torres frowned, confused.

"Give me the phone," she said.

The sat phone buzzed as Tate handed it to her. She tapped the receive button and quickly pulled the phone away from her ear as Roman's voice screamed from the earpiece.

"Boss, it's me," she said.

Roman stopped shouting and she put her ear back to her phone. Tate watched her as she listened.

"Yeah," she said. "Yeah, okay. What do you want me to do with...?"

Torres glanced at Tate then quickly away. He saw her tense, but only for an instant, then tried to look relaxed.

He didn't react, but his instincts were yelling at him that she was preparing for something and trying to hide it from him. Tate moved his feet under his chair and shifted his weight slightly forward. His legs tensed, ready to move.

As she was listening, Torres's free hand casually disappeared under the table and alarm bells went off in Tate's head.

"He wants to talk to you," she said, offering the phone to Tate.

As he reached for the phone, Torres's free hand appeared with a gun.

Tate launched himself forward, punching her in the jaw and grabbing the gun. The blow rocked her back and her chair tipped over, dumping her at the Vix's feet.

The Vix moved like a coiled spring and grabbed the girl, wrenching her to its jaws. Its rotted face twisted as its mouth gaped open, ripping into her.

Torres's scream was cut in a flash of light and an ear-splitting crack. The Vix's head snapped back, half its face shattered in a spray of gore. Its talon-like hands went slack, dropping Torres who scrambled away in whimpering panic.

She looked up to see Tate standing over her. His grey-blue eyes stared at her, cold and grim as he pointed the smoking barrel of the gun at her face.

"Stay," he said flatly and picked up the sat phone.

Trembling and breathless, she looked at gun then the stony expression behind it and nodded in agreement.

6

NO GOOD DEED

"Roman," said Tate.

"You aren't dead?" said Roman. "What the hell am I paying those people for?"

"It's been a rough week and I'm trying really hard not to take your psycho BS personally," growled Tate. "But can you can try, for just a second, not to go Scarface on me?"

"I love that movie," said Roman excitedly. His mood instantly changed. His rage and violence vanished. "The way that dude smoked those punks at the end."

"He died at the end, you know," said Tate.

"Huh? Hey, you okay?" asked Roman. "You know, sorry about that. I was pissed off and my temper, it gets away from me sometimes. But you're okay, right?"

"You just tried to have me killed," said Tate, sounding angrier than he felt. From his first face-to-gun-to-face meeting with Roman, he learned a lot about him and had started to compile a loose profile. It matched up closely with other's Tate had met during his time in Delta.

Unstable was the operative word.

"I said I was sorry," said Roman. "Get over it."

"I'll let you know when I'm over it," said Tate.

"You caused me a lot of trouble, you know?" said Roman. "My reputation's taken a serious hit. People are saying I can't take care of my own business. They think I let a couple of punks push me around and take my number one man. I want him back and you're going to get him."

"Do you know if Dante's alive?" asked Tate.

"Yeah. He's alive," said Roman, sounding bored. "I got a tracker on him. His bio-whatever says his heart's still pumping."

Tate was surprised to hear Dante was tagged. He seriously doubted Dante would have accepted that willingly. He supposed it was possible Roman could have drugged him and done it without Dante knowing.

"You screwed up and you gotta fix this," said Roman.

"Does your tracker show you his location?" asked Tate.

"Yeah, I got all that stuff," said Roman proudly. "You think I live in the stone age? It's not my style."

There was a small part of Tate that felt responsible for Dante's predicament. Compounding that was there was no way Roman would take no for an answer, and if Tate refused to rescue Dante he was sure Roman wouldn't rest until Tate was swinging from a tree.

"I'll need some of your soldiers," said Tate.

"I'm not losing my people because of your screw up," said Roman.

He knew he wasn't going to win this argument with Roman.

"Send me all the information you have about the Brotherhood and Dante's location," said Tate.

"Good," said Roman. "Hey, tell Torres she's fired, then shoot her."

"There's already people investigating the three you hung," said Tate. "If you keep stacking up bodies, they'll leave a trail right to the smuggling operation you're running on base. Is that what you want?"

"See?" chuckled Roman. "This is why I like you. Always looking out for me."

The connection clicked as Roman hung up.

Tate put down the sat phone and turned his attention to Torres, who looked at him with deepening fear.

"You gonna shoot me?" she said.

"You did try to kill me," said Tate. "You can see how I might take that personally. I'm not going to shoot you."

Torres's expression wavered between relief and confusion as he kept the gun pointed at her.

"But you're not working for Roman anymore," he said. "Before I put this down, you need to accept that's not going to change. Killing me won't put you back in his good graces, if he has any. Are you going to be a problem for me?"

"No," said Torres.

Tate put the gun on the table. There was no scheming in her eyes and he knew she wouldn't be a threat.

"So, what now?" she asked.

"Now?" said Tate, extending his hand and pulling her to her feet. "I'm getting something to eat. Hungry?"

"I'll drive," said Torres.

Tate two, Roman zero.

It was evening and Tate was going over the intel Roman had sent him. Thankfully, the air conditioning had finally caught up with the heat and knocked it down to a comfortable temperature.

A rap at the door made him grimace, wondering if Colonel Wade and Roman were taking turns with him.

Opening the door, his expression lightened as he saw Kaiden standing there.

"Every time I see you, you look like your warranty's expired," she said, admiring his banged-up face.

"Women like a rugged looking man," he said.

"There's rugged and then there's looking like you tried to French kiss a belt sander," said Kaiden.

Tate stepped inside and she followed him to the table where he'd been going over the sparse info from Roman.

He told her about the failed meeting with the Brotherhood, losing Dante and Roman's demand to save him, then sat back, giving her time to turn it over in her mind.

"You've got a new base commander who you've managed to piss off and wants to tie you to three murders," said Kaiden, counting off the situation on her fingers. "Then there's the prepubescent, cartel whack job you also pissed off, who will absolutely hand over evidence that you're spying for him if you don't get his man back. So that's the rest of your life in prison, or they hang you. And now you have an entire gang that will kill you on sight."

Tate smiled awkwardly, but only shrugged.

"Saving the colonel's life, uncovering The Ring's plan and offering a peace treaty," said Kaiden. "All of your troubles come from doing the right thing."

"No good deed goes unpunished," said Tate.

"Did I miss anything?" she asked.

"You always know how to cheer me up," he smirked, but his humor was snuffed out as his mind returned to the bleak reality. "Things are bad. I'm feeling boxed in and the walls are closing in on me."

"That's called a coffin," smiled Kaiden.

Tate didn't smile back and she leaned forward, her cool grey eyes looking serious.

"Not helpful, I get it," she said. "There's a lot going on and it's too big to tackle at once, so...?"

"Break it down and prioritize the problems," he said.

"Who makes the top of your list?" asked Kaiden.

Tate paused, sorting through and weighing each situation until he had organized the chorus of thoughts all yelling for his attention.

"Roman," he said.

"You can't take him on alone," she said.

Tate frowned and he let out a heave sigh.

"You never told the team about him," she stated. "Or the deal you made with him."

Tired, he rubbed his face, feeling even more weight settling on his shoulders.

"You don't have to drag out all the ugly details," said Kaiden, reading his thoughts.

"I don't want to lie to them," he said. "They put everything on the line for me. I owe them the truth."

"Come on," she said. "You were Delta a long time. Slave runners, gun merchants, butchers, the worst scum there is. Sometimes you have to get dirty to get the job done. We know how that is. The people on your team? That's a world they've never had to live in. You can't judge yourself against their ignorance."

"We can drape it with all the justification," he countered. "But it's still lying."

"It's not lying. It's compartmentalizing," said Kaiden. "Why are you beating yourself up over keeping them safe? If they got involved with Roman, they could be in the same fix you're in."

Tate could only nod in agreement and Kaiden was content to let silence hang in the air. She sat back and looked around the room with disinterest as he stared at a stain on the table.

After a few minutes, Kaiden looked at Tate, sizing up his mood.

"When you're done dragging out your pity party, let me know," she said. "I'll be ready to help."

"I'm done," he said, looking up at her.

"You sure?" she asked. "Because I can come back. Give you time to have a good cry, maybe..."

"Do you ever stop rubbing in the salt?" he grumbled.

"Only after I hit bone," grinned Kaiden.

Tate laughed and it felt like the weight was lifting from his shoulders. His conflicts cleared away and clarity set in. The pieces of a plan began to take shape.

"You know," she said, "Roman's got to go."

"I'm way ahead of you," he said.

"I didn't take you for the assassination type," said Kaiden, cocking her head with a grin. "I like this side of you."

"Sorry to disappoint you," he said. "Killing him isn't the answer. Getting rid of the evidence, whatever he's got that ties me to him, that's the answer."

"Do you know where he is, or where he keeps his evidence?" she asked.

"No," he said. "I also don't know what kind of security he has guarding his house, but I know someone who's going to give me all that information."

"Dante," said Kaiden.

"How'd you guess?" he asked.

"Please," she said with disappointment.

"Right," agreed Tate. "Dante knows everything about Roman."

"Why would he help you?" she asked.

"Because he wants the same thing I do," he said. "He wants to get out from under Roman's thumb."

Kaiden propped her elbow on the table, putting her chin in her hand. "I'm listening."

"Before we met with the Brotherhood," said Tate, "Dante told me he was only there as an observer. I figured Roman wanted to keep an eye on me, be sure I didn't make any deals behind his back. We show up and I'm talking to the leader, Samuel. It's a rough start, but I'm thinking we might actually work something out. Then Dante steps in. He starts making threats, talking about Roman going to war with them. Derails everything."

"I thought you said he was a public relations guru," said Kaiden. "He had to know that would throw gas on the fire."

"I think he was planning on it," he said. "He showed up in an armored car. I thought he was being cautious, but now it makes sense. He wanted to provoke them and had the car to make a safe exit. Then he'd report back to Roman they tried to kill him, and psycho nature takes its course."

"How does a war help Dante?" asked Kaiden

"Roman doesn't earn loyalty. He creates it with blackmail, or ransom," said Tate. "Dante came into the job thinking Roman was just another crime boss. By the time he knew he had to get out of there it was too late. Roman must have some kind of leverage on him."

"So, Dante starts a war between Roman and the gang," she said, connecting the dots. "Roman eventually wipes the gang out, but it'll cost him in soldiers and resources."

"That leaves him vulnerable to his enemies," he said. "They off Roman, take over his operation and Dante is free."

"Sounds like Dante's no stranger to toppling regimes," said Kaiden. "I'm getting the sense he's got other skills he hasn't shared with you."

"There's only one way to know," said Tate.

"Let's break him out and ask him," she said.

"Easier said than done," he said.

"Thanks captain obvious," said Kaiden. "Everything is easier said than done."

"I'm in," said Ota.

"Me, too," said Rosse. "I'm in."

"In what?" asked Monkhouse, baffled. "All he said was 'gang'. We don't even know what he's got to say."

"I'm bored," smiled Ota, shrugging.

"He doesn't have to say nothing else," said Rosse. "I got a special place in my heart for gangs. Hate' em."

"I get that," said Monkhouse. "But before you go committing us to I don't know what..."

"Nobody's committing you to nothing," said Rosse, as a warning grumble edged into his voice. "You can stay home with the wo..."

He felt Wesson's pale green eyes drill into him and his words stumbled to a halt.

"Eh, workers," he finished. "Like in the kitchen."

"Nice save," chuckled Monkhouse.

"What's wrong with kitchen workers?" asked Fulton.

"Anyone mind if I continue?" said Tate.

The room quieted down and the team turned their attention back to him.

It was early morning when Kaiden had finally left. Tate still faced the struggle of how much of his involvement with Roman he'd reveal to the team.

He was exhausted, sore and on everyone's hit list. That sort of combination was like paint stripper on self-delusions.

He cleared his throat, unsure how many would still be sitting in the room after he finished, but at the very least it would be one less load stone around his neck.

"Several months ago I started using a local drug lord, Nesto San Roman, as an intel source," said Tate.

The look of surprise from the group wasn't lost on him.

"Did you say drug lord?" asked Monkhouse.

"If he was giving you information," asked Rosse, "what were you giving him?"

Everyone in the room groaned, exasperated with Rosse's implied accusation.

"What'd I say?" he asked defensively.

"Settle down," said Tate.

"I wasn't helping him run drugs, if that's what you're asking," he said.

"But you didn't shut him down," pressed Rosse, eliciting another round of protests from the group.

"You were a prison guard," said Tate. "Did you shut down every card game and confiscate every piece of contraband you found?"

"Are ya kidding me?" scoffed Rosse. "Not unless I wanted to start a riot."

"So you broke the rules," said Tate.

"The people who wrote them rules never stepped foot in my world," said Rosse. "They don't know how things really work."

"Well Sergeant," said Tate, "do you know how things work in my world?"

Rosse's mouth opened then shut as he realized he had nothing to say.

"Roman was an important source of information," continued Tate. "Without him we would have never known the truth about The Ring. But over time, Roman has been expanding his operation, getting more powerful and becoming more dangerous."

"So now you're gonna shut him down," smiled Rosse, vindicated.

"That's the plan," said Tate. "But I can't do it without all of you."

"Like I said from the very beginning," grinned Rosse at Monkhouse, "I'm in."

Tate couldn't help but smile at Rosse's contrary nature. One minute he's grousing at you and the next he's helping you.

Ota, typically the least talkative of the team, was looking at Tate with a grin.

Tate couldn't square how Ota was nearly monk-like in his practice of Zen and also be a sniper, and a frighteningly good one. It was a puzzle Tate didn't expect to solve.

"I'll need your skills, Ota," he said, "but this won't be an assassination. For obvious reasons, Roman's kept the location of his operations a secret, making it a hard target to hit. The only other person who knows that location is his right-hand man, Dante Barrios. This is where we come in. There's a new gang looking to take over the city. As a show of force, they kidnapped Dante a couple of days ago. We're going to get him back."

"How's that help us get at Roman?" asked Rosse.

"Dante wants out, but Roman doesn't take rejection well," said Tate.

"So, if we rescue Dante," said Fulton, "you think he'll tell us where Roman is?"

"Yes," said Tate flatly.

"Hitting a gang and a drug lord?" smiled Rosse. "This team is finally shaping up to make something of itself."

"We're not taking on the entire gang," said Tate. "Just the ones between us and Dante."

"That sucks," said Rosse. "But taking their trophy will wreck their street cred and make them look like punks and losers. Someone'll wipe 'em out before the year's over."

"This isn't a typical mission," said Tate.

"Hey, Top," said Monkhouse with his hand in the air. "Can you remind me when we ever had a typical mission?"

"Fair enough," said Tate. "We're going to do some house cleaning. Are you in?"

Everyone in the room nodded in agreement, filling Tate with a sense of pride and friendship.

"All I have is where they're keeping Dante," he said. "It could be a few guards or the whole gang."

"So, we're going in blind," said Monkhouse.

"Yes," said Tate, getting frustrated.

"Thanks," said Monkhouse. "Just wanted to, you know... Going in blind."

"You wanna shut up?" said Rosse.

"Both of you shut up," barked Wesson.

The room went quiet.

"They don't know we're coming," said Tate, nodding thanks to Wesson. "If we exploit that advantage, we'll be in and out of there before they know what's happening."

Nobody spoke and Tate didn't see any questions in their faces.

"Anyone wants out, now's your chance."

The team traded looks, but nobody moved.

"We'll leave tomorrow night at zero one hundred," said Tate. "I'll arrange transport. We'll stage behind the motor pool. I think it's a good idea to avoid drawing any attention from Wade or his MPs. Stagger the times you collect your gear from the arms room. That's it. See you there."

"Say that again, Corporal," said Tate, as the anger began to boil inside him.

"We're closed," said the corporal in charge of the arms room. "Sorry, Top. I have my orders."

A knot started in the pit of Tate's stomach an hour ago when Fulton told him his weapons authorization form was denied. When the same thing happened to Wesson, the knot tightened. Now it was happening to him.

"Check it again," he said.

With a sigh, the corporal studied the master authorization list for a moment, already knowing it wouldn't change anything.

"You're not on the MAL," said the corporal. "The base commander updated who's authorized to check out weapons a couple of days ago. You're not on it."

"Who is on it?" asked Tate, feeling his hackles rise.

"Well, nobody," said the corporal.

Tate's face went slack in disbelief.

"Nobody? Why did you look for my name?"

"You told me to," said the corporal, beginning to perspire.

Tate forced himself to calm down. Pressuring the corporal wasn't going to help the situation.

"Corporal Westcot," he said, reading the clerk's name on his uniform, "How long has it been since you had a good cup of coffee?"

"Real coffee?" asked Westcot.

"California coffee," said Tate. "A bag of it."

The west coast state, at least the areas that were habitable, included much needed agriculture and one of the few areas growing coffee. Its scarcity made it worth its weight in gold.

Since the Vix first appeared, commonly referred to as the outbreak, trade with other countries was nonexistent. It wasn't that foreign ships were turned away; they simply stopped coming. The US had sent cargo ships abroad, but only a handful returned. The rest were never heard from again.

Those that came back told similar stories; ports deserted or overrun with Vix. Burnt out city scapes, buildings in ruins, and everything abandoned. No signs of living anywhere.

"Don't lie," said the corporal. "A bag?"

His wistful expression faded away. "I'm sorry. I mean really sorry, but I don't want to risk it. The new commander is serious bad news. Word around the base is he's got it out for you. If I got caught helping you..."

"It's okay," said Tate, trying to calm the corporal. A sudden thought came to him and the knot in his gut disappeared.

7

A NEW WAY OUT

"Yeah, I got some stuff I could trade," said Rosse reluctantly. "Why?"

"I want you to tell your friend, Dr. Jer, we're in the market for guns," said Tate.

"I don't think so," said Rosse. "He uses the black-market strictly for medicine. Those gun dealer types make him nervous."

"He doesn't have to be there for the deal," said Tate. "Just set it up."

"Yeah, but it's his name," muttered Rosse. "If the deal goes bad, he's the one they'll take it out on."

"Tell him he's got my word," said Tate. "Nothing's going to blow back on him."

"I'll talk to him," said Rosse. "He's not gonna like it."

"This is what we need," said Tate, handing Rosse a list of weapons.

"Geez, Top," said Rosse. "This is gonna put a big dent in my inventory."

Rosse's time as a prison guard had taught him a lot about the nature of human beings, mostly bad, but he also picked up a few skills that were proving very useful in the over regulated world of the military.

Trading for hard to find items had become a part time job for Rosse. Unknown to Tate, Rosse had been snagging things of value whenever they went out on missions. Abandoned cities and towns were an unlooted gold mine of stuff that would easily sell on the black-market.

As the team's medic, he needed to supplement the lean medical supplies of Fort Hickok. His conduit to the market was an intelligent but odd veterinarian named Dr. Jer.

Medicine for animals suffered the same shortages Rosse was facing and the two naturally fell into the black-market business together.

"If you ever needed to take one for the team," said Tate, "now's the time."

Rosse arched an eyebrow and shook his head at the obvious manipulation.

Tate grinned, admitting to himself it was a weak move, but he knew it would work.

"Aw right," grumbled Rosse. "I'll talk to him."

"Thank you, Sergeant," said Tate. "Let me know when the meet's set up."

"Yeah, yeah," said Rosse.

"In the meantime," said Tate, "I'm going to see what I can do about getting Wade off my back."

"If you can pull that off, you're a miracle worker."

———

"Colonel Wade?" repeated Hewett. "I know the name from somewhere."

Tate listened to static on the satellite phone as Colonel Hewett went quiet as he searched his memory.

"He's starting to dig into my nonexistent backstory," said Tate. "How worried should I be?"

Colonel Earl Hewett was the covert sponsor behind the creation of the Grave Diggers, and Tate's unofficial commanding officer.

For Hewett to pull off Tate's promotion and sanction for the creation of the Grave Diggers, he must have twisted the arms of some very powerful people.

Hewett had spent most of his career working in the murky darkness of the intel community. Over time, he had built up a network with assets that didn't exist on any military or governmental records. It was a cutthroat swamp riddled with politics and people eager, yet cautious, to make alliances in order to move up in their organizations.

How well Hewett's smoke and mirrors would hold up under close examination was an uncomfortable question hanging in Tate's mind. Especially now with Colonel Wade taking a keen interest in him.

"Ah, I remember now," said Hewett. "And this is your base commander?"

"Yes," said Tate.

"Well, hell," sighed Hewett. "You have a real ball buster on your hands."

"That bad?"

Hewett laughed. "You'd be lucky if it was just bad. Wade used to be in the JAG."

"A lawyer?"

"No," said Hewett. "He was a judge."

The Judge Advocate General Corp was the military's justice system.

"He's what you'd call a hanging judge," said Hewett. "He always went for the maximum punishment, and if that wasn't enough for his tastes, he'd stack on extra. The man has an axe to grind."

"Base commander is a big step down," said Tate.

"Someone had their own axe to grind against him," said Hewett. "They got him for judicial misconduct and since nobody liked the guy they added as many secondary charges as possible to make sure they sunk him with one blow."

"Kicked out of the JAG," said Tate.

"I could try to find out more, but the records are probably sealed," said Hewett. "He was their problem, now he's yours."

"A resentful ex judge," said Tate, "with a God complex and he's got his sights on me? That's a big problem."

"The last thing you want is to get on his radar," said Hewett.

"Thanks for the warning, but you're a little late," said Tate. "Kidding aside, he has a lot of questions about me, the Grave Diggers, who we report to, how we got approved... everything."

"You know I can't do anything about this," said Hewett. "If he links you to me, things will unravel damned fast."

"My file's a dead end," said Tate. "And I'm not telling him anything, but if he knows the right people to dig around for him..."

"That's a possibility," said Hewett. "Maybe I can run some interference. I can't make any promises."

Tate was silent as he thought through his options and the possible outcomes that lay in his future. He didn't see any that were good.

"How much time do I have?" he asked.

"The JAG made an ugly example of Wade," said Hewett. "Enough that a lot of his friends cut ties with him. There might be some die hards that think he could return, and he'd show them special favor for being loyal."

"This just keeps getting better and better," said Tate, blowing out a long sigh.

"It's a crap shoot that he's got the right person in the right place," said Hewett. "But..."

"But what?"

"Hunkering down and hoping it'll all work out is a lousy tactic," said Hewett.

"I was thinking the same thing," said Tate. "Any suggestions?"

"Well," began Hewett.

"Besides a body bag," chuckled Tate.

"I never said that."

"Okay, seriously," said Tate. "You've got a lot of experience playing politics. What would you do?"

"Create an ambush," said Hewett. "Know you know the guy breaks rules that get between him and what he wants. Dangle something he wants."

"And place a lot of rules in his path," said Tate.

"There you go," said Hewett.

"Honestly, it feels underhanded," said Tate.

"Not every battle is fought with guns," said Hewett. "It doesn't make the enemy any less dangerous."

Tate was alone in the storage shack. All that remained of the Vix were the chains and a dark stain on the concrete floor.

He checked his watch again. He'd been there for thirty minutes, but this was important. He'd wait as long as it took. He was out of options and hoped his instincts were right.

His thoughts were interrupted by the sound of approaching footsteps crunching on the dead grass and gravel.

He shifted his weight in the chair, feeling the comforting weight of the Colt .45 holstered on his hip. It wasn't the sexiest gun and didn't have all the bells and whistles of newer weapons, but it did possess two of his favorite features; it was reliable and it made a big hole.

Sunlight spilled in as the thin, metal door scraped open and Cruz walked in. Tate had made sure to sit where he was well lit and easily seen. He wanted Cruz to know he wasn't walking into a trap.

Suspicious, Cruz paused in the doorway, weighting his doubts before coming inside. He scanned the shack for anyone else as he walked to the table and sat down across from Tate. Cruz stared at Tate, trying to look bored, saying nothing.

This time the talking was all on Tate.

"I need your help," he said.

Cruz didn't respond or react.

Tate blew out a sigh, trying to fend off his annoyance.

Why did people insist on the same tired tactics?

The answer was because they worked, but only with someone less experienced than Tate.

Do these guys all take notes from the same tough guy book?

"I need to come and go from the base without being seen," he said. "You're going to show me how."

"Don't know what you're talking about," said Cruz. His chair creaked as he sat back and folded his arms across his chest.

Tate drew a circle in grit on the table, considering his next move.

It was an obvious lie and they both knew it, but the lie was a bargaining chip. If Cruz was going to help Tate, he wanted something in return.

They had just formed a vague alliance and Tate understood that it didn't mean Cruz would be a willing partner in everything Tate wanted.

But the clock was ticking and he needed things to start going his way fast.

In his younger days he would have cut to the chase and been smacking this punk around until he got what he wanted. Fortunately for everyone involved, Tate had gotten wiser over the years. He wasn't opposed to beating the help out of Cruz, but he decided to make it a last resort, alliance be damned.

"You're moving drugs through here, sight unseen," said Tate. "You sure as heck didn't drag those three soldiers through the main gate before hanging them. You have a tunnel that goes out of the base."

A hint of a smile curled the corner of Cruz's mouth then quickly disappeared.

"Maybe I do," he said, sitting forward. "Maybe I don't."

"I need to use it."

"You killed my Vix," said Cruz.

Tate leaned forward, across the table. Cruz didn't move away, but Tate could see him tense up.

"I think what you meant to say," said Tate, "is thank you for saving Torres's life, *and* not shooting her for trying to kill me."

"She was off the crew the second she didn't shoot you," said Cruz. "She stopped being my concern after that."

"That so?" Tate murmured. "Is she still alive?"

"I guess so," said Cruz. "Like I said, she's not my problem."

"I think she is," said Tate. "Roman's the poster child for trust issues. He's got a secret pipeline, smuggling drugs through here and an ex-employee walking around that knows about it. The two things don't make sense."

"It's a big mystery," said Cruz, grinning.

"I know a great way to clear up this mystery," said Tate. "Get your sat phone and I'll ask Roman about it."

The grin turned stale on Cruz's face. "He don't want to hear your noise," he said.

"What you mean is you don't want him to know she's still alive," said Tate. "Because he told you to kill her, and you disobeyed his order."

Cruz didn't say anything, but shifted uncomfortably in his chair, feeling like Tate was dissecting him.

"What do you would happen if someone, I'm not saying me," said Tate, putting his hand on his heart, "because you and me, we're on the same side, but if somebody told Roman you ignored his order?" asked Tate.

"You're pushing your luck, man," hissed Cruz. "Something could happen to you, too."

Tate leaned back in his chair, chuckling.

"Oh, you are gutsy. I'll give you that," he said. "You lied to Roman. He thinks you smoked her."

"So what?" said Cruz. "Torres isn't a rat. She wouldn't tell anyone about the tunnel."

"So there is a tunnel," grinned Tate. He looked at his watch then back to Cruz.

His expression turning grim and serious. "Listen to me carefully. I have a lot going on and not a lot of time. We can work together, or I can burn you to the ground."

"That a threat?" scowled Cruz, sitting up and bristling.

"Go on, push your luck."

"I'm just shining a little reality on your situation," said Tate. "You don't want to end up swinging from a tree with a sack over your head, and I need access to your tunnel, *anytime* I need it."

Tate backed off, giving Cruz room to cool down and think clearly. There were pros and cons to telling Roman that one of his people was lying to him. But the idea of being Roman's snitch left a bad taste in Tate's mouth. Having Cruz as an ally and the use of the tunnel would make his life a lot easier and right now easier would be a welcomed change.

"When you look at it," said Tate, "not telling Roman about you means I've saved two lives. Torres's and yours. Hang on, I almost forgot your families lives."

Cruz's jaw clenched with anger.

"I told you about my family because I thought I could trust you," he said. "Now you gonna turn that around on me?"

Tate dropped his smile and fixed the MP with a hard stare.

"You need to get your head around this," he said. "I'm not looking to knife you in the back, or have Roman kiss my butt for turning you in. You're making this a lot harder than it needs to be. As soon as you stop making my life difficult, I stop being a threat to you and your family."

"You threatened my family," spat Cruz, jabbing the table with his finger.

"And I showed you the respect of being honest about it," said Tate. "You lied about not knowing there's a tunnel. That makes me a man and you a liar."

Cruz flamed with resentment and Tate locked eyes with him, not backing down until Cruz blinked and turned away in frustration.

To his surprise, Tate put his hand out.

"Man to man," said Tate.

Cruz looked at the offered hand for a long moment.

Tate was content to wait this time. The reward for his patience was more important than his pride.

Cruz reached across the table and shook Tate's hand.

"Man to man," said Cruz firmly.

"All right, my friend," said Tate. "Show me the tunnel."

It had been three days and each time Tate had seen Rosse he had to fight the gnawing urge to ask if Dr. Jer had found them an arms dealer.

Each minute of inaction felt like a steel band cinching tighter around his chest. The world wasn't static. While he waited, doing nothing, Wade, Roman, and the Brotherhood were all moving closer their own goals.

He had a slippery relationship with patience. Unlike many of those he'd known in special operations, Tate had not mastered a stoic attitude of time.

On the fourth day he caved to his restlessness. Immediately after breakfast he'd find Rosse and find out what was going on.

Halfway through his meal, Rosse sat down, awkwardly close to him and leaned over.

"Everything's set with the you know who," he murmured. "We meet tonight."

"Oh, right," said Tate, crunching a piece of fake bacon. "I almost forgot about that."

"Yeah?" said Rosse, impressed. "All this waiting's been driving me nuts."

"You need to relax a little," said Tate. "Here. Have some bacon."

Later that night, the buzz of crickets suddenly stopped as Tate's head emerged from the ground. Shafts of moonlight threaded though the dense woods, creating a world of shadows. He watched and waited, scanning his surroundings for any sign of danger or detection.

"We gonna stay in this hole all night?" groused Rosse from the bottom of the ladder.

Tate clenched his jaw, biting back the urge to swear at the husky sergeant. He lowered himself down the ladder, his face etched in pale light and frowned at Rosse.

"All right," whispered Rosse, getting the message. "Small spaces make me jumpy."

Tate turned around and quietly went up the ladder. With a last look he climbed out and waved Rosse up.

Half a mile from the base, the lights lining the walls were barely visible. A short distance away they found the footpath Cruz had described and followed it until they came to a clearing. There was something odd about the way the trees abruptly ended, making Tate squint into the gloom until he recognized that it wasn't a clearing at all, but a landing strip.

Hard packed dirt and clumps of grass made up the crude runway. Any pilot landing on that was either brave or a fool.

The final piece of how Roman was getting his shipment to the camp fell into place.

The landing strip was still close enough that the sound of a plane could attract attention. Tate rightly guessed the pilot was cutting the engine and gliding in. He shook his head, grudgingly marveling at the guts that took.

"Over here," called Rosse in a horse whisper.

Tate followed the voice and saw Rosse standing next to a tarp-covered car. They pulled it off, revealing a Ford Clear Sky sedan.

Tate was surprised, expecting to find a rust-streaked beater. Instead, the car was clean inside and out.

They got in and tapped in the security code Tate had gotten from Cruz. The dashboard displays came to life. The only indication that the motor was running was from the screen next to the speedometer.

"Pretty upscale for drug runners," said Rosse. "Nobody's gonna hear ya in this thing."

"Or see you at night," said Tate, picking up a pair of military issue night vision goggles.

He fitted the goggles over his eyes and adjusted them. The surrounding gloom changed into a well-defined landscape of whites, grey and blacks.

He put the car into gear and turned onto the dirt road that snaked its way through the woods until it joined up with the smoother, paved road leading to town.

"Have you met these guys before?" asked Tate.

"Nah," said Rosse. "I only deal with the ones that have medicine. First time for gun runners."

Tate's thoughts couldn't help but consider how badly things went the last time he met with an unknown group. The meeting with the Brotherhood was still fresh in his mind. There was no reason for tonight's meeting to blow up in his face, but he'd learned to never underestimate Murphy's law.

"I've done this kind of thing before," said Tate. "They don't know us, so they'll be suspicious."

"Hey, Top," said Rosse. "This ain't my first dance. I know how it goes. Ya don't need to give me a lesson."

"Prison guard?" asked Tate.

"You'd be surprised the kind of crap I had to deal with," said Rosse. "Prison's got its own culture. I worked a couple of places where the warden didn't do jack. The convicts ran the place, we were just spectators. A couple of times we was on the brink of a civil war in there. I had to step in and be like a go between. Everybody was pissed at everybody else, an' everybody else was pissed at me."

"Sounds fun," said Tate.

"If you like homemade knives shoved your my face," said Rosse.

"At least they didn't have guns," said Tate.

"They had them, too," said Rosse. "They didn't want to waste a bullet on me. Now that I think about it, that's kinda insulting. So I got this idea that I'd make guns like money."

"Currency?" said Tate.

"Yeah, that," said Rosse. "I made it so they could buy stuff with their guns."

"How did that go?" asked Tate. He couldn't see why a convict would give up something like that.

"I didn't think they'd go for it," said Rosse. "But the first time they saw a guy with a big screen TV in his cell, they were lining up to trade in them guns."

"That must have scored you some major points with the warden," chuckled Tate.

"Not really," said Rosse. "Turns out he was the one bringing them in. He was making all kinds of money and they still shot the crap outta each other, but it was mostly quiet when their favorite shows were on."

8

ARMS DEAL

The lights from the city glowed against the low hanging blanket
of clouds, but their destination lead them away from the
nightlife of everyday people. Their dealings were better done in the
quiet, dim shadows.

Tate drove a long stretch of road that took him to the industrial
area of the city. Soon he was navigating between the hulks of abandoned factories and warehouses. Splotchy, red brick buildings sat
broodingly, their windows shattered, looking like jagged teeth.

The Ford stuttered over the damp, potholed roads as they neared
their meeting location. A long, low row of buildings lined one side of
the road. Chips of white paint peppered the large, rust-covered, metal
doors.

Tate didn't like the feel of this place. The memory of his meeting
with The Brotherhood was still fresh in his mind. *This meeting's
happening outside or it's not happening at all.*

A large factory shouldered the edge of the road, its cracked,
stained face looming over them like an ancient monument long
forgotten. On the other side, moss and dead weeds clung to a four-
story high, slab-sided brick wall. Tate didn't like the way it made him
feel hemmed in. It didn't matter how many times he'd done it; these
encounters never got easy.

Once past the factory, the road opened into a large, storage lot. The Ford's headlights swept over the rusted husks of steel containers cluttered in the far corner before illuminating a group of people standing by three cars.

"Show time," said Rosse.

Tate stopped the Ford a short distance from the group. He left the car running while he took a moment to study the group. The car doors were closed, which he took as a positive sign; at least none of them were thinking they'd need to dive in for cover or make a quick getaway.

Getting out, Tate took a moment, scanning his surroundings. In the distance, a tin-clad silo rose above the empty hulks of buildings. Looking like a derelict robotic spider, it stood on a network of skeletal metal legs. Pieces of its rickety skin had rotted away, exposing the bones of struts holding it together.

Tate and Rosse walked halfway to the group and stopped.

"We're ready when you are," said Tate.

The lights of the three cars snapped on, lighting up the center of the lot like an arena.

He counted eight people in the other group as they all walked across toward him and stopped in the wide pool of light.

"I hear you're looking for guns," said the group's leader.

Business must have been good. All of them were well groomed and wearing expensive looking clothes. Many of them wore rings on all their fingers and oversized watches that glittered in the headlights.

"What are you looking for?" asked the leader.

"I need six assault rifles," said Tate, getting to the point. "Single fire to full auto. Eight magazines each and ammo."

The leader looked at Tate a long time before speaking. Tate could smell the man's cologne. All the signs were pointing at this being a lot more expensive than he had planned.

"Yeah, I can make that happen," said the leader. "I do some business around here, but never seen you before."

"First time for everyone," said Tate, avoiding the veiled question. He wanted to get this deal over quickly and disappear like smoke.

"You don't look the gang banger type I normally see," said the leader.

"There's a type?" said Tate. "I'm just someone who's looking to buy."

Now it was the leader's turn to size up Tate and Rosse. He studied them, putting together a picture of these two strangers, if they were setting him up, or telling the truth; as much as anyone did buying illegal guns.

He was taking longer than it felt right. Something was making the leader's nose twitch with suspicion.

"What kind of guns do you have?" asked Tate, trying to keep the leader's attention.

"Depends on what you have to trade," said the leader.

Rosse reached into his back pocket and froze as guns instantly appeared in everyone's hands.

"I'm get'n a list," he said, his voice tight with caution.

"I thought you said this wasn't your first dance," hissed Tate.

"Come on," grumbled Rosse. "You dummies think I'm stupid enough to pull a gun on eight of you?"

Oh great, thought Tate, gritting his teeth. *Here it comes.*

"Who you calling stupid?" said one of the group, walking up to Rosse. Before Rosse could answer there was a gun in his face.

"Say the word," said a voice in Tate's ear.

"Standby," whispered Tate, barely audible, as he glanced at the tall silo from the corner of his eye.

"Copy," said a voice only Tate could hear. Quiet static returned to the small, flesh-colored radio tucked in his ear.

Folded into the deep shadows, Ota peered through his sniper scope from high up in the silo. Adjusting for wind and bullet drop, the cross hairs hovered slightly above the head of the man pointing the gun at Rosse.

Ota's body was braced but relaxed, his breathing steady and smooth. He flowed with the Zen of the moment.

His aim would put the bullet right though the brain stem, ensuring no posthumous reflex or muscle twitching, especially since the guy had his finger on the trigger.

Tate could feel the mood of the others shifting. Some were heating up, grumbling threats under their breath.

"You don't come into our town, mouthing off," said the leader, striding up to Rosse. "Maybe I let Little Jimmy show your boy how to be respectful."

"It's the last lesson you ever get, punk," sneered Little Jimmy.

"It's looking pretty tense," said Ota, clicking off his rifle's safety. He eased his finger onto the trigger of the Remington M30. Part science, part art, he felt when he reached half the pressure needed to fire. The chambered 7.62 round would hit before the sound of the gunshot ever reached them.

"Not yet," whispered Tate.

"Everyone hang on," he said as he slowly raised his hands. "We're all here to do business. Just look at the list of things we have for trade. It's a good deal."

The leader took his gaze off Rosse and considered Tate for a moment, then held out his hand, gesturing for Rosse to give him the list.

"Better be good, my man," said the leader, as he unfolded the paper. "It's going to take a lot to put my boys in a good mood."

Tate hoped so, too. The terrible thought just occurred to him that he didn't know what Rosse had scavenged from their missions. His treasure trove might be enticing to black marketers trading in medical supplies, but an insult to gun runners.

Tate watched the leader's face as he read down the list. If this all went bad, Tate knew Rosse could be a dead man. Ota would drop Little Jimmy and that would buy Tate a couple of precious seconds to get to his car before the surprised group started shooting at him.

It was the botched meeting with the Brotherhood all over again, except this time his car wasn't bullet proof, he wasn't in it, and his gun was a long way away.

Tate could see the leader's lips move as he read down the list, then stopped. Whatever he saw on the list made him look again, making sure he wasn't mistaken.

"La Barbosa Saint Reys?" said the leader. "The real thing?"

He walked up to Tate and showed him the list, pointing at the item.

"My grandfather made cigars for La Barbosa," said the leader. "In Columbia. They haven't made Saint Reys since the Vix. Are you trying to pass bogus cigars onto me?"

"Rosse," said Tate. "Those are the real things, right?"

"Course they are," gruffed Rosse, in spite of the gun in his face. "Remember that mission in Cartagena?"

"Nobody goes into Vix country," said Little Jimmy.

"What's he mean, on a mission?" asked the leader.

He stepped back from Tate, eyeing him with renewed suspicion.

"Check these guys out," he said.

Several of the group walked towards Rosse and Tate.

"Best I can do is three," crackled Ota through Tate's earpiece.

"Get ready," whispered Tate.

"Copy," answered Ota.

He took a deep breath and let it out slowly as he snugged the rifle against his shoulder.

The group surrounded Tate and Rosse as a couple patted them down. They had left their military clothing back at the base, opting to fit in better with civilian clothing and shoes. Tate didn't carry any form of identification and assumed Rosse would do the same. But then again, he also assumed Rosse wouldn't call a crowd of arms dealers stupid.

"What's this?" said the guy, patting down Rosse and pulling something out of his back pocket.

Tate sighed, not believing things could get any worse. He glared at Rosse, who only shrugged his shoulders in response.

"You better see this," said the guy, handing his find to the leader.

Tate couldn't see what the leader was looking at, but the way the leader kept looking from Tate to what he was holding was making him nervous.

One of his men was looking over the leader's shoulder and Tate heard him say, "It's them."

Crap, we're screwed.

Tate kicked himself for not thinking of it sooner. The Brotherhood must have put out the word on Tate and offered a reward to anyone that brought him in.

The leader walked over to Little Jimmy, staring oddly at Tate. To his surprise, the leader put his hand on Jimmy's gun and lowered it away from Rosse's face.

"Are you guys really the Grave Diggers?" asked the leader.

Tate's mouth fell open in utter surprise as the leader showed him the Grave Diggers signature card with their skull and dagger emblem on it.

After the formation of the team, Monkhouse thought it would be cool to leave a calling card behind. "Like in the movies," he'd said.

"Like the Lone Ranger," agreed Rosse.

Everyone loved the idea except Tate, who thought it was the dumbest thing he'd ever heard.

"Covert teams, running secret operations don't leave behind cards with their names and addresses on it," he'd fumed.

After making his point, they agreed to drop it. But, in the tradition of never letting a bad idea go to waste, Monkhouse had them made and passed them around to the team. They didn't use them on missions, but still carried a couple as a point of pride.

What shocked Tate was how these gun runners knew who they were.

"No way!" said Little Jimmy, seeing the card. "You dudes are badass. Respect." And he gave Rosse a friendly punch on the shoulder.

"How do you know about us?" asked Tate. There was no point in trying to deny it. Thanks to Rosse, that ship had sailed.

"We been hearing about you guys on the radio," said the leader.

"Radio?" said Tate.

"Yeah," said Little Jimmy. "White Hat. It's all about..."

"I know," said Tate, remembering Fulton playing that station non-stop. "The deep state."

"So, it's real," smiled the leader. "I told you guys," he said to his friends. "They're the ones who started the Vix. The White Hat guy..."

"Revolution Terry," chimed in Little Jimmy.

"Revolutionary?" asked Rosse.

"No," said Jimmy. "Revolution. Terry."

"He's been talking about a black ops group," said the leader. "You guys. He says you're making moves to wipe out the deep state."

If everything they said was true, he and his team may have been completely exposed. How long had Revolution Terry been broadcasting about them? More importantly, what was he saying? Tate felt like Terry had just nailed a target to their backs. But that was only half the problem. Where was the information coming from? He had discovered a mole in their group once before and plugged that hole. Imagining someone in the team leaking information filled him with bitter anger. He trusted his people with his life.

Groping for answers, he could think of only one person with a tie between the team and White Hat radio.

Fulton.

"The deep state's got eyes everywhere," said the leader. "But you're safe with us. Nobody here would sell you out."

"Let me get this straight," said Tate. "The guy on the radio said our name?"

"He's too smart for that, you know?" said the leader. "He speaks in code. Everything he says has a double meaning. One time he said something about being six feet under. Couple weeks later he said, 'secret shovel'. See what I mean? Not everyone understands what he's saying, but my guys are hard core when it comes to following White Hat. They worked it out."

Tate was trying to process the conflict of emotions. He felt relief that they hadn't been directly outed, but someone knew about the Grave Digger's activities and was passing that information out. That was a problem.

"Hey, Lucy," called the leader. "Bring the showroom."

Lucy pulled down her hoodie, revealing long, red hair and a small crescent moon tattoo on her cheek. Tate watched as she murmured into a radio and the sound of big engines grumbled to life in the distance.

The mood of the arms dealers had become friendly and relaxed. Rosse was a celebrity.

"I can't say too much," he said, "but there's stuff going on out there that you wouldn't believe."

"You already said too much, sergeant," warned Tate, then turned to the leader. "I'm guessing our deal's still on?"

"For you, my man," grinned the leader, "you can pick anything you want."

Two big trash trucks lumbered around the corner and pulled into the lot. As they stopped, a couple of the group hopped up, standing on one of the tires and grabbed the handle to the access door of the garbage compartment. Metal squeaked as he pulled the handle and opened the door to the dark interior.

"Let me show you around," said the leader.

As they neared the first truck, they were hit with the pungent stink of garbage, making the leader grin even more.

"Really helps sell the disguise."

He climbed up and disappeared through the door.

As Tate followed him inside, a light came on revealing clean, white walls covered with guns. Almost all of them were older models, but each of them were spotless, oiled and rust free.

"Holy crap," said Rosse, entering the door. "You guys don't mess around."

"Hey," said Little Jimmy, following behind Rosse, "You guys want some espresso?"

"Most of the people we deal with are crooks and bangers," said the leader. "They get the other truck. That's got the cheap stuff in it, but this is what I call the executive showroom."

Rosse and Tate watched in fascination as Little Jimmy opened a cabinet revealing a polished brass and copper espresso machine. He started working the machine and taking out cups.

"He used to be a professional coffee maker," said the leader.

"Barista," said Jimmy, pressing coffee grounds into the filter.

The leader took them on a tour, the selection and quality of weapons was impressive. There was nothing here that was run of the mill. This dealer had top of the line connection. He checked Rosse's list of trade items and did a mental calculation.

"Your stuff is good, but not enough for what you're asking," he said, "but I'm gonna give you a discount."

"Thank you," said Tate.

"Thanks," said Rosse, accepting the tiny cup of espresso.

Little Jimmy offered the other to Tate, who politely refused. He didn't need any help losing sleep.

"I'll take his," said Rosse, downing the first cup with relish.

"What about me?" said Ota in Tate's ear.

"On second thought," said Tate, taking his cup back from Rosse. "Can I get this to go?"

Crestfallen, Rosse watched Little Jimmy leave with Tate's cup.

With their attention turned to selecting their weapons, they quickly picked out what they needed.

Tate listened as Rosse and the leader made arrangements for the trade and deliveries. The weapons and ammo would be left near the tunnel entrance near the drug smuggler's landing strip and Rosse's items would be delivered to a derelict factory.

The deal was finally done and Tate's only thought was to get some much-needed sleep, but before they left, the gun dealers insisted on shaking their hands. The Grave Diggers were celebrities.

The drive back to the tunnel was mostly quiet as Tate ticked over everything that had happened, including the revelation about their notoriety.

"Sergeant," said Tate, breaking the silence. "About that unit card you're carrying."

"That was a lucky break, right?" said Rosse, hoping to cast his mistake in a positive light. "That whole deal could'a gone south."

"This time it was lucky," said Tate.

"I know. I know," said Rosse. "Sorry about that, Top. It was stupid to carry it."

"No," said Tate. "Calling arms dealers stupid is stupid."

"I didn't call'em stupid. I said they were dummies. Big difference."

"Maybe the next time you can explain the difference, if they don't blow your head off first."

"People are too thin skinned," said Rosse.

"What do you think about that radio station talking about us?" asked Tate.

"Right?" smiled Rosse. "We're famous. Those guys treated us like movie stars."

"How do you think our enemies will treat us once they know who we are?" asked Tate.

"Oh, yeah," said Rosse, as realization set in. "But it's not like there's a big sign say'n 'Grave Diggers live here'. Those gun runners even said Revolution Terry talks in code. Like them English spy radio shows in world war two. They used code words the whole time and the German's never caught on."

"You know about that?" asked Tate, sounding more impressed than he should have.

"Why wouldn't I?" said Rosse. "I read stuff."

"Sorry," said Tate. "I didn't mean it like that. I didn't know you liked history."

"Nah, not really," said Rosse. "I seen it in a' old movie."

"Someone's leaking information about us," said Tate, getting back on topic.

"I'd bet money it's Kaiden," said Rosse.

Tate stopped himself from disagreeing out of reflex. He knew Kaiden better than anyone in the team. She was capable of a lot of things, but compromising their security wasn't one of them. At least that's what he was telling himself.

"Maybe," he said, his voice neutral. "Fulton's the only one who listens to that radio station."

"He's a good kid," said Rosse with a dismissive wave. "He don't have it in him to rat us out. Besides, we've all heard him play'n that station. Could be anyone of us decided to reach out to that Terry guy."

Tate grunted in agreement. Rosse was right. Instead of narrowing down the field of suspicion, it just opened up.

"I know this is bugging you," said Rosse, "but, if it helps, if that radio show was giving any details about us or the ops we're running we'd already be up to our eyeballs in bad guys."

Tate nodded, admitting that it did help ratchet down his concern. Not by much, but enough. He dropped the subject for now, but he wasn't about to let it go.

9

CONSPIRACIES

I t was going to be several days before the weapons were delivered. The puzzle of who was giving information to Revolution Terry pushed its way to the front of Tate's thoughts like a nagging itch. He forced himself to equally consider every member of the team, what he knew about them, and how likely they would be the one who was leaking information about the team's activities.

Questions piled up faster than he could answer them.

Who else knows this information? Just the White Hat radio DJ, or is he getting it from someone else? Why would one of our own do this?

He forced himself to stop before he yelled in frustration. He'd had traitors in his teams before. It didn't matter why they did it; the end result was they were trading the lives of their teammates, people who would and had risked their own lives to protect them, in exchange for something else.

They were traitors. There was no other word for it and that excluded them from any mercy in Tate's book.

In an endless loop, he went through the faces of his team, examining what he knew about them, looking for any tells that could be a clue, but like a powerful magnet, he kept returning to Fulton.

Fulton was in his early twenties; just a kid to Tate. Kids do stupid things. It's an historic fact. Most of them haven't lived long enough to earn the wisdom of experience. They don't look beyond the here and now and they feel invulnerable.

Tate stopped himself. Was he making excuses for Fulton?

It pained Tate to think it was him.

Fulton was a fan of that radio show, and proud to be a member of the Grave Diggers. The things Tate and his team did never made the news; never got the praise of the Army. No awards, medals, or citations. The work was its own reward, but that wasn't enough for some people. They felt their sacrifices and risks should be recognized by others. They wanted to be seen as heroes.

It wasn't ego, or maybe it was. Tate had never experienced the desire to be celebrated for what he'd done. His reward was the bond shared with his brothers and sisters who had been on those missions with him.

What was the point of telling someone that's never lived through that insanity?

You could tell an outsider every detail of a mission, but they'd never get it. The constant battle in your head to keep control, fighting the paralyzing fear that wants to root you in place.

Someone spills their coffee and thinks it's the worst day ever. How could they comprehend leaving the only cover you have to run into the open, knowing there's a sniper somewhere out there. Fearing they're lining you up in their crosshairs. Willing the rest of your team to see everything, especially the tale tail signs of an IED hidden in their path, or the guy in the shadows with an AK47 or bomb vest.

Tate shook his head to clear it of the speeding flashes of memories and bring himself to the here and now.

Fulton.

The name kept coming back. Tate couldn't avoid it. The kid was what his mind was fixated on and he'd have to confront him. He weighed the option of taking Kaiden with him. She had an uncanny ability to see into people.

No. That's a bad idea.

Kaiden didn't take prisoners when she was after the truth. If Fulton was innocent, the damage Kaiden would do couldn't be repaired. The kid would be a wreck and hate Tate for the rest of his life. Kaiden was best left for the ones he was sure were guilty.

Giving in, he resigned himself to talking to Fulton. His mind now made up, he considered how he was going to approach him; how he'd phrase his opening words.

Tate threw all of that away.

There was only one way to do this. Right to the point.

They were three miles into the jungle. Tate had taken Fulton out under the excuse to practice his fieldcraft.

Tate felt a small ache over the deception and how completely Fulton trusted him. He never questioned Tate about the request, how strange it was, that it came out of left field.

Tate made sure to run Fulton hard, make him tired and draw him away from the comfort and familiarity of anything he could use to ground himself when the questions came.

That plan backfired.

Tate had been so occupied with the questions he would ask that he entirely overlooked the obvious. Fulton was younger and fitter than him. He was the one who had to stop, gasping for breath, while the kid, even though panting and dripping with sweat, was game to keep going.

Tate grunted curses at himself for being so old. Being a soldier demanded things of your body that stacked extra years on you.

He took off his boonie hat and wiped the sweat from his face. Their water was supplemented with electrolytes to help against dehydration, but it made the water feel thick and robbed any sensation of feeling refreshed. Necessity and comfort were not mutually exclusive.

"Good run," said Fulton, a smile cracking his dust-streaked face. "What's next?"

How about trying to stop my heart from exploding?

Tate waved him off as he fought to bring his heaving lungs under control.

He ran his hand though his short ash-blond hair, which he regretted, as his hand acted like a squeegee, pushing the accumulated sweat over his face, stinging his eyes.

So far, none of this was going the way he had seen it in his head.

He wiped his face and took another drink.

I'm stalling, he thought. He didn't want to know the truth, if the truth was the kid was guilty as hell.

What if he confessed?

Tate's brain went blank. He didn't want to think about what happened next.

Maybe he'd just send the kid to some far-flung camp where he could spend the rest of his tour of duty. Out of sight, out of mind.

He clenched his jaw in annoyance. Now he was negotiating with himself.

"What's wrong, Top?"

Lost in his own thoughts, Tate didn't realize he was glowering at Fulton and the kid was looking at him with a mix of concern and worry.

It was as good a beginning to a bad situation as Tate was going to get.

"The other night," he said, "when I met up with the gun dealers."

"That must have been intense," said Fulton. "I wish I could have been there."

"No," said Tate. "You don't."

Fulton looked at him quizzically but said nothing.

"They knew who we were," said Tate.

"You met them before?"

Tate found a large rock and leaned against it. He adjusted his holster. The big Colt .45 felt heavier than before.

"Not like that," he said. "They knew about the Grave Diggers."

Fulton only looked at him in confused surprise.

"They said they heard about us from the same pirate radio station you listen to," said Tate.

He let that hang in the air.

Fulton's face changed from surprise to confusion as his eyes wandered in thought. They came to rest on Tate who was frowning at him. The pieces came together and Fulton almost yelped in alarm at the unspoken accusation.

"Top," he stuttered, trying to sort through his collision of thoughts and emotions.

"Be honest with me," said Tate firmly.

Watching Fulton begin pacing with growing distress churned Tate's gut, but he ignored it. The truth had to come out.

"No," said Fulton, sitting down on a tree stump. "I'd never do that. Never."

"You understand how the connection between you and that radio show..."

"Yeah," said Fulton, getting to his feet. He started pacing again, trying to expend the nervous energy buzzing though his body. "But lots of people listen to that show."

"Not lots of people know about us," pressed Tate. "Or our missions."

"Yeah," said Fulton. "I mean... I don't know what I mean."

Tate could see the rising panic in Fulton. Was it the guilt of being caught, or the fear of being wrongly accused?

"It wasn't me," he said, coming to a stop. "I'd never do that in a million years. You guys... you're my friends."

Out of anyone else's mouth that would have sounded feeble, but from Fulton it was as honest a proclamation as Tate could ask for.

Sighing heavily, Tate felt a huge weight slide off his shoulders. "Okay."

He got up and put a reassuring hand on Fulton's shoulder. Now that he was closer, he saw Fulton was quaking with grief and worry.

"Okay, I believe you," assured Tate. He felt the tug of an apology for putting the kid through this but stopped himself. That will come later.

For now, he wanted this experience to sink in; let Fulton understand the gravity of secrecy.

"What are you going to do now?" asked Fulton.

"*We* are going to find out who's talking about us."

"How do we do that?" asked Fulton, looking much calmer.

"We're going to ask Mr. Pirate Radio," said Tate.

"Revolution Terry?" said Fulton, his face lighting up in excitement. "We're going to meet him?"

"Right now, he's the only lead we have," said Tate. "Before you break out your autograph book, we have to find him first."

"Oh," said Fulton, his smile fading. "Right."

"This could be hard," said Tate. "We'd have to find someone with the right equipment to pick up the signal he broadcasts on. That's specialized gear and tough to come by. If Terry is using repeaters, that multiplies the difficulty. He could be sending that signal all over the place before it's rebroadcasted."

The more he thought about it, the more he saw their success dwindling.

It was a lot easier when he was in Delta Force. He had all technology of the military and intelligence community behind him.

"There's another way," said Fulton, breaking into Tate's thoughts. "There's a huge movement that follows Terry."

"Movement?" asked Tate.

"Okay, well, community," said Fulton. "Like, millions of people talk about him online."

Tate didn't question him about the 'millions' but moved on to the important details.

"Like in a chat forum?" he asked.

There was a time people spent hours on the internet, sharing pictures of their dog, or food. If he had ever posted a thing called a selfie, his friends would have laughed him out of the military.

After the outbreak, the internet was never the same. Many of the server farms and network infrastructure that supported it went down. They might have still physically existed, but the people that ran them didn't.

Pictures of butt implants were replaced with pictures of missing loved ones. The self-titled 'influencers' disappeared. In their place grew organic collections of people acting as conduits to connect people in need of food and medicine with others who had some to spare.

But human nature being what it is, some things never changed. The fascination of chasing conspiracies was one. It had been around since the first tales of Atlantis, and perhaps longer. In ancient times, conspiracy fans rallied around Plato. Now it was Revolution Terry.

"What do they talk about in this forum?" asked Tate.

"Everything," said Fulton. "You wouldn't believe the stuff going on in the world they keep hidden from us. Human trafficking, shadow governments."

"Deep state," said Tate, remembering the phrase from one of Terry's broadcasts.

"Yes!" said Fulton, lighting up. "Terry knows about all this stuff, but he doesn't come right out and say it. He drops clues, gives hints."

"Like a code."

"Exactly," said Fulton. "There's people in the community that are really good at piecing together what Terry's saying. They decode it then explain it to the rest of us."

"Doesn't it concern you that they could be making up the translation?"

"Making it up?" asked Fulton. "Why?"

"They have a huge audience," said Tate. "Eager to act on whatever they're told. The translators could use this as their own platform, spreading whatever personal agenda they have."

"Oh right," said Fulton. "I see what you're saying. No, they're all legitimate. A lot of the people decoding Terry's messages are embedded in the government. Secret patriots who have joined the cause."

"Who are they?" asked Tate.

"They don't give their names. That would be too dangerous," said Fulton. "

But they drop clues about their identity in their posts, too. They'll give hints about things before they happen."

Tate swatted the back of his neck as something bit him. He looked at his hand but saw nothing.

"Okay, let's get back to real... uh, stay on track," he said. "How do we find out Terry's location using this...?"

"Community," said Fulton.

"Right."

"We read the community posts," said Fulton with growing excitement.

"Is that the only way?" asked Tate.

"You are going to have your mind blown," said Fulton.

Tate's eyes ached from staring at the computer screen and his tortured sense of reality screamed for relief from reading the unhinged posts of the community.

There were thousands of posts from people, all talking about every conspiracy that could possibility be dreamed up.

Every event, human or natural was suspect. A building fire was a cover to destroy incriminating evidence against a home realtor, which they used as a front to create an underground railroad for moving sex slaves. A train crash had been the work of deep state operatives using the death of fifty people to cover the one death of someone who was about to testify before a secret intel sub-committee.

Even clouds weren't free.

One person claimed that clouds were being shaped to form coded symbols so agents could communicate across the world.

Tate felt like there'd never be enough showers to feel clean again.

"I can't do this anymore," he said, rubbing his tired eyes.

"I told you," said Fulton, his eyes glued to the screen. "This stuff's mind blowing."

"Something like that," said Tate.

Fulton continued to read the endless posts, writing notes and intermittently blurting out, "I knew it."

"How do you make sense of this?" asked Tate.

"I know my way around here."

"That's probably the most disturbing thing you've ever said," smirked Tate.

Fulton mumbled in response, lost in the parade of human mental disorders on display.

Tate closed his eyes against the growing throb of a headache and fell asleep.

Out of the comforting darkness he felt himself being roused. Stretching, he rubbed the grit from his eyes.

"Yeah, I'm up," he said. "What is it?"

"I got him," said Fulton, triumphant.

"Yeah, okay," said Tate. "Are you sure this time?"

"A connection to Terry," said Fulton, sitting back down in front of the computer.

He waved Tate over and pointed to the screen.

With a groan, Tate rolled off the lumpy couch and stood behind Fulton, looking over his shoulder. The glare of the screen assaulted Tate's eyes and he squinted to filter out some of the light.

"You're going to wreck your eyes," he said. "How much time do you spend reading this stuff?"

"Tuesday," said Fulton, distractedly. "Here he is."

Fulton clicked on a posted message. The screen changed, filled with a seemingly endless manifesto, punctuated with strings of all caps.

"This guy, Sword of Gabriel," said Fulton, "says he knows Terry. Lots of people come on here saying that and get flamed."

"Flamed?" asked Tate.

"Yeah, you know," said Fulton, shrugging. "Jumped on. Beaten up. Trolled. This guy was showing off, saying he knows Terry. Most people get run out of the community and never come back. Total losers. But Sword's not backing down."

Tate started reading the post. It was clear Sword was on the losing side of the mob attack he'd kicked off. There was a lot of pressure by the rest of the forum to prove his claim or forever be branded as a heretic.

It all sounded like a sad attempt to garner prestige, but the next sentence changed Tate's opinion.

"You bums feed off Terry," wrote Sword. "I'm the only one that feeds him."

Tate had years of experience surveilling messages, communication, and chatter between bad guys. Even in those groups there was always someone who wanted to sound more important than they were and made claims to be connected to someone in power.

Sometimes the person bragging was telling the truth but trying to walk a fine line between saying too much and too little. Most of the time, ego overrode good judgement and revealed too much.

To the masses of this conspiracy group, Sword was just another loudmouth.

To Tate, he was the link to Terry they were looking for. He had just admitted to being Terry's grocery supplier.

"We need to find that guy," he said.

"How?" asked Fulton. "Nobody uses their real name. Everyone goes though underground servers that mask their information."

"Masks can be removed," said Tate. "We're going to need someone with the right tech to get this information."

"Are you talking about Nathan?" asked Fulton.

"Yes," said Tate. "He's not going to like this."

"I'm insulted," said Nathan, his irritation clear over the phone.

"You're the only one I know who can do it," said Tate.

There were only two people who had the resources to track down Sword. Kaiden would have to go through someone else, and Tate wasn't keen on having to explain she was going through all this work over a conspiracy guy.

She'd have to call in a favor or involve someone in her intelligence ring. Each step up the ladder would be another barrier of resistance she'd have to convince to her side.

Nathan was a well-placed tech mercenary, highly skilled with an overkill of resources for this particular work, and better still, he could do it without involving anyone. The one advantage Tate had going for him was that he'd saved Nathan's life. He wasn't going to wave that in Nathan's face; it wasn't the sort of thing someone could forget.

Sooner or later, Nathan would get fed up and tell Tate he had cashed that chip one time too many. Tate could accept that the time was coming, but he wouldn't let it be now.

"I know this isn't up to your level," he said.

"My level?" said Nathan. "I infiltrate polymorphic security arrays in my sleep and you want me to find someone's IP address. Want to see me use a light switch too?"

"If it's that easy," said Tate, "then you could of had it done in the time we were talking, or is it harder than you thought?"

"Louis Shoemaker," said Nathan, as Tate scrambled for a pen and paper.

"Twelve, seventy-five, Mercer street," said Nathan flatly.

"Hang on," said Tate. "Can you repeat that?"

"Now I'm dictating? Never mind. I'll send you the information."

The line clicked dead in the middle of Tate saying thank you.

He considered his next step. If Shoemaker lived far away, it wasn't like he could hop in a car and take a road trip on a whim.

The sat phone chipped and the display lit up with Nathan's message. Tate's eyebrows rose as he read the address.

"Where is he?" asked Fulton.

"Looks like we're going on a road trip," smiled Tate, showing Fulton the message.

"Panama City?" said Fulton. "Revolution Terry's that close?"

"Don't get ahead of yourself," said Tate. "Shoemaker lives there. It's a good bet that he's no more than a few hours away from Terry. Groceries are perishable.

"Maybe he's got a refrigeration truck," said Fulton.

Tate frowned, considering that as a possible wrinkle.

"Either way," he said. "We find Shoemaker, we'll find Terry."

10

ROAD TRIP

"This is so cool," said Fulton, vacillating between excitement and worry. "What if we get caught?"

Tate had told Fulton to wait until that night. When they left their quarters, they'd carefully but easily navigated the patrolling MP's to the abandoned shed where Tate revealed the tunnel leading out of the base.

"We're going AWOL?" said Fulton. "We can't do that, can we?"

Tate smiled as they uncovered the Clearview SUV. Discovering the drug smugglers operation was paying off in ways he hadn't expected.

"We're the Grave Diggers," chuckled Tate. "We make our own rules."

It was chest beating bravado, even by Tate's standards, but he knew humor would ease Fulton's reservations more than trying to explain the truth.

The truth was Fulton was absolutely right. They were officially AWOL and could be court-martialed, possibly sent to prison for desertion. Something Tate was convinced the new base commander would make happen.

That guy was on a serious power trip and clearly took pleasure in exercising his authority. In Wades world, everyone was his inferior.

Admittedly, leaving the base was a gamble, but Tate told himself there was more than enough things dysfunctional about Fort Hickok to keep the base commander busy.

———————

It wasn't long before they connected to the Pan American highway and the road opened before them. He pressed the accelerator and the SUV sped up with no effort.

Tate thought it was a shame they had to make the trip at night. The highway traveled through some of the most richly forested and dramatic landscapes he'd ever seen.

A few miles later, the edge of his headlights revealed the sides of the highway were bordered by a wall of jumbled scrap and he realized it was a barricade to keep the Vix wandering onto the road.

He shook his head for not thinking about that. Fort Hickok was established to stop the masses of Vix from traveling north from South America. Some of them still got through, but nobody wanted to admit it. Maybe it was wishful thinking on Tate's part that he didn't have to worry about Vix in this region.

Other than a couple of freight trucks, they hadn't seen any other cars. He switched on his high beams and eased off the accelerator.

The highway went on for a hundred and eighty miles, and if there were gaps in the barrier there could be Vix on the road.

Smashing into one of them wouldn't be healthy for their car. Hitting a pack of them would be a disaster. They'd likely survive the impact, but then they'd be stranded in the middle of nowhere, at night, in wild country. It was not an image Tate wanted to see play out.

Fulton had been happy to listen to his radio over his earbuds; a recent acquisition he was still reveling in.

He mumbled and took out his earbuds.

"I can't get a signal out here," he said disappointedly and turned off the radio.

"It'll probably be that way for the next couple of hours," said Tate. "Sorry to be the bearer of bad news."

Fulton tried to entertain himself by looking out the window, but in the moonless night, all he could see were featureless shadows of the distant hills above the barrier.

"This reminds me of when my dad used to drive from our farm to the stock auctions," he said. "We'd have to leave in the middle of the night to get there early, before the good animals were already spoken for."

"You worked on a farm?"

"For a while," he shrugged. "I couldn't get into it. My dad told me that the farm had passed through all these generations and I should be proud to be part of that history. I knew he was disappointed that I didn't want to carry on the family legacy. I mean, yeah, I did, but farming?"

"Dads," said Tate. "They're the same wherever you go. They've already figured out what their kid's going to do with their lives before they've started walking."

"Right?" agreed Fulton.

"Their dad's dad did the same thing," said Tate. "And on and on since the beginning of time."

"I promised myself if I had a son, I wouldn't do that to him," said Fulton.

"Every son ever born makes that promise," chuckled Tate. "Then they grow up, experience life and when they have a son realize the world is full of pitfalls. Then they plot out their son's life, so they'll be safe and happy."

"Don't make the same mistakes I did," said Fulton in his dad-voice.

"Have no fear," said Tate. "There's a whole world of mistakes still left to choose from."

They both laughed over that one.

"What kind of mistakes did you make?" asked Fulton.

It was a complicated question for anyone who had lived a normal life. Tate's life couldn't have been more distant from normal.

Things like locking your keys in the car or spilling your coffee didn't even register in Tate's world. He'd lived in a life of frenetic combat, life and death decisions. He'd killed people and watched the life disappear from his friend's eyes.

He'd overheard someone at a party talking about getting a bad haircut. 'Worst day ever.' Everyone had stared at him when he laughed out loud.

"Sorry," said Fulton, seeing Tate's expression in the glow of the dashboard. "That was a dumb question."

"No, it's fine," he said, shaking off the memory. "Worst mistake. Hmmmm, I'd say ignoring my gut. I wouldn't trust my instincts because I didn't believe in myself. I always thought the other guy was smarter, more experienced than I was. The truth was they felt the same way I did."

"I feel like that all the time," said Fulton.

"You're a kid," said Tate. "Everyone knows more than you do."

Fulton looked at him, wounded until he saw the mischievous grin on Tate's face.

"You changed a lot, Top," said Fulton. "When I first met you, you were... different."

"Remember asking me about mistakes?" said Tate. "I was carrying a lot of baggage from one."

"I guess you let go of that," said Fulton.

"Yes," said Tate. "Looking back at it, it's surprising how hard it is to let go of something that does so much damage."

"How do you do it?" asked Fulton. "I mean, even when you know it's no good for you, but you still hang on to it. How do you let go of it?"

"That depends on how long it takes to come to forgive ourselves for being imperfect," said Tate. "Something bad happens. Maybe something we had nothing to do with, but you'll find a way to blame yourself. 'If only I did this or didn't do that'. It's a trap that'll drag you down."

He sighed, noticing he was gripping the steering wheel. He flexed the stiffness from his fingers. "I didn't learn to let go until I hit rock bottom."

"No offense, Top," said Fulton, "but I hope I never screw up that badly."

Tate's laughter rolled through the car, infecting Fulton and making him smile.

"Me, too," said Tate. "Look at it this way, failure is a bruise, not a tattoo."

"Yeah," said Fulton. "I'll remember that."

They drove for a while in silence and he realized that Fulton had cleverly steered the conversation away from his own story. There was a lot Tate didn't know about the people on his team. This seemed like as good a time as any to learn about Fulton.

"What made you leave the farm?" he asked.

Fulton paused, looking thoughtfully out at the black nothingness.

Tate felt like he'd touched a nerve but didn't say anything. Fulton was an adult, he thought. It's his decision if he wants to answer or not.

"I didn't like it there," said Fulton.

It sounded like that was all he was going to say and Tate was fine to let it go, but then Fulton continued.

"We lived outside of town, you know, farms," said Fulton. "When the Vix came, everyone learned fast that the only way we'd all survive was to fight together. Kind of like our volunteer fire brigade. If Vix showed up at someone's farm, they'd sound an alarm and the whole town would get their guns and drive out there."

"You were all spread out," said Tate. "Walling off the town's one thing, but everyone's farm?"

"There wasn't enough siding or trees to cover all the acres of farm to do that," said Fulton. "We tried ditches."

"That makes sense," said Tate. "With nothing else, it sounds like the only option."

"It worked sometimes, but not always." There was a note of sadness to Fulton's voice that hinted at a tragic story. "Little by little the town was losing. We could kill a lot of Vix, but..." He paused as the memories surged in. "Sooner or later, more would show up. Every time we lost a family, we all got a little weaker. If you ever saw blight kill off a field of crops, it was like that. Most people, they kept saying we could beat them. It was our lands and we made it through worse things."

Fulton's hands were squeezing his legs. "But see, I knew they were wrong. I tried telling them, but nobody listened. I don't know why they couldn't see it. We could have saved so many people if they…"

His words trailed off and he shook his head.

"People want to believe in things," said Tate. "It gives them hope."

"My dad didn't want to hear what I said. He had hope. That changed when he had to shoot his brother."

"I'm sorry," said Tate. "The Vix got him?"

"No," said Fulton. "My uncle was stealing our food. We didn't know who was doing it for a long time, but we were running out pretty quick. My uncle was selling it. Dad saw someone in our barn, but it was dark and he didn't know who it was. Not until after he shot him. I guess Dad didn't have much hope after that. We packed up and left the same night."

There was nothing Tate could say. The outbreak had been like an acid bath, stripping away civility and revealing the darker side of people.

Not all of them. Sure, some had sunk to terrible lows, but others embraced selflessness, rallying people to work together for the greeting good.

"We drove all night," said Fulton. "Kind of like this. But back then you'd see a small light from someone's home, way off in the distance. I'd think, there's someone who's staying put, but only because they haven't lost enough yet."

Tate could see the experience had aged a part of Fulton. Like so many people, the Vix had torn away his innocence too young in life.

"But then I joined up with the army and met you guys," he said, his mood brightening.

"I'll bet joining up wasn't what you expected," said Tate.

"It was better," said Futon. "We don't lose people."

"Yeah," said Tate, forcing himself to smile.

Now it was his turn for his words to falter. He'd lost people before. What the Grave Diggers did was dangerous. They'd come this far with only a few scratches, but he knew in his heart that it was only a matter of time before their luck ran out.

This team of misfits had bonded into family, but death didn't care about bonds, or age, or the power of hope.

The conversation dwindled out and Fulton fell asleep for the rest of the drive.

Dawn broke over the horizon as they neared the edge of Panama City, revealing the makeshift defenses that bordered the city.

Sheets of plywood, tin siding, and anything else that would act as a barrier had been constructed in a patchwork wall that shouldered the highway leading into the city.

The early light backlit small figures patrolling the top of the wall and Tate was surprised at how many people were up there.

He rightly guessed there was a checkpoint at the entrance of the city from the string of cars stopped ahead of him.

Fulton woke up as they came to a stop and looked around with bleary eyes.

"What's going on?" he asked.

"They want to know that the people coming in aren't sick or a danger," guessed Tate.

"Yeah, but what about the rest of us?" said Fulton, feeling exposed. "We're just sitting here. What if a swarm of Vix showed up?"

"There could be one or two wandering around," said Tate, "but you're not going to see swarms around here. That's what Fort Hickok is for. We're the stopper in the bottle. We keep the swarms from moving north."

"Oh," said Fulton. "Yeah."

He looked calmer until he remembered it wasn't that long ago they'd been in Texas and ran into hundreds of Vix. His face paled at the memory and he looked at the glass windows surrounding him with shrinking confidence.

"Texas?" grinned Tate.

"Yeah."

It was their turn at the checkpoint. A sturdy barrier blocked their way and a knot of armed people moved to both sides of the car.

Tate rolled down his window as a guard walked up to the driver side door.

"Hi," said Tate, with his best 'I come in peace' smile.

The guard was unimpressed and studied Tate's face.

"Lean forward," he stated flatly.

Tate leaned towards the guard who pointed a light into his eyes. The scanner beeped and the guard glanced at the readings indifferently.

Satisfied, the guard walked around to Fulton, who rolled down his window.

The guard grunted and waved Fulton closer, then pointed the light in his eyes. Instead of the beep, the scanner gave a shrill chirp. It was not a good sound.

Fulton intuitively knew whatever test he'd just been given, he'd failed.

"What's that mean?" he asked. "There's nothing wrong with..."

The guard's surly air of boredom never changed as he smacked the scanner with the side of his hand.

The chirping stopped and he pointed the light in Fulton's eyes again.

The scanner beeped and the guard stuffed it back into his pocket. He walked away, nodding. Others shoved the barrier out of the way and the guard waved them through.

"Welcome to Panama City," chuckled Tate.

"I thought they were gonna arrest me," said Fulton.

"Don't be silly," said Tate. "They would've shot you."

Fulton paled and looked over his shoulder as the guards shuffled the barrier back into place.

There was never a middle ground when it came to how the Vix outbreak effected cities. For some, everything changed. Everyone was edgy, impatient, wrapped in their own bubble. You didn't have to see it to feel the shift in the atmosphere.

Other cities went on as if the Vix never happened. Once you were passed the walls, the general mood of Panama City was just like that. People waved and there were smiling faces everywhere you looked.

The warm disk of the sun had just cleared the ocean's edge and the sky was taking on a brilliant blue. Sunlight winked off the stunning, glass high-rises that lined the beaches.

The city was waking up and the smell of food wafted through the SUV's windows.

"Do you smell that?" said Fulton, feeling his stomach grumble.

Tate nodded as his appetite began to demand attention.

Street vendors and small open-air shops were already in full production to feed the morning migration of people on their way to work.

The smells were too good to pass up and Tate turned off the highway at the first off-ramp he came to.

"You don't have to twist my arm," he said as Fulton smiled at him.

As soon as they left the broad open highway, they entered another world. People, cyclists, scooters and carts clogged the narrow streets.

"I think we're swimming against the tide," said Tate.

Fulton was one step ahead and pointed to a dirt spot they could park the car.

Neither of them complained about the walk as they got out and stretched their legs.

Fulton homed in on the first breakfast cart and fished into his pocket for money.

Tate hung back and checked out what the other vendors were selling. Fulton changed his mind and followed Tate's example.

The smell of Columbian coffee, sizzling ham and baked bread was intoxicating.

They stopped where three carts had formed together, each making part of a breakfast.

Fulton was grinning and pointing at what he wanted. His enthusiasm was infectious and the woman grilling sausages chuckled as she handed him a flimsy paper plate with the savory links.

He started to leave and she called him back, adding an extra two sausages to his plate.

"Thank you," gushed Fulton.

The woman said something in Spanish and he looked at Tate quizzically.

"She said you're too skinny. You need fattening up."

Fulton took a sausage off his plate and popped the whole thing in his mouth.

The woman elbowed her friend and they both cackled as Fulton chewed with wistful bliss.

"Come on," said Tate, "before they adopt you."

"You say that like it's a bad thing," mumbled Fulton around the wad of food in his mouth.

With full plates, they looked for a quiet place to eat without being jostled by the flow of people.

They tucked themselves against a wall, between a stack of weathered pallets and an old pickup truck.

Tate inhaled the earthy aroma of his coffee before taking a sip.

"I don't know what the rest of the city is like," said Fulton, "and I don't care. I'm never leaving this place."

Tate chuckled as he spread a generous slab of butter on a wedge of hot bread.

"What about being AWOL?" he said.

"What?" grinned Fulton. "I can't hear you over the sound of this awesome tortilla"

"Every man has his price," chuckled Tate.

Both stopped talking and dug into their breakfast with relish.

It wasn't long before Tate had cleaned his plate. He lingered over his coffee, lost in his own world as his senses enjoyed the aroma.

He marveled at the sight of so many people, all going about normal lives. In contrast his life was bland army green, hot, unwelcoming jungle and horrific ghouls trying to kill you.

The only thing on the minds of the people here were the day's responsibilities and demands of the clock.

This jumble and chaos had a renewing effect on Tate. Not everything was rot and blood and death. He speculated there were probably places like this all over the world. Regular lives being lived.

They watched the stream of people from their pocket of calm, feeling a restored connection to the human race.

Fulton burped loudly, bringing Tate out of his thoughts.

"Gimmie," said Fulton, holding out his hand. "I'll throw these away."

Tate handed him his plate and Fulton waded into the throng of people and disappeared.

Peering at the remains of his coffee, Tate swirled the contents and took the last drink.

"I'm ready," said Fulton, appearing out of the crowd.

"Same here," said Tate. "Let's see what Shoemaker has to tell us."

Returning to the highway took several minutes, a lot of turns down side streets and a little patience, but the good cheer of their breakfast made the time go quickly.

After the stop and go of the surface streets, the open highway felt like a playground for speed.

Whatever Tate asked of the SUV's motor, it gave with more to spare. They both felt a tinge of regret as the off-ramp for Shoemaker's street came into view.

"I bet you this guy's a typical troll," said Fulton.

"Is that like the creature that lives under a bridge?" asked Tate.

"Kind of," said Fulton. "Except this kind of troll lives in his mom's basement and spends his life on the internet."

"That must make mom proud," said Tate.

"Not really," chuckled Fulton. "How do you think he ended up in the basement?"

"Here we are," said Tate, pulling to a stop.

It was a startling contrast to the neighborhood where they'd stopped for breakfast.

The house sat, unremarkable, among a row of unremarkable houses. The street was empty of people. The only sound was the barking of a dog.

A chain-link fence ran around the patchy, brown and green yard.

The driveway gate was open and they walked up the lumpy asphalt drive to the front door.

"You're up," said Tate.

Fulton pressed the doorbell, but they didn't hear anything. He shrugged his shoulders, not knowing if it was broken or rang in a distant part of the house.

Nothing happened.

Fulton looked at Tate for direction.

"Afraid you'll make his mom angry?" teased Tate.

If it was possible for a knock to sound apologetic, Fulton succeeded.

"Moms can be scary," he said.

They heard a shuffle on the other side, but nothing happened for a moment.

"Hello," said Tate, letting the person on the other side know he'd heard them.

Locks clacked as they were unlatched. The door squeaked and a pair of watery grey eyes critically examined them.

"Yes?" she said with guarded politeness.

"We're here to see Louis," said Fulton.

"Does he owe you money?" she asked.

"No, ma'am," said Fulton. "We want to ask him about Revolution Terry."

"Well, hell," said the woman in disgust. She walked out of sight, leaving the door open.

Tate and Fulton shared a look of confusion.

11

GATE KEEPER

"Do we go in?" said Fulton.

"The door's open," said Tate.

Fulton tentatively opened the door a bit more and leaned in. The entryway lead down a short distance and he saw the woman had returned to the living room where she was watching an old movie.

He shrugged and walked inside with Tate following him.

Pictures of people smiled at them from photographs on the wall as they walked into the living room.

"Down the hall," said the woman over her shoulder. "It's the door with the stupid picture on it."

"Uh, thank you, ma'am," said Fulton.

He pointed at the only hallway they could see and invited him to lead the way. Without another option, they headed down the hall.

They stopped at the third door where a poster of Rambo glared down on them. Under his smoking M60 machine gun was a red sign with bold white lettering, 'Enemies of the state will be shot'.

Tate looked up and saw a camera looking down on them.

"Paranoid much?" he said.

"What do we do?" asked Fulton. "Knock? Go in?"

"This is my first troll," said Tate. "Go with your gut."

Fulton shrugged and raised his hand to knock.

"Who are you?" growled a deep voice.

Both of them looked at the keypad next to the door, where the voice came from.

"Hi," said Fulton. "We're, uh..."

"We're fans of Revolution Terry," said Tate.

"Yeah," said Fulton. "We're part of the community and..."

"So what?" said the voice. "Who are you?"

"We want to meet him," said Tate.

"Leave," said the voice.

"Hey, Louis," began Tate.

"Sword of Gabriel!" boomed the speaker.

"Knock it off down there," yelled the mother from the living room.

"I don't know you," hissed Louis. "You don't have a legal right to be in my house."

"It ain't your house," yelled the woman. "Not until I'm dead."

"She's definitely his mom," smirked Tate.

"Your mom let us in," he said. "That makes it legal."

"This is your last warning," said the voice. "You don't want to mess with me. I know a lot of people. We have eyes and ears everywhere. You mess with one of us, you mess with all of us."

"We just want to talk to you," said Fulton.

Tate tried the door and wasn't surprised to find it was locked.

"You're wasting your time," said the voice. "That door is steel reinforced and bullet proof."

"Just a minute," said Tate, leaving Fulton at the door.

He walked back into the living room and laid several bills next to her on the side table.

"For your trouble," he said.

She only nodded, her eyes never leaving the television.

"I've already uploaded your faces to my associates," railed Louis. "You'll never..."

Tate leaned back and kicked in the door.

Louis yelped and the speaker switched off.

A short flight of stairs led down, opening into the basement.

"How about that," said Tate. "You were right."

He led the way down the stairs into a wide room. One wall was completely bare and used to project a computer screen on it. The other walls were a cluttered mix of action hero posters, newspaper clippings, costumes, packaged toys and stacks of books.

"It's like nerd heaven," said Fulton in wonder.

"Hey, Shoemaker," said Tate, looking for the missing occupant. "We just want to talk about..."

Louis appeared from behind the overstuffed couch with a strange looking gun, aimed at Tate.

In a fluid blur of motion, Tate pulled out his Colt .45 and leveled the sights on Louis.

"Crap," said Louis, dropping his gun. "Is that real?"

His gun clattered to the floor, pieces of it breaking off.

"Aw, damn it," he said. "That was a limited edition."

"A toy gun?" said Tate, scowling down the big barrel of his Colt. "Are you stupid?"

"I panicked," said Louis, looking miserable.

Calming down, Tate sighed and holstered his gun, disappearing from sight.

"Sit down," he said, not leaving room for debate.

Louis quickly came around the couch and took a seat.

Tate and Fulton crossed the room and Louis shied away.

"Calm down," said Tate, reaching out to show his hands were empty.

"Deep state. Deep state!" blurted Louis.

Tate looked at Fulton, exasperated.

"We saw your post about Revolution Terry," said Fulton.

"Yeah, so?" said Louis, eyeing him suspiciously.

"We believe you," said Fulton.

"Yeah?"

"Most of the people on the community are wannabes," said Fulton. "We knew you're legit."

Louis tentatively straightened, reevaluating the two strangers. "Most of those posers don't know jack."

"But you do," said Tate, causing Louis to flinch.

"We want to talk to him," said Fulton. "We have information, but it's only for him. We can't trust it to anyone else."

"He trusts me," said Louis. "I'll give it to him."

"We need to give it to him in person," said Tate. "Where is he?"

"You can't make me talk against my will," said Louis, looking nervously between Tate and Fulton. "I have my rights."

Tate stood to pace the room and let Fulton take over.

"Deep state! Deep state!" yelped Louis.

Tate put his head in his hand and walked away.

"We're not one of them," said Fulton, hoping to calm Louis down.

"I'm an American citizen," said Louis. "You're violating my constitutional rights. I have the right to remain silent."

"We just want to know about Terry," said Fulton.

Louis glared at them in a transparent show of strength, but his watering eyes and trembling hands told another story.

Tate sighed, walking back to the couch and leaned in close to Louis.

"You're going to tell me what I want to know," he said, "or I swear..."

"Revolution Terry lives on an oil rig, eighty miles due west off the coast," blurted Louis. "I deliver supplies to him every two weeks. He likes apples. Not the mushy red ones, but the hard, green ones."

Tate leaned back, nodding to Fulton to take over.

"Okay, that's helpful," said Fulton. "Thanks. We need you to take us to him."

"I can't do that," said Louis. "He made me promise I'd never reveal his location. He'll never talk to me again."

"We can pay you," said Fulton.

It was like someone had thrown a switch in Louis's attitude. The panic and fear vanished.

"How much?" he asked.

"Enough," answered Tate.

Louis considered Tate for a moment, thinking over the offer.

"Okay," he said decidedly. "But I don't go for another three days."

Tate glanced at his watch then back at Louis.

"We'll go tonight."

"What? No," said Louis with sudden alarm. "If I show up early, he'll know something's up. The man knows everything."

"He's going to figure out something's up when we're standing in front of him," said Tate. "A few minutes won't make a difference."

Doubt and suspicion clouded over Louis's face as a new thought came to him.

"Wait a minute," he said, renewed suspicion in his eyes. "How do I know you're not hit men, hired to kill Terry?"

"Seriously?" said Tate with a lopsided grin.

"And when you say you're going to pay me, you shoot me and dump me in the water?" said Louis working himself into a panic.

"Come on," said Tate dismissively. "Can we get back to reality?"

"Honestly," said Louis, nearly pleading. "I wouldn't tell anyone about you. I can keep a secret."

"Like not knowing where Terry is?" chuckled Tate.

Louis sprang to his feet and started pacing the room, mumbling to himself with worry.

"I'm a dead man," he repeated to himself, nearly in tears.

"This is hopeless," said Tate, exasperated.

"We're the good guys," said Fulton. "We're..."

Tate glanced at him with a stern expression, guessing where Fulton was going with this, but then softened his stare and nodded agreement.

"We're the Grave Diggers," said Fulton.

Louis stopped as if he'd been slapped and his mouth fell open in utter surprise.

"Shut up," said Louis. "You guys?"

He glanced around the room as if he expected to see someone listening in on him.

"The Grave Diggers?" he whispered excitedly. "Here in my lair?"

"A lair?" scoffed Tate.

"This is amazing," said Louis. "Hey, can I get a picture with you guys? The community's going to lose their minds when I tell them..."

"Hey!" snapped Tate. "There's not going to be any pictures, and you don't breathe one word about us."

Louis recoiled, getting a hold of himself, but still tingling with excitement.

"Right. Yeah, of course," he agreed. "Not a word."

His ability to keep a secret didn't inspire Tate's confidence.

"I want you to take a reality check," said Tate. "Our anonymity is worth killing for."

"Oh yeah, sure," said Louis, his head nodding in agreement.

"And we know where you live," said Tate.

"Right," said Louis.

Tate held him in his humorless stare until understanding dawned on Louis.

His head continued to nod but slowed as he connected the dots of Tate's implication.

"Not a word," said Louis. "I'll take it to my grave."

"We can agree on that," said Tate.

"Okay," said Fulton, hoping to get the situation back on track. "I'm guessing you have a boat to get us to Terry."

"Yeah," said Louis, happy to look away from Tate's discomforting smile.

"Keys. Keys," he said, patting his pockets as he looked around the room.

"There they are," he said, crossing the room and brushing away the clutter to reach them. "It gets cold out there. If you need a sweater, you can borrow a couple of mine."

"We're good," said Tate.

Louis finished collecting what he needed, until he stood in front of them.

"Yeah, done," he said. "Oh. Can you guys drive? My car's, you know, in the shop."

"Sure," said Tate.

"And maybe some lunch?"

"We can do that," said Fulton. "Right?"

Tate rolled his eyes.

Louis gave Tate directions, guiding him to a dirt parking lot near the shore. Dingy boats bobbed in the water, tied to a row of weather-stained docks.

Louis unlocked the rusted gate and held it open for Tate and Fulton to pass through. Locking it behind him, he shuffled past the two and led them to his boat.

During the drive, Tate had imagined having to cross eighty miles of open sea in whatever rust bucket Louis ferried his groceries in. He was weighting the option of renting anything more seaworthy when Louis stopped in front of a clean, sleek cabin cruiser.

Sunlight bounced off the polished chrome and immaculate gloss white hull.

"Uh," began Tate, at a loss for words, "that works."

"Something isn't it?" said Louis proudly. "It's not mine," he quickly added. "It's Terry's."

"Oh," said Tate, feeling the world was making sense again.

The cruiser gently moved with the swell of the water and Louis paused at the side of the boat, timing the movement between the dock and the boat.

Fulton and Tate followed easily behind.

Louis made his way to the boat's console and switched on the power.

"Fuel. Oil. Fresh water," he said, checking the gauges. "Looks good."

He pressed a switch and the engines rumbled to life. Louis waited for the engines to warm up and they settled into a thrumming purr.

"Hey, can you do that rope thing?" he said, waving to the mooring line.

"Cast off?" said Fulton.

"Yeah, that," said Louis.

Fulton made his way to the bow of the boat and untied the cleat as Tate stepped next to Louis.

"You got this okay?" asked Tate, feeling a twinge of doubt about Louis's piloting skills.

"Oh sure," said Louis. "I do this all the time."

Fulton gave a thumbs up and Tate steadied himself against the console, expecting the boat to lurch into the dock. He watched in mild surprise as Louis smoothly throttled up the engine and steered the boat away from the dock with ease.

It didn't matter how well Tate thought he could read people, they always surprised him.

Louis competently navigated the boat with an almost causal confidence. He was a different person behind the wheel of a boat.

They cleared the small, artificial cove, leaving the dock behind. The skyline of the city began to dull in the haze of distance.

Slivers of light reflected off the water in a hypnotically rhythmic motion and Tate yawned, thinking he might go below for a nap.

"Everyone down," said Louis, as he cut the boat's engine and squatted down behind the console.

"What's going on?" asked Tate, feeling a surge of adrenaline.

Louis pointed to the starboard from under the console. In the distance they saw a white boat with a broad red stripe on its hull.

"They're looking for Vix," he said. "They make sure none of those things wash up on shore."

"Vix float?" asked Fulton.

"Just the gassy ones," said Louis.

"Why are we hiding?" asked Tate.

"I dunno," said Louis. "Just seemed like the thing to do. You know, stealth."

Tate pressed his lips in exasperation and stood up. "You know they can see our boat, right?"

"It's not the boat," said Louis, pointing to his face. "Facial recognition."

They drifted for a few minutes until the patrol boat turned away and headed off. Satisfied the coast was clear, Louis emerged from his hiding spot and started up the engines.

The late afternoon sun was tinted with orange and Louis announced they were getting close.

Tate and Fulton looked towards the flat edge of the horizon and in the distance saw a tall, thin blur standing on the water.

"That's it," said Louis.

As they approached, the blur became more defined, growing in size until they were at its base and the enormous oil rig towered over them.

Fulton gaped in disbelief, craning his neck to look up at the platform a hundred feet above. Seagulls wheeled overhead and peered down at the new intruders from their nests.

"How can something this big float?"

"Hard to believe," said Tate. "Hey, Louis, stop here."

Whoever was on the rig had a bird's eye view for miles in every direction. They would have spotted the bright white of the boat on the blue water long ago.

Tate knew their presence did not come as a surprise. He stepped out from behind the console, certain someone up there was watching them. He hoped that by putting himself on full display they'd understand that he wasn't a threat.

Louis nodded and dropped the engines to a murmuring idle.

"We're here to talk to Terry," yelled Tate through cupped hands.

The boat bobbed in the low chop of the ocean as they waited for a reply, but none came. There was only the hiss and sigh of the water rising and falling against the giant pylons supporting the rig's platform.

"Do you think they know we're here?" asked Fulton.

"They know," said Tate. "See that ladder?" He pointed to a set of rungs that traveled up one of the pylons.

Louis nodded and Tate directed him to bring the boat closer to them.

As they neared it, the rise and fall of the pylons was much more dramatic. The column plunged deep into the water then rose high above their heads, water and froth cascading off like a waterfall.

"We're not climbing that," said Fulton, with growing concern.

"Yes," said Tate. "We are."

"You guys are crazy," grinned Louis in admiration.

"Make sure you secure everything you don't want to lose," said Tate to Fulton. "We might get a little wet."

They inched closer to the ladder. Metal bands formed a safety cage that incased the length of the ladder.

At the bottom of the ladder was a sturdy grate locked in place and blocking access to the ladder.

"What now?" said Fulton.

"We'll have to use the cage," said Tate, liking the situation less and less.

"What do you want me to do?" asked Louis.

"Do you have a key to that lock?" asked Tate.

"No," said Louis.

"Stick around until we're finished," said Tate. "We'll need a ride back."

Louis looked around. Besides the massive pylons, there was only miles and miles of open water. "Uh, I guess."

"Or you can come with us," grinned Tate.

Louis laughed nervously and waved off the invitation.

Tate guided Louis closer to the pylon as it plummeted and the deck of the boat rocked in the churning water.

"The trick is to wait until it's just starting to rise out of the water," said Tate, wiping his hands on his pants. "Then get on and climb. Very fast."

Fulton paled green as his mind flooded with all the reasons this was a bad idea.

"That's got to be going thirty feet down," said Fulton.

"Forty," said Louis.

"I said you might get wet," said Tate, as he swung his legs over the boat's chrome railing. "If you go under, hang on and hold your breath."

Fulton's mouth was dry as dust. He'd never been this close to something so big, moving so much, so fast.

"You've done this before," said Fulton. "Right?"

"First time," said Tate and jumped.

12

STEEL CASTLE

He'd been tracking one of the cage's crossbars. It was bent with chipped paint, making it easy to find as the came out of the water. His feet had barely left the boat when he realized he had badly misjudged how fast the pylon was moving. He was in the air and the crossbar was already out of reach.

This is going to hurt.

Tate pulled his knees up, adjusting to land on a different crossbar which was rapidly zooming up to meet him.

He dropped his hands to catch the crossbar and smacked into the cage. The crossbar slammed into his open hands and he gripped it for all he was worth.

The crossbar flew upwards, moving faster than Tate who peddled his feet in the air, trying to plant them on the safety cage before his arms were dislocated.

He snagged a crossbar with the tip of his boot but slipped off. With a grunt of effort, he hooked the crossbar with the tread of his other boot.

The next instant his arms were yanked upwards with breathtaking force. Explosions of pain went off in every joint of his arms and shoulders. As he squeezed his eyes closed, clenching his jaw against the pain it suddenly all stopped.

Tate opened his eyes in confusion as he felt a sensation of weightlessness. His eyes went wide in sudden realization.

The pylon had reached its high point and was starting its plunge into the white froth of the ocean below.

Now he realized the full danger if he should ride the pylon underwater. The force of the rising pylon had nearly wrenched his grip loose. With the added weight of the water, he wouldn't be able to hold on. If he got tangled in the cage he would drown.

What was supposed to be a simple jump and climb had become a battle of survival. Tate almost laughed at the ridiculousness of it.

His beaten body protested as he scrambled up the cage in a burst of speed. The cage fell away, making him feel like he was staying in one place.

Breathing hard, knuckles and shins banged against the dropping cage. Tate slowed as his energy drained, bringing him closer and closer to the water.

The pylon slowed then stopped, his boots only inches above the water. Relief flooded through him as it began its rise again. Once again, the fates had forgiven his stupidity and allowed him to live.

He saw a streak of white as a seagull flew past; its cawing sounded like it was laughing at him.

He looked across at Fulton whose face was a pale mask of dread and knew it would be reckless to expect the kid to attempt the same harebrained maneuver.

"You guys are freaking awesome!" shouted Louis.

"Get a rope," called Tate as he rode the pylon upwards.

"There's one under the passenger seat," said Louis.

Fulton lifted the seat cushions and took out a coil of rope. He made his unsteady way across the bobbing deck, back to the railing.

"When I reach the water," called Tate, "throw me the end of the rope."

Fulton waited as Tate rode the pylon down and tossed the end to him.

"Let the rope run out," said Tate, catching the rope as he began his ride up.

He began climbing up, keeping the rope gripped in his hand. He pushed away his aches, but a new sensation was rising to the top. He was getting seasick.

An ironic smile spread across his face as he wondered how awesome Louis would think of him when he threw up.

Tate kept his eyes focused fixed on the cage, forcing himself to breathe deep and slow. The rising queasiness thankfully subsided.

At the top of the ladder, he tied off the rope with a secure knot. Testing his weight on it, he nodded, satisfied it would hold Fulton.

"When the pylon stops going down," called Tate from high above, "grab the rope, high up, and get your feet planted on the cage. Understand?"

Fulton paused, thinking through the body mechanics. "Yeah, got it."

Tate really hoped he did, because if Fulton got it wrong and fell into the water, things were going to get real ugly real fast. Tate would go after the kid, there was no question in his mind about that, but he also knew this could end with both of them dead.

Tate watched, suppressing the urge to coach Fulton's every move. Times like this, the best help was to shut up.

As the huge pylon drove into the sea, Fulton climbed over the boat's railing and tensed, ready to grab the rope.

The pylon reached its limit and paused. Fulton grabbed the rope, stepped off the boat and onto the cage. He'd gone from the boat to the cage in one easy step. The pylon began to rise and Fulton grinned, giving Tate a thumbs up.

Tate released the lung full of air he didn't know he'd been holding and returned Fulton's smile.

"I'm not worthy," shouted Louis, bowing.

Tate cringed as Fulton began climbing up to him.

"Don't wander off," he reminded.

"Are you kidding?" Louis scoffed. "And miss this?"

"Right," sighed Tate under his breath.

The ladder opened up to a landing and he wriggled through the slats of the cage and waited for Fulton.

Fulton joined him and together they climbed the stairs to the rig's main platform.

The rig looked big from below, but now they were on the platform they could take in the full scope of this city on the sea.

At nearly three-hundred-thousand square feet and two football fields wide, the buildings on the oil rig rose another eighty feet above. Over a hundred-thousand tons of structures, scaffolding, stairs, railings and pipes meant they could spend days looking for Revolution Terry and never find him.

"I don't even know where to begin," said Fulton, mirroring Tate's thoughts. "If he's hiding, we'll never find him."

Tate's eyebrows knitted together as he tried to break down the problem into a manageable plan. Terry likely knew this rig like the back of his hand. If he didn't want to be found, they could climb all over this rig while he easily slipped by them using any number of catwalks and crawlspaces.

Another thought, more troubling, surfaced. What if Terry had set booby traps on the rig?

One thing at a time.

Tate considered splitting up, but even if there weren't any traps, once they were separated who knew how long it would take to find each other again.

He saw another streak of white from the corner of his eye, at first taking it for a diving seagull, but the shape and size was wrong.

"Did you see that?" he asked.

"What?" said Fulton, glancing around.

Tate walked to the rail and scanned the sky for birds, but it was empty. Below, in the water was a cluster of white dots and he instantly recognized them as golf balls.

"Where would you go if you wanted a driving range?" he asked.

Fulton's brows knitted together at Tate's strange question.

"Someplace flat," he said as he puzzled over it, then his face lit up. "The helipad."

"Exactly," smiled Tate.

Eight floors above them, they saw the shelf of the helipad stretching far out over the edge of the platform.

The two began climbing the zig-zagging flights of stairs until they the landing which opened onto the windswept deck of the helicopter pad.

On the other side of the wide pad stood a lone figure; his colorful, Hawaiian shirt contrasted against wide, blue horizon.

His back was to them as he bent down and picked a golf ball out of a tin bucket and carefully placed it on a tee.

With a fluid motion that comes with long practice, the figure brought the club in a backswing then downswing. The club connected with a clack, sending the ball into the air.

"Is that him?" asked Fulton.

"It's your radio show," said Tate. "What's a conspiracy nut look like?"

"He's not a nut," grumbled Fulton. "Anyway, people like him don't spread around pictures of themselves."

"Let's introduce ourselves," said Tate.

"Hello," he called out over the gusting wind.

The figure put another ball on the tee before briefly looking at them.

The wind blew the ball off the tee and the man watched his ball disappear over the edge of the helipad with a curse.

He bent over and put another ball on the tee, then adjusted his grip on the driver.

Tate and Fulton stood to the side, giving the man a respectful distance. His tanned arms contrasted with his white golf glove as he dropped his shoulders and lined up his swing.

The ball rustled on the tee as the wind threatened to take it away. The man stared at the ball, daring it to move. He swept the golf club over his shoulder and swung. The driver hit, sending the ball into the air where the wind caught it, hooking off to the side.

Tate quickly studied the man, sizing him up and looking for the telltale bulge of a weapon.

His shorts and t-shirt hung loosely on his thin frame, flapping in the tug of the wind. From what Tate could see, the man's only weapon was a well-worn golf club.

The stranger propped his hand on his driver and turned to Tate and Fulton with a look of bored disinterest.

"Hello," said Tate. "Are you Terry?"

The man dropped his chin and peered at them over the top of his sunglasses. "You aren't fans, are you?" he asked, his brown eyes looking them over.

"No," said Tate.

"In that case, yes," said Terry.

"I'm a fan," blurted Fulton.

"I don't do autographs," said Terry, pointing his club at Fulton.

"You don't seem surprised to see us," said Tate.

"You knew we were coming," said Fulton. It was more of a statement than a question. "I told you. He's got a whole network. He probably knew about us the minute we got to the city."

"A true believer," said Terry, looking at Fulton with mild contempt. "What about you?"

"Not really," said Tate.

"That's refreshing," said Terry.

The tin bucket of golf balls rattled as the wind dragged it over the rough surface of the helipad.

"It's getting too windy," said Terry, picking up the bucket. "Come on."

He led them off the helipad and down a flight of stairs. Sheltered from the roar of the buffeting gusts, the mood took on a somber feeling as the wind moaned around them.

They followed him down another flight and through a door into a surprisingly spacious room. Judging by the furniture, Tate guessed this must have been the crew's communal area.

Terry put the bucket in the corner then wiped down the head of the golf club before putting it on a rack on the wall.

Tate took a seat, and Fulton followed his example.

Fulton watched Terry's movements with anticipation, as if waiting to see a magician's grand finale, but as the minutes ticked by, Fulton was becoming doubtful. This was not the conspiracy genius he had imagined and began to suspect they had the wrong person. Maybe this was a decoy Terry.

Finished with putting away his things, Terry sat down. He leaned back, crossing his bandy legs and looked at his two visitors, saying nothing.

"You are Terry, right?" asked Fulton.

"Yes," he said.

"If you don't mind, we'd like to ask you some questions," said Tate.

"I don't suppose it would matter if I did mind," said Terry.

"Well..." began Fulton.

"No, not really," said Tate.

"Louis brought you, didn't he," said Terry.

Tate nodded.

"It's always the weakest link," he grumbled. "Not like I have my pick of followers who are willing to bring me supplies."

"How do you know about the Grave Diggers?" asked Tate, deciding to get down to it.

"I hear things," said Terry, his hazel eyes giving away nothing. "People like to talk. A man of your experience knows that."

The comment sounded like Terry was familiar with him and made Tate take a closer look.

"Have we met before?" he asked.

"You guys know each other?" said Fulton, brightening up.

Terry's expression faded away and a sly smile curled the corner of his mouth.

"You're in special forces," said Terry. "I'd recognize your type anywhere."

Fulton's mouth dropped open in surprise.

"Wow," he said. "He's good."

If Terry had been in special forces it was a long time ago, but he must have been around them enough to know what he was talking about.

There was something about him that nagged at Tate. He had seen this man before. It was another time; another place.

As Terry shifted in his chair, Tate caught a brief wink of light reflected off of the front of his shirt. Hidden in the colorful pattern of Terry's shirt was a small, round pin. The edge of the pin was ringed in gold. In the red center was the coat of arms of the United States. It was a pin exclusive to members of congress.

"You're Congressmen Baskins," said Tate, finally making the connection.

"You know me?" asked Terry.

"I worked security for you on a couple of your trips to Germany."

"You worked for Revolution Terry?" gaped Fulton.

"Fulton," said Tate. "Keep it in your pants."

Fulton blushed and clapped his mouth shut.

"I thought you were dead," said Tate, turning his attention back to Terry. "Your detail was trying to get you out of the city. The news reported you were all overrun by Vix. They never recovered your body."

"That was the plan," said Terry.

"You planned your death?" asked Tate, baffled. "Why?"

"About four months after the first reports about the Vix started trickling in, we began losing contact with our intelligence assets everywhere. I mean all over the world," said Terry. "There was a lot of bickering in Washington about what was happening. The military was pointing fingers at different terrorist groups, claiming it was a coordinated attack. Really?"

He waved his hand with a dismissive eye roll. "Granted, I didn't have the same kind of boots on the ground insight like you guys, but hell, even I could put the pieces together. It wasn't terrorists."

He stared at the arm of his chair, sweeping away imaginary dust, as he collected his thoughts.

"We were getting reports of people getting sick. Hysterical. Becoming violent. It was mostly background clutter as far as everyone was concerned. Contact with our people in the field dropped to nothing. Then our contacts in other governments stopped answering our calls. It was eerie."

"Like the way a busy street would be deserted just before you got ambushed," said Tate.

"Exactly," said Terry. "Everyone had their heads up their butts about terrorists. I don't know if they really believed that, but it didn't make sense to me. That night, or maybe it was later, I don't remember, someone sent me security footage from a South Korea hospital. One of the patients, a woman, was trashing her room. Scared the staff half to death. They were all hiding down the hall. Then the cops show up."

Terry looked up, meeting Tate's eyes with a look of cold fear.

"She came out of her room and charged them. This one cop, you could see how nervous he was. Well, she's almost on top of him and he shoots. Blood flies everywhere." Terry rubbed his face as the weight of the memory played out in his mind. "Yeah, it was horrible. Anyway, he shoots her... and she just stands there. I'm thinking she's dead, right? Her brain just hadn't caught up to the fact that this cop had just emptied his gun in her chest."

He went quiet, circling his finger on the arm of the chair.

"She never dropped," said Tate.

"No," said Terry. "No, she didn't. Her face twisted into something unnatural. But in that expression was lust and hunger. Another cop shot her in the head. That's when her lights went out. Then I got what was going on."

"What did you do?" asked Fulton.

"What politicians are good at," scoffed Terry. "I formed a committee to investigate what was really happening. I mean, I knew what was happening. I was using the committee as a platform to get the other members to listen to me. By then there were reports of this *fever* springing up in America. I had to convince the committee if I had any chance of convincing the president. Time wasn't on our side, but the others came around. We took our findings to the president. I really thought we could get measures in place to lock down the country," he said. "Contain it."

The history Tate had lived through didn't align with Terry's version.

"That's not how it played out," said Tate.

"No," said Terry. "I was overseas the day before the president was going to sign off on our plan. My aide calls and tells me the committee members are withdrawing their names."

"Why?" asked Fulton.

"That's what I wanted to know," said Terry. Most of them never took my call. The couple I did reach were evasive. They sounded frightened. I'm a logical man. I don't believe in conspiracies."

Fulton and Tate both blinked in surprise. By all rights they were sitting in front of the king of conspiracies.

"Meaning, I don't easily jump to conclusions," continued Terry, "but I believe someone had gotten to them. Intimidated them to back out. Yes, it could have been politics. What would you have thought if your congressman had called a news briefing to announce that zombies were real?"

He chuckled. "But why they did it was unimportant. Our only chance to save lives was gone. I'd seen movies, you know, last man standing in a post-apocalyptic world. I mean, I didn't picture people wearing scraps of metal and leather, tearing around in cars covered in spikes."

Terry nervously tapped his sandaled feet and looked at his two visitors. "Hey, would either of you like a beer?"

"No thanks," said Tate.

"Sure!" said Fulton.

Terry walked out of the room, leaving Tate and Fulton looking bewildered.

"He's not what I expected," said Tate. "You?"

"Not even close," said Fulton. "But how cool is this place?"

Terry reappeared with two cans of beer and handed one to Fulton.

"We'll have to pick this up later," said Terry, glancing at the clock. "I have a show to do." He headed for the door and stopped halfway out. "You can come if you'd like."

"The show?" stammered Fulton, coming out of his chair, heading for the door.

Tate had to admit he was curious to see Terry at work. He stood up to follow and felt a brief whirl of dizziness as the room tilted. Then he remembered he was in a floating city.

They followed Terry outside. The stiff ocean breeze was refreshing but cold. They crossed a long gantry to another set of buildings with large windows looking out in every direction. A small forest of antennas crowded the top of the building's roof.

They walked into what had been the operations room of the oil rig. The large glass windows provided an impressive vantage point of the rig. Several fold out tables had been set up against one side of the room, each with a hodgepodge of radio gear. A tangle of wires spilled over the back of the equipment and snaked up into the ceiling.

Terry sat down in a swivel chair and pushed off, rolling across the floor to the opposite end of the tables. He began flicking switches, pressing buttons and turning dials, working his way down the line of radio gear.

"Pretty serious gear for a radio show," said Tate.

"A lot of it's single boosters," said Terry. "I use it to step over existing broadcasts and ride their singles like a wave. They try to stop me from doing it, but I got a lot more power than they do. That's how my show's able to reach so far."

Terry wheeled himself back to the middle where a boom mic was clamped to the table. He put his finger to his lips and pointed at the mic.

Tate and Fulton nodded in understanding and remained quiet.

Terry rested his finger on a blue switch as he followed the second hand on his watch.

He flipped the switch with a flourish and put on a set of headphones. The boom mic squeaked as he pulled the mic in front of his face.

"Calling all patriots! You are listening to the voice of truth," said Terry. His voice changed to the gravely, fast clipped persona they knew as Revolution Terry. He flipped another switch and a dead metal version of the National Anthem. Terry turned down the volume and leaned into the mic.

"This is White Hat radio," he boomed. "And I am your host, the keeper of the keys of truth, the all-seeing eye, the Paul Revere of freedom. Revolution Terry." He pressed a button and speakers filled with the screech of an eagle.

"I have a message for the deep state. We know who you are. We know your secrets and your days are numbered. You can't silence us. We are many and we're coming for you!"

Terry tapped a keyboard and a monitor lit up, scrolling row after row of text.

"That's from the community," whispered Fulton excitedly in Tate's ear.

"There's been a lot of discussion among you patriots about my last coded message," said Terry. "We know the deep state is listening. They're scared of us, but be warned, they will strike, so never let your guard slip. I see a message from Minute Man five zero five about the train that derailed last week. He believes that was a planned attack by forces within the deep state to cover the assassination of one of our secret operatives. Minute Man, I can't name names, but you are closer to the truth than you know."

Fulton watched in rapt attention while Tate could only shake his head in amazement.

13

PUZZLE PIECES

Over the next twenty minutes, Terry read and commented on comments from the community. Theories ranged from death cults to UFOs. Tate was awe struck at the breath and width of paranoia and self-delusion on display.

"Take a breather people," said Terry. "The revolution will continue."

He turned the time over to playing music and took off his headphones as he turned around in his chair to face Tate and Fulton.

"That was amazing," said Fulton. "Is all of that true?"

"Some is," said Terry. "Some I don't know. Some I make up."

"Aren't you worried your followers will figure out you're lying to them?" asked Tate.

"It's not lies," said Terry to a baffled Tate.

"It's all about disinformation," said Fulton. "You mix the truth in with all this other stuff."

"The deep state doesn't know how much we really know," said Terry. "It keeps them confused and off balance."

"Is there a deep state?" asked Tate.

"I can't tell you if there is or isn't," said Terry. "You have to look at the information and make up your own mind."

"But," stammered Tate, "you just spent thirty minutes telling everyone there is a deep state."

"That's my truth," said Terry. "Your truth might be different. It's all based on what you know."

It sounded like a lot of circular logic to Tate. He wondered what happened to the rational man he'd been talking to before the show. This wasn't the same Terry.

"So, there is a deep state," said Tate.

"You mean a shadow government made up of globalists that have spent generations slowly seizing power to create a one world government?" asked Terry. "No, that's a fairy tale."

"Like the Illuminate," said Tate.

"Oh no, that's real," said Terry, looking very serious.

"He's new," explained Fulton.

"How long have you been doing this?" asked Tate.

"This?" said Terry, thumbing over his shoulder to the radio equipment. "A couple of years. But I started it mostly out of boredom, but then I got an idea. Remember when I told you about all the committee members pulling out? I knew then all of us, the country, were finished. I decided I better hurry up and die before one of those creatures ripped me apart. Looking back on it, it was being overly dramatic. I'm not saying it wouldn't happen, but it was only a matter of time. Well anyway, I couldn't decide how to kill myself, so I went out and got blind drunk. That'll help me think clearly, right?" He chuckled. "After a lot of expensive scotch, I thought why wait. I'd go outside and step in front of a truck. Perfect, except I knew self-preservation would take over and I'd jump out of the way. But if I was drunk enough, I wouldn't jump. Just let it flatten me."

"I guess you couldn't get drunk enough," said Tate.

"Not enough scotch in the world," said Terry. "Instead, I paid my bill, walked into the middle of the street and I kept going. Next thing I know I woke up on an oil freighter. One thing led to another and here I am."

"What about all of this?" asked Tate nodding to the radio equipment.

"Surprisingly, swinging a golf club gets old after a while. I found I had a lot of time on my hands," said Terry. He looked around the room and sighed. "Maybe too much. But you know," he said, wagging his finger at Tate, "it always nagged at me, the way everyone pulled out of the committee. I wanted to believe it was about optics. How their voters would think they were crazy, but the longer I thought about it the more I knew I was lying to myself. Someone got to them."

"You were trying to save lives," said Fulton. "Save the country. Why would someone want to stop you?"

"Let me show you something," said Terry.

He walked out of the control room and down a stark hallway, through another door. Tate and Fulton walked in as he turned on the lights.

They were standing in what had been the crew's movie theater. The chairs had all be removed, but the plush carpet and sound deadening ceiling tiles were still in place.

Tate and Fulton could only gape as they looked around. The large walls were covered with pages of notes, photographs of objects, hand scrawled papers, black and white photos places and newspaper articles. Portions of maps were visible under the clutter with circles around various locations of interest. Colored string ran back and forth in a crazy spiderweb, connecting events, places and individuals.

Tate had never seen a more tangible expression of a man in the grips of paranoia and insanity.

Fulton began examining the wall, fascinated. He was getting a behind the scenes look at the bible of conspiracies.

"I know," said Terry, reading Tate's expression. "Looks crazy."

"You could say that," said Tate.

"I could look at this for days," said Fulton.

"All of this," said Terry, "is how I'm trying to answer that question. Living on a steel island in the middle of nowhere, it's not like I can pop over to the library on a whim. I needed information and for that I needed a network."

"The community," said Fulton over his shoulder.

"One thing I learned doing intel oversight is that someone always talks who shouldn't have," said Terry. "They always do. If I could cast a net wide enough, I knew I'd find something. That's why I stared the show. The conspiracy crowd is a huge, untapped resource. I needed them to see me as one of their own, but more than an equal. I had to be what they wanted to be. Using different aliases, I started seeding rumors about Revolution Terry. That he was deeply embedded in the government, all that. It ignited curiosity and speculation until everyone had convinced themselves I was going to save the country."

"You caught on," said Tate.

"Like a match to a flame," said Terry. "People began sending me messages about everything you could imagine and a lot you don't want to. Every few shows I'd drop something about good guys outwitting shadowy bad actors, just general stuff, but buried in the haystack of responses I'd find a needle."

"This is a lot of needles," said Tate, looking at the walls.

"It's a lot to keep track of," said Terry. "The information is fragmented, but the real story about who's behind disbanding the committee will come out."

"It's about your net that we're here," said Tate.

"Of course, sorry," said Terry. "I haven't had a real conversation with a rational human being in, huh..." Terry paused to consider how long he'd been alone on the oil rig. "Well, a long time."

"How did you hear about the Grave Diggers?" asked Tate.

"About who?" asked Terry.

"Fort Hickok," prompted Tate. "South America."

"Oh yeah. I got it now," said Terry. "That's you, right? Never mind. You don't have to answer that. To be honest, finding you was a lucky shot in the dark. It was just chatter in the community about something going on here or there in South America. Nothing interesting, but worth filing away. A while later, something else would come up. Same area. I knew it had to be military. There's nobody else down there."

"How do you go from vague rumors to knowing our unit name?" asked Tate.

"I have a frequency scanner I use to look for anyone broadcasting from outside the US," said Terry. "I have to believe we aren't the only ones that survived the Vix."

"Did you hear from anyone?" asked Fulton, tearing himself away from the wall.

"No," said Terry. "But it's not the best equipment. Maybe it's too weak to pick up their signals."

"What about your scanner?" asked Tate.

"It got a hit. A local one," said Terry, looking disturbed. "What made this special is that the frequency doesn't exist on the charts. It was hard to keep a lock on it and it kept cutting out. Two people were talking. They were angry but sounded scared. They had lost a package, down south?"

"Vulcan..." began Fulton and Tate waved him off.

"What's Vulcan?" asked Terry.

"Nothing you want to repeat to *anyone*," said Tate, his face turning dark and grim.

"Hands off," said Terry, nodding. "I understand. So you know the rest of the story."

"I'd like to know what you heard," said Tate.

"They sent people who found it, but lost it," continued Terry. "It would expose everyone. The other one asked what happened. The first guy said, 'Grave Diggers' and the other guy swore, saying it wasn't a secure line. The signal dropped."

"And you thought it was a good idea to put our name out there to see what would happen?" asked Tate.

"Nothing that black and white," said Terry. "Blurting your name would have put a big red X on me and I don't want that kind of attention. For all I knew you could have been the bad guys. Either way, I didn't want to get on anyone's radar."

"But here we are," said Tate.

"How did you find me, anyway?" asked Terry.

"Easy enough that you shouldn't feel safe," said Tate. "I don't know about UFOs and white slavery rings, but I think you tapped into something a lot more real and dangerous. You should leave this alone."

"Hey, Top?" said Fulton.

His finger was pointing to a scribbled note on the wall where several threads all came together.

"What is it?" asked Tate, getting up.

"That," said Terry, excitedly, "is where the breakup of the committee began. Past that is a black hole. I can't find ..."

Terry's voice faded into the background as Tate read what Fulton was pointing to.

The Ring.

He could feel the bottom fall out under his feet and Tate's mind reeled as the pieces fell into place with shattering clarity.

He had thought The Ring had formed *after* the outbreak. They'd seen an opportunity to take advantage of an already weakened United States.

No. The Ring was older than that. They had existed before the outbreak and were responsible for sabotaging the country's single chance to save millions of lives.

"What is it? Do you know about that?" asked Terry. His answer was etched on Tate's face in anger and malice.

If The Ring could provoke this reaction from a man hardened by combat, it should have been a glaring warning to Terry that he'd stumbled far more dangerous than he could handle.

"Tell me about them," said Terry.

"Congressman," said Tate, fixing him with his eyes. "You trusted me on your security detail to keep you alive. Trust me now. Stop pulling on this thread."

"Why?" asked Terry.

"You won't survive what's waiting for you at the other end."

———

Two days later, Fulton was still buzzing with excitement from meeting Terry, but Tate had made him swear he would not mention it to anyone outside the team.

Tate struggled over what he would do with the new information about The Ring. He had no way to authenticate it, which he knew meant it was nothing more than a rumor. But what if it was true?

His questions were pushed to the side when Rosse told him the arms dealers had made good on their deal. The crates of weapons were ready and waiting in the woods near the landing strip.

The team had maintained their readiness, knowing they would be called on to rescue Dante as soon as their gear had arrived. Tate passed the word to assemble at the smuggler's shack the following morning.

It was zero two thirty when Tate entered the shack. The team had gotten there before him, but something didn't feel right. The cover concealing the tunnel was moved away, revealing the dark entrance, and they were restless and uncomfortable.

"Is there something I should know?" he asked.

"Permission to speak freely," said Wesson, stiffly.

Tate cocked a curious eye at the rare formality of request. "Of course, Sergea..."

"To hell with that!" snapped Wesson, pointing at the tunnel.

Dumfounded, Tate could only blink.

"I uh..." was all he could utter as his mind tried to make sense of what she was talking about. The expressions from the rest of the team told him they knew what was going on... then it hit him.

"Cuba," he said.

"Damn right, Cuba," said Wesson, looking flushed and pale at the same time.

It all came flooding back to him. They were on a mission to sneak into Cuba, observe and report on the activities of an ex-Spetsnatz. The island was overrun with Vix and the only way in was underground, through the sewers.

Tate was the only one with night vision goggles and was the team's eyes in the pitch-black tunnels.

They were moving single file, Tate in the lead and Wesson bringing up the rear. The walls of the sewer resonated with every sound, echoing down every side tunnel for hundreds of yards. Like the vibration of a spider's web, any noise they made would alert the Vix.

Everyone had frozen at the sound of a low growl from behind. Tate cautiously scanned for the threat; he saw the Vix and his heart stopped. It was standing right next to Wesson, unaware she was there.

Wesson, who could see nothing in the dark, knew exactly what was inches from her as its breath tickled her neck.

Silence wanted to root Tate in place. He couldn't shoot, couldn't move towards her for fear of making a sound. Wesson's face had been taunt and wet with sweat as Tate pulled his tomahawk from its sheath.

There was only the faint rustle of his clothing as he threw. Wesson hardly flinched as the blade whispered past and sunk into the Vix's skull.

Wesson never talked about it, but Tate knew she would have nightmares for a long time afterwards.

Now they stood with the mouth of another tunnel at their feet. To Wesson, it must have looked like a living maw, waiting to consume her.

"I'm sorry," said Tate.

He'd been caught up with everything else and overlooked something that should have been obvious.

"You don't have to go. No one will judge you if you stay," he said, knowing none of the team would hold it against her.

For a brief moment, Wesson looked relieved, but it quickly passed and she set her jaw, rebuking herself for a weakness nobody else there would have done.

Tate saw it play out on her face and recognized that she would only be harder on herself.

"Sergeant," he said firmly. "I'm ordering you to return to your quarters."

Technically, he was not an officer, but he was in command.

The mixture of emotions was clear as Wesson between relief and self-contempt and back again, over and over.

She looked at the black void of the tunnel entrance for a long time before speaking.

"I'm going," she said, looking at Tate, defying him to argue with her.

"I got yer back," said Rosse, clapping her on the shoulder.

"And I got your, uh, front," fumbled Monkhouse. "I mean, in front, not your... I'm leading, okay?"

Wesson smiled as the team rallied around her.

"Looks like that's settled," grinned Tate. "Let's go."

He climbed down the ladder with the team following behind. Wesson never faltered or said a word.

At the other end, he pretended not to notice her face streaked with sweat.

They easily found the two crates of weapons and divided up the guns and ammo. Everyone did a quick pre-check.

Rule one of going into a mission was never to take untried gear. It was a rule burned into every soldier that had faced the gut-wrenching experience of having the single most needed piece of equipment be the one that hadn't been tested and it didn't work. There was no way around it this time. Tate had to break the rule.

Time didn't allow them to test their weapons and he couldn't risk the sound of gunfire drawing Vix, or the attention of someone from the base. This was supposed to be a clean zone, but nobody wanted to put that to the test.

They uncovered the SUV and with Tate at the wheel, they climbed in.

It wasn't long before the city walls came into view and he turned off to a long disused road that skimmed the cities parameter. Their destination was outside the wall's security.

The Brotherhood were smart. They were using the Vix as a lethal buffer zone. If anyone wanted to attack the gang, they had to want it pretty bad because even rival gang members weren't hardcore enough to leave the protection of the city walls.

Tate followed the planned route, using the weed-choked and cracked roads.

He kept the headlights off in the pre-dawn night, using the night vision goggles to steer by. He never saw any Vix but didn't know if that was because there weren't any, or the noiseless Ford wasn't attracting their attention. In a way, he would have preferred to see some just so he knew one way or the other. It was the 'not knowing' that made it hard.

"We're coming to the half mile point," said Rosse, watching their progress on the dashboard's trip screen.

The tires crunched over dried grass as Tate pulled off the road and stopped.

Everyone looked out the windows for any signs of movement among the shadows but saw nothing.

"This is supposed to be a cleared area," said Tate, "but we know what that's worth."

Everyone in the car chuckled, having run into Vix in officially designated 'clear zones'. They knew better than to let their guard down.

"There's a half mile of wild country between us and our objective," said Tate. "Wesson's on point. Rosse brings up the rear. Check your comms."

Each took their turn testing their communications without any issues.

There was nothing left to do but get out of the car and leave its protective steel shell.

"Let's go," said Tate, opening his door.

They quickly lined up in order, Tate behind Wesson, and began their move on Dante's position.

They quickly settled into their familiar rhythm of moving as a single entity that came from countless patrols hunting Vix in the Columbian jungles.

Alert but comfortable, they moved along the side of the road, staying in the concealment of the deep shadows.

They covered the half mile without incident when Wesson whispered over the radio for the team to halt.

Everyone stopped and crouched as Tate quietly moved up next to her.

"Were you expecting that?" she said, carefully pulling back a branch, revealing a wide parking lot, ringing a modern looking, square-sided glass building.

Just in front of them was a crisscrossing metal web of chain link fencing. The building was completely dark; no lights shown from within it or the surrounding light poles that dotted the parking lot.

"Think it's electrified?" asked Wesson.

"Let's see," said Tate, casually touching the fence with his finger.

Wesson gasped at his recklessness, choosing caution above all else.

For Tate it wasn't foolishness, but observation. Thick weeds were intertwined on the fence and Tate knew that plants could ground the electric charge. Enough plant growth could short out a fence. He seriously doubted the fence was hot, but there was always that small nagging doubt.

The rough wire was cool to the touch and nothing more.

"See anyone?" he asked.

"No," said Wesson.

The parking lot was barren except for clumps of overgrowth that had pushed up through the cracked asphalt.

"Let's give it a minute," said Tate. "See if anyone sticks their nose out."

He radioed to the rest of the team to stand by while he and Wesson watched for any of Brotherhood patrolling the grounds.

"What's this place doing in the middle of nowhere?" she said.

"No company name on the outside of the building," observed Tate. He leaned over to get a better view of the entrance to the parking lot and saw a sturdy gate next to a security gate.

"Looks like they were pretty serious about security," he said.

There was nothing unique about the squat, glass building and, in fact, he couldn't help but get the impression it was designed to look unremarkable.

"I wonder what they did here," said Wesson.

"We're about to find out," said Tate. "Monkhouse, bring the cutters."

As the team's engineer, Monkhouse was a jack of many trades, and master of few. The sort of things he was skilled at and his ability to jury rig gadgets on the fly impressed Tate, but also gave him reason to wonder if Monkhouse's previous life had been a little shady. Like everyone else, Monkhouse had joined the AVEF to start a new life or leave an old one behind. Tate didn't even know if Monkhouse was his real name, but the man came through where it really mattered. He'd proven himself to the team and that's what mattered most to Tate.

Monkhouse knelt next to Tate with his compact bolt cutters in hand.

"Open sesame," he smirked, putting the cutter's jaws around the first wire of the fence.

"Careful, it's hot," hissed Tate.

Monkhouse blanched, pulling back the cutters.

"Just kidding," grinned Tate.

Monkhouse's eyes narrowed in annoyance.

"I liked you better when you were sullen and depressed," he grumbled. "You know, trust is an important quality in a real leader."

Tate put his hand on his shoulder and looked at him sincerely.

"You're right," he said, "and I do trust you."

Monkhouse gave him a mock smile and turned his attention back to the fence. The cutters made quick work of the wire and they quietly peeled back the fence.

"We're moving," said Wesson over the radio.

She slipped through the fence and moved to the side, making room as the rest of the team came through and lined up behind her.

Coming through last, Tate followed Monkhouse and joined up next to Wesson.

"Anything?" he asked.

"No sounds or movement," she said.

The parking lot was devoid of any concealment or cover. If someone was watching them from the shadows of the building, all they'd have to do was wait until the team was in the middle of the lot. It would be the perfect time to spring an ambush.

"Okay," said Tate. "Stagger formation. Move quick, but quiet."

He squeezed Wesson's shoulder and she stood, followed by the rest of the team. They fast walked across the parking lot, spread out, each aiming at the windows of the building.

14

INTO THE DARK

Surrounded by darkness, Tate still felt exposed. He'd lost count how many times he had done something just like this, but it always made his heart beat faster. Every time he wondered if the last thing he'd see would be a flash of light from a hidden sniper and all would go black.

The stillness of night remained undisturbed as they reached the outside of the building and crouched down.

"What next?" asked Wesson. "Door or window?"

The glass walls of the building were wide and tall. Breaking one of those was out of the question.

Looking down the line of his team, Tate saw that Fulton was nearest the door and motioned to him to test it.

Crouching next to the door, Fulton reached up and grasped the weathered handle. With a gentle pull, the door cracked open.

"There you go," said Tate to Wesson, smiling.

"Check for traps," he radioed to Fulton.

Taking a small flashlight from his pocket, Fulton shined the beam along the inside of the door then snapped it off.

"It's clear, Top," he said.

"I'll lead inside," said Tate, getting up with Wesson behind him.

The rest of the team prepared and he nodded to Fulton to open the door.

Tate slipped inside and moved to the right as the rest of the team followed. The light was murky and the inside smelled of damp, cigarettes and urine.

"We're in the right place," said Wesson, wrinkling her nose.

"They've been here a lot longer than a couple of weeks," said Tate.

"Do you think this might be their headquarters?" asked Rosse.

"Why aren't they guarding it?" asked Monkhouse.

"Yes," said Tate, "and I don't know. Maybe they are." He made a slow scan of their surroundings, looking for anything suspicious. "We just haven't stepped in front of their sights yet."

"You sure?" asked Samuel.

Shy Girl nodded. "Yeah, Big Money said there's six of them."

"Another gang?" he asked.

"No way," she said. "They're loaded up. Looks like a SWAT team."

Samuel let his gaze drift as he considered his options.

"We could move some of our guys around behind them," said Shy Girl. "Get them front and back."

"No," he said thoughtfully. "We could take some of them out that way, maybe all of them, but how many of us would it cost? We'll use the guard dogs."

"They creep me out," she said, looking nervous.

"Go tell Spider we're using the dogs," said Samuel.

Shy Girl nodded but didn't hide her reluctance.

"It's okay," he said. "We'll stay inside until we know they're asleep."

Shy Girl quietly pushed open the steel door leading to the stairwell. A large sign marked Emergency Exit pointed up and displayed a simple map of the fire exits.

She was small, but lithe, making her the perfect messenger for running up and down the stairs. Her legs carried her quietly up the long flight with little effort.

It wasn't long before she stopped at the topmost landing next to the door marked Rooftop Exit. The sign had be crossed out with spray paint with 'Spider's Hut' above it.

She pushed past the heavy door, and out into the night air. Her feet crunched on the gravel as she walked past rows of solar panels to a large utility room.

"Hey Spider," she said, before going in.

She knew he had a thing for her, but he looked at her in a strange way that made her uncomfortable. Samuel said he wouldn't hurt a fly, but it didn't make her feel any better about being alone with him.

As she walked in, he put down a worn-out magazine. The cover had a muscle car with a dragon painted on the side.

"Hi," said Spider, a wide grin spreading across his pockmarked face.

"Yeah," said Shy Girl, looking around the small utility shed.

Thick ropes of wire snaked through the roof and spread out across a wall covered with banks of circuit breaker switches. A desk, chair and couch made up the rest of Spider's home.

He got up and shoved a pile of clothes aside, making an empty space on his lumpy couch.

Shy Girl glanced at the couch but pretended not to notice.

Spider took off his headscarf and dusted the couch seat.

"That's okay," she said. "Samuel wants you to wake up the dogs."

He stopped his dusting, looking back at her with a shine in his eyes.

"What's up?" he asked.

"Cops..."

"Yeah?" said Spider, getting to his feet. "Oh man, those fools are gonna get messed up."

Grinning, he rubbed his hands together as he searched the wall of circuit breakers until he found the switches he was looking for.

He put his thick palm under the first lever.

"I don't like those things," said Shy Girl.

"You want to stay up here?" he asked. "They don't come up here."

"It gets hot up here when the sun's up," she said after thinking about it. "I'll hang out underneath."

"Your call," said Spider with a sniff of annoyance.

He pushed up on the wide lever. It made a loud clack as it snapped in the *On* position, making Shy Girl jump.

"I'm outta here," she said, walking out of the utility room.

She heard three more sharp clacks behind her and she sped up as she threaded her way thought the solar panels to the stairway door.

The sky over the horizon was a dark grey against the black of the tree line. Sunup was still a while away. She had time, but fear made her hurry and she rushed down the stairwell.

"What's that?" said Fulton.

Everyone stopped and listened. Somewhere within the building they heard the faint echo of running on metal. It quickly faded away until there was nothing but shadows and silence.

"Big rats," said Monkhouse.

"Do you think they know we're here?" asked Wesson.

"Count on it," said Tate, easing his grip on his assault rifle.

They moved into the center of the first floor where they found an open staircase with glass railings leading up. The once tastefully glass and wood stairs were streaked and worn.

Wesson knelt down and ran her finger over the stair tread and examined the layer of dust on her finger.

"They're not using this to get around," she said.

Tate reached into his pocket and took out the simple note he'd made from Roman's tracker information. The numbers suggested Dante was underground.

"There must be another way they're getting around," he said. "He's below us. Everyone spread out. Look for another way down."

After searching the floor, they came to the double doors of an elevator. To the right of the doors was an inactive keypad and card scanner.

Before Tate could call him, Monkhouse appeared, pulling a small pry bar out of this tactical pack.

"You called?" he said.

"You're a mind reader," said Tate.

"I charge extra for that," grinned Monkhouse.

Rosse and Tate took up position on either side of the doors as Monkhouse wedged the bar in the seam and twisted. As the doors began to move apart, Rosse and Tate grabbed each door and pulled them open, revealing an empty elevator shaft.

Cables disappeared into the darkness above and below.

"We go down," said Tate, shifting his rifle behind his shoulder.

"Hang on," said Rosse. "We don't know how deep this shaft is. There could be Vix at the bottom. How do we know those cables aren't broken? We could be sliding down, fat, dumb and happy and next thing you know the end of the cable slips through your hands with a whole lotta nothing under your feet."

Tate heard Fulton behind him swear under his breath as he imagined free falling through the dark.

Flicking on his flashlight, Tate stuck his head inside the shaft and looked at the walls to either side of the door. His light played over rows of metal rungs bolted to the wall.

"Maintenance ladder," he said, showing them to a relieved Rosse. "Feel better?"

"I do," said Fulton.

Wesson reached around the elevator door until she felt a solid ladder rung. She reached out her boot, finding another rung and pulled herself onto the ladder.

As she climbed down, Tate followed.

"Hey, Top?" said Fulton.

Tate stopped, his head level with the floor and looked up at Fulton.

"We didn't train for combat on a ladder," he said, looking concerned. "What happens if someone shows up below us and starts shooting?"

"Climb up," said Tate, disappearing below the floor. "Very fast."

"Uh..." muttered Fulton.

"C'mon," said Rosse, gently elbowing Fulton. "I'll go ahead of ya. If anyone starts shooting, I'll take care of them."

"No greater love than to use your butt to shield your fellow team-mates," said Monkhouse, as he reached inside the elevator shaft and pulled himself onto the rungs of the ladder.

"Funny guy," grumbled Rosse, climbing out onto the ladder. "Nothing outta you," he growled, wiping the grin off Fulton's face.

Several feet down, Wesson felt her boot brush against something and turned on her flashlight. She found the elevator which had stopped, blocking the bottom half of the doors leading to the next floor.

She swept her light below and saw the rungs of the ladder had been cut.

"Looks like this is our floor," said Tate, gesturing to the elevator.

"Whether we like it or not," said Wesson.

"We'll have to pry those doors," he said.

"Will the elevator take our weight?" she asked.

Tate used his light to examine the cables and touched the dried grease that coated them.

"There's no corrosion and the cable isn't frayed," he said. "It should be okay, but let's not linger longer than we have to. Rosse and Fulton, you stay on the ladder until we get the doors open."

Rosse grunted in acknowledgment.

Using the pry bar, Monkhouse, Wesson and Tate opened the doors with little trouble. Stale air wafted into the elevator shaft.

Wesson's nose wrinkled.

"I smell it too," said Tate, nodding in agreement.

The air was tinged with the odor of death and rot. There was something dead inside.

The change in the group was palpable. Everyone became hyper alert, stretching out their senses for the smallest hint of danger.

Wesson shouldered her gun, aiming into the blackness.

"Ready," she said.

Tate switched on his flashlight. The blue-white light stabbed through the darkness, illuminating a long hallway bordered by several doors. The distant edge of the flashlight beam brushed over a crumpled heap on the floor.

Wesson held it in her sights as Tate gently tapped on the edge of the elevator.

To the rest of the team, hidden in the dark and quiet, his tapping sounded like a sledgehammer on metal.

Nerves tight, they watched the thing in Tate's beam of light, expecting at any moment the obscure pile would spring to its feet and charge.

It never moved.

Wesson sighed and lowered her gun.

"Lights on," said Tate, climbing down from the elevator into the hallway. "I want to see what's coming before it's on top of us."

Everyone gratefully switched on their flashlights and snapped them into the bracket attached to their gun barrels.

Outside, the sun was breaking over the horizon. Life giving, warm light crept over the ground.

Spider watched from the edge of the roof, impatiently shifting his weight from one foot to the other. When the light reached the base of the building he jogged over the rows of solar panels. Several of them were cracked and broken, their surfaces caked and streaked with grime, bits of dead insects and bird droppings. The few remaining unbroken panels shone like mirrors, even in the dim light.

Using his headband, Spider wiped them down with loving care.

The edge of sunlight spilled over the top of the building and glistened off the panels.

"That's it, baby," he said. "Time to wake up."

He trotted into the utility shed and fixed his stare on the power meter.

Columns of small, dead LEDs lined the board like glassy, black eyes; one column for every solar panel.

His face stretched into a grin as the bottom most lights flickered to a bright red. Only five panels were working, but it was enough. It wasn't long before all the columns glowed with life as the panels began converting the light to energy. Trickles of electricity began flowing through cables that snaked down into the bowels of the building.

Far below, in the power room, rows of dormant fuel cells began a low hum as they received the first drops of energy.

It wouldn't be long before the cells would reach their minimum capacity. The building was about to wake up.

Wesson and Rosse returned to the group after checking the mysterious object.

"It's a body," she reported.

"And just a body," said Rosse.

"There weren't any visible signs of death," said Wesson. "It's been here for a long time."

"Okay," said Tate. "Let's find a way down."

The team cautiously approached the first door and spread out on either side.

Something caught Fulton's attention by his boot. A small, two-foot square black panel at the bottom of the wall. It seemed oddly out of place.

"Fulton," said Tate.

"Yeah. Copy," he blurted, realizing Tate had been talking to him.

"Focus," said Tate. "Ready?"

"Yes," said Fulton. "I'm uh, I'm good."

He forgot about the panel, turning his attention to the door.

Everyone nodded as Tate put his hand around the doorknob, turned and pushed it open.

Tate and Wesson leaned around the corners of the doorway, scanning the interior with their lights. An empty office. Desks, computers, scattered papers. The air was stale but untainted by rot.

"It doesn't feel like the Brotherhood is around here," said Monkhouse.

"I'm know what you mean," said Tate. "I don't think Dante is on this floor. He's got to be somewhere below us."

"The elevator's a no go," said Rosse.

"They're using another way to move around the building," said Wesson.

"We're going to find it," said Tate.

"There's a lotta doors," said Rosse. "We're gonna be doing this all day."

"Sounds like you have a suggestion," said Tate.

"Well, yeah," said Rosse. "We split up in teams of two."

Tate sniffed. The subtle tang of death was in the air. If it was stronger, there'd be no doubt Vix were definitely roaming the floor. But it wasn't. He weighed the risk of breaking up the team. They had seen action, but not enough to give him the confidence they were prepared, or able, to survive a serious situation.

On the other hand, Rosse made a good point. Time was a factor. The risk seemed minimal.

Shrugging, Tate decided. "We'll do it," he said. "Your idea. You decide how we split up."

"Sure, okay," smiled Rosse. "Ota an' Wesson. You an' Monkhouse. Me and the kid."

Fulton was the youngest and lowest rank of the team. Rosse had taken him under his wing almost from the beginning. Part stern mentor and part protector, Rosse had helped Fulton come a long way.

"Sounds good. Final words, Sergeant?" said Tate, prompting Rosse to take the lead.

"Same as before," he said. "Keep the chatter down on the radio. Call out if you get in trouble or find another way out. Everyone pick a door."

The three teams spread out, each picking a door.

Moving from room to room, they quickly cleared the remaining doors in the first hall. The end of the hallway opened into an intersection with other halls branching off into several directions.

"Whoa," said Monkhouse. "How big is this place?"

"What kind of companies have underground complexes?" said Tate.

"Creepy, dangerous ones?" said Monkhouse.

With every office they found empty, Tate felt the level of risk dropping and his concern for the separate teams to move further down their chosen halls and away from each other.

"If the hall splits off on the other end, let me know," he said. "Come back to this position and wait for me."

Everyone agreed and set off into the darkness.

Tate and Monkhouse had gotten into the rhythm of clearing the offices and the end of their hall was in sight with only three doors left.

It was beginning to feel they were wasting their time. If they couldn't find the stairwell, their only option was to return to the elevator and figure out how they could get down to the next floor.

Monkhouse was poised at the door with his weapon shouldered and nodded to Tate; he was ready.

Tate tried the doorknob. This one was locked.

"I need the pry bar," he said.

"Coming up," said Monkhouse.

Swiveling his rifle out of the way, he reached over his shoulder and searched for the tool.

Far below, in the power room, the fuel cells reached their operating capacity. The computerized energy regulator checked the current power levels and compared the levels against its programmed setting for essential building operations.

All settings met their required parameters.

The regulator sent a pulse of energy to a bank of large relays, opening circuits, which allowed the flow of energy to the building above.

Monkhouse pulled out the pry bar and held it out to Tate when the hall lights snapped on.

Both of them flinched, blinking the spots out of their eyes as the pitch-black of the hallway filled with dazzling light.

His senses were overwhelmed by the glaring light and Tate was barely aware of the low hum of an electric mechanism unlocking the door, or the hiss as the vacuum of the air-tight door pulled it open.

A puff of air brushed over his face and his eyes went wide as he staggered back. The stench from inside slammed his senses, making him gag.

Pry bar still in his hand, Monkhouse froze, gawking, as the door opened into a room filled with Vix.

The Vix turned towards the sound of the door. With guttural snarls, they charged.

"Contact. Vix!" grunted Tate into his radio. "Shoot," he yelled at the stunned Monkhouse.

Tate grabbed the pry bar and swung, catching the lead Vix across the face with a vicious blow. Bone crunched as the metal rod destroyed the Vix. It reeled backwards into the rest of them and they spilled to the floor in growling tangle.

Monkhouse woke from his daze and grabbed his gun.

Before he pulled the trigger, Tate pulled the door closed which clicked into place.

"What the...?" stuttered Monkhouse, shaking. "What just happened?"

The inside of the room had looked like a typical office.

"It's a security door," said Tate. "It seals the room from the hall-way. No sound. No vibration. No eavesdropping."

"What the heck kind of company needs security like?" said Monkhouse.

"One that wants to keep its secrets," said Tate.

15

DEATH SWITCH

F ulton and Rosse were trying to adjust to the sudden light when
Tate's voice snapped in their ears.

"Contact. Vix!"

Fulton clenched his gun and brought it up to his shoulder, scanning for threats.

"I don't seen anything," he said.

Rosse squinted down the hall as the door next to him unlocked with a click.

The sound made Fulton flinch. He swung his gun at the door as it seemly opened by itself. He forced his eyes open, expecting a wall of Vix to crash down on him.

Bland office furniture sat dormant and nothing more.

Rosse looked back the way they'd come. Previously locked doors began to open. Low moans seeped into the hallway.

"I think we better get in this office, kid," he said, bringing up his rifle and backing towards the open door.

Fulton looked at him, confused as Rosse put his firm hand on his shoulder, pushing him through the door.

Rosse closed the door, leaving a small crack to peek through. As he searched the length of the hall, he saw a small, black panel at the base of the wall. He took it for a maintenance access panel, nothing more.

As he looked away, the sound of a soft electric whine brought his attention back to it.

The access panel flipped up and receded into the wall. Out walked a small, four-legged robot. Except for the lack of a head and tail, it looked like a dog. Its metallic grey body was angular, a couple of feet long. A wink of light bounced off the camera, mounted in the front of the body. The robot's eye panned up and down the hall until it heard the sounds of grunting and moans.

Rosse watched through the crack in the door, fascinated. With a drone of motors, the robot turned towards the sound, its legs strangely prancing in place.

It walked forward a few feet and stopped, continuing to look down the hallway.

Rosse's hand squeezed the doorknob as several Vix shuffled out of a door, milling aimlessly in the hall.

The robot approached the Vix who suddenly stiffened as they heard the sound of the robot coming closer. A narrow beam of cool green light came out the robot and painted across the chest of the closest Vix in a thin, horizontal line.

The green light swept up and down the Vix four times, then turned off.

"This is a restricted area," said the robot in a flat but stern voice. "Remain where you are. Security has been notified and will arrive soon."

Triggered by the sound of the robot's voice, the Vix began moving towards it. The robot bent its rear legs, tilting the front of its body upwards.

Rosse grinned at the sight of the small robot trying to stand its ground.

"Any attempt to leave will be met with force," said the dog.

One of the Vix screamed and dashed at it, electrifying the others who charged after it.

Rosse was curiously entertained to see what the Vix would do when they tried to eat the dog.

A small plate opened on the top of the dog's body, near the front followed by the sound of a series of rapid, sharp cracks. Rosse's jaw dropped as the head of the leading Vix shattered into a cloud of gore and bone.

Crack, crack, crack.

Within seconds there was nothing left of the Vix but a pile of ruined corpses.

"To all employees," said the dog, "the security breach is over. Clean up has been notified. Please continue with your normal tasks."

"Holy crap," gasped Rosse.

"What?" asked Fulton. "Let me see."

Hearing the noise, the dog turned around, searching the hallway.

Rosse pushed Fulton back and closed the door.

"Shut up," hissed Rosse. "Ya wanna get us killed?"

He peeked out the door and watched the dog disappear into an office.

"What are we going to do?" asked Fulton, looking worried.

"Come on, kid," said Rosse, after checking the hall was clear. "We're getting out of here."

He keyed his radio. "Guys, there's a killer dog robot thing in the hallway. If you see one, don't let it shine a green light on you."

"What?" asked Wesson into her radio. "Rosse, make sense."

At the other end of the hallway, Wesson and Ota saw a peculiar, small, headless dog appear from a hole in the wall.

Ota only shrugged, a bemused smile in his blue eyes as the robot turned in the other direction and began looking into each of the open offices.

"It's a robot," said Rosse over their radio, "but it looks like a dog, kinda."

At the last office, the dog turned around. Its glass eye saw Wesson and Ota and began walking towards them.

"Think it saw us?" she asked.

Ota, never long on words, only shrugged again.

"It just chewed through a mob of Vix," said Rosse.

As it got closer, they could hear the quiet whine of the dog's motors. Its grey body was smooth and shaped like a hexagon.

The similarities to a dog were close enough that Wesson felt the ridiculous urge to talk to it like it was a real animal.

Just as the dog stopped a few feet away from them, they heard Rosse's urgent voice over their radios.

"Guys," he said into his radio. "The things got guns. Don't let it scan your face."

Wesson saw a sharp beam of cool green light shoot out from the dog. Without hesitating, she turned her back to the robot and Ota quickly did the same.

The green light scanned up and down Wesson's back a few times and turned off.

"Hello," said the robot in a cheerful voice. "I apologize for the interruption. Please turn around and display our employee identification."

Wesson and Ota exchanged glances at each other, silently agreeing. The last thing they were going to do was turn around.

"This is Wesson," she said in her radio. "We have one of those robots, but we're not letting it scan us."

"Can you move?" asked Tate.

"I think so," she said.

"Everyone meet back where we split up," said Tate. "Wesson, just keep moving and don't let that thing see your face."

"Copy," she said.

She and Ota began walking, ignoring the robot.

"Hello," said the robot. "I cannot read your identification. Please stop and turn around."

"Keep walking," whispered Wesson.

Facing straight ahead, Ota gave a thumbs up as he kept pace with her.

Behind them, the dog followed. Every few seconds its green light would come on, panning up and down their backs.

"Excuse me," said the dog, "you're required to follow my instructions. Please turn around for identification check."

Wesson and Ota picked up their pace to a quick walk. The whirrs and clacking of the dog's feet on the floor picked up speed as it kept pace with them.

Tate and Monkhouse were the first to reach the meet up location, quickly joined by Rosse and Fulton.

"You seen them things?" asked Rosse.

"No," said Tate.

"Scary as hell. They got guns," said Rosse, his voice rising in disbelief. "Dogs with guns. What kinda sick brain comes up with stuff like that?"

Glancing at a nearby open door, Tate got an idea.

"Everyone inside," he said.

He followed them in and, scanning the room, grabbed a jacket hanging over the back of one of the chairs.

"Hide behind the desks," he said, as he peeked out around the corner of the door. "Don't shoot. There could be more Vix and we don't need to add them to our troubles."

He stuck his head into the hall just as Wesson and Ota came into view.

Tate motioned for them to keep walking and go past his door. Ota calmly nodded while Wesson gave him a curt nod, stress pulling at her face.

Tate disappeared into the office, hugging the wall next to the door and out of sight.

Listening, he heard whirring motors getting closer. He gripped the jacket as Wesson and Ota passed the door.

"Stop," the dog commanded in a hard voice.

Just as the dog passed the door, Tate wheeled into the hall and dropped to his knees, pulling the jacket over the dog.

Tate flinched from the sound of sharp cracks next to his ear. Smoking holes appeared in the jacket and plaster shattered off the wall as the dog fired blindly. Tiny, hardened ceramic darts zipped past Wesson and Ota.

"Take cover," yelled Tate, as the dog's surprisingly powerful legs kicked, trying to break free.

Wesson and Ota dove through a door as chunks of the wall blew out next to them.

The robot was heavier than Tate expected and he threw his body over the struggling form as it wrestled against him. Through the jacket, Tate could feel the dog trying to squirm around towards him. He tried to grab its legs, but the dog wrenched free of his grip.

"Move yer head," said Rosse, suddenly appearing, standing over Tate.

Rosse lifted his foot and Tate pulled his head out of the way as Rosse smashed his boot down on top of the dog.

Its legs buckled under the force and the dog paused for only a moment, then began to fight back again.

Tate's face was flushed and sweating. "It's getting stronger."

He lost his grip on the jacket and the robot began to scramble free of the jacket. Just before the dog's camera appeared, Tate yanked the jacket over it.

Rosse pummeled down on the robot again and again, but the robot only shook it off and continued to fight.

Tate's knuckles were white and his forearms burning. He was tiring out and losing his grip. He had to do something fast.

"Back!" he said. "Get back."

Rosse hurried out of the way as Tate fought to his knees. Getting his feet under him, he squatted over the dog. Grunting, he heaved up the jacket, scooping up the dog in its folds like a sack. Swinging it over his shoulder, he slammed it down to the floor.

The robot hit with a metallic thud. Tate lifted it over his head again, hearing the sharp cracks of its gun. With all his might, he smashed it into the floor again, cracking the tiles.

Smoke and fluid started leaking out of the jacket.

Breathing hard, he lifted it again, the smell of burning electronics stinging his nose. He was fast running out of energy, but he knew he had enough for one more swing.

He heaved the robot over his head and with a growl, he swung the robot down for all he was worth. The robot bashed into the floor. Bits of it fell out of the jacket, scattering on the floor.

The dog twitched and smoldered but didn't get up.

Sweat poured down Tate's face as he gulped air.

Everyone came out of cover and stood around the mangled dog.

"Bad dog," panted Tate.

"Stay!" said Monkhouse, pointing at the still jacket.

"Anyone see where it came from?" asked Tate, wiping his face.

"A hole in the wall," said Rosse.

Fulton looked a couple doors down the hall and pointed. "Like that?"

Everyone looked to a small, black panel at the base of the wall, except Monkhouse who kept staring at the robot.

"Yeah," said Rosse. "Just like..."

That front panel flipped up.

Tate bolted towards the panel just as it was beginning to recede into the wall. He stomped down on the lid and bent it down, making it impossible to retract. The motor strained, but the cover wasn't going anywhere.

Robotic feet appeared in the small gap below the edge of the cover. The dog probed around the opening but could not get out.

Sighing with relief, Tate returned to the team to work out their next move. He glanced up as Monkhouse reappeared from the office.

"I stuffed the bot in a desk drawer," said Monkhouse. "Just in case the thing woke up."

Tate saw the empty jacket and shrugged.

"What kind of company uses lethal security?" asked Wesson.

"One that's serious about its secrets," said Tate.

"We need to get off this floor before another one of those dog things show up," said Monkhouse. "They may have other tricks besides facial scanners and guns."

"Like that?" said Fulton, looking nervously at the bent cover.

They turned just in time to see an articulated claw extend from under the lid. It clamped around the bottom of the lid and attempted to bend it out of the way.

"Are you kid'n me?" said Rosse.

"It's okay," said Tate. "It's not strong enough to bend that metal."

"No disrespect," said Rosse, "how would you know that?"

"That arm is only meant for opening doors and picking up small things," said Tate.

He sounded more confident than he felt and stared at the robotic arm, willing it to fail. The next couple of seconds felt like hours as they watched the dog struggle against the lid, until finally the claw disappeared back inside. Everyone breathed a collective sigh of relief.

"What next?" asked Fulton.

"I'm open to suggestions," said Tate.

"If we run into Vix, the sound of guns will attract another dog," said Wesson.

"If we run into another dog," said Fulton, "we better shoot before they do."

"That'll attract Vix like a dinner bell," said Rosse.

"This place is huge," said Monkhouse. "We hardly covered a third of this floor. We're going to run into one or the other if we go out there looking for that stairwell," he said.

Everyone looked at Ota for his thoughts; he only smiled back at them.

"Really?" said Rosse, annoyed. "We got our butts between a rock and hard place and you're gonna do the silent Zen monk act?"

"I thought it was obvious," said Ota. "We go back out the elevator."

"It ain't moving," grumbled Rosse. "Or did you miss that part while you was meditating?"

"Isn't the power back on?" said Ota.

"What's that...?" Rosse stopped, his mouth hanging for a moment. "Right. The elevator."

"You heard the man," said Tate.

They turned back down the long hall towards the elevator, which soon came into view.

"Didn't we leave the doors open?" asked Fulton.

"Weren't you listening?" said Rosse. "The power's on."

"Yeah, I heard," said Fulton. "I just thought... never mind."

"Well, that's just great," said Rosse as they reached the doors.

Next to the buttons that controlled the elevator was a card scanner.

"No problem," said Tate, patting Monkhouse on the shoulder. "We have our own master key."

"What?" said Monkhouse.

"Use the pry bar," said Tate, slightly confused.

"Oh, that," said Monkhouse, shifting the straps on his tactical pack. "You left it buried in the face of a Vix back there."

Tate swore, mentally kicking himself for such a stupid mistake.

"Can you rewire it?" he asked. "What else do you have in your pack?"

"Sorry, Top," said Monkhouse. "That's out of my skillset."

"Wait a minute," said Fulton. "That's a card reader."

"We know that," said Rosse.

"That robot," said Fulton, undeterred by Rosse. "You said it had facial recognition, but I don't think so. When we saw it scanning those Vix, it wasn't scanning their faces. It was scanning their chests."

"Where employees would wear an ID card," said Tate. "You're too smart for a private."

Rosse looked at Fulton dubiously.

"What? I was looking over your shoulder," said Fulton.

"Good catch," said Tate. "We need to find a card."

"I think I know where one is," said Fulton.

Leaving the group, he trotted down the hall towards the long dead corpse.

"Fulton!" hissed Tate.

"Too smart for a private?" scoffed Rosse.

Fulton reached the body and aimed his gun at it, nudging the corpse with his boot. Satisfied there were no surprises, he slung his rifle over his shoulder, reached down and rolled the body over.

His face screwed up in disgust as he rifled through its clothing. In the folds of its coat he saw a plastic-coated ID badge. His rifle slipped off his shoulder and clattered loudly on the floor.

He stopped cold. Several seconds passed as he listened for anything coming. Finally content, he let out a long breath. He pulled off the ID card and waved it over his head to the others.

He heard it before he saw it. Something running around the corner, coming up behind him.

Fulton looked over his shoulder. A lone Vix was almost on top of him. There was nowhere to go, nothing to do.

Fulton cringed, bracing for the Vix to slam into him.

Its ragged fingers latched onto him as a loud crack echoed through the hall. The Vix's head snapped back, bone and black ooze splashing the wall. The thing rag-dolled, tumbling into Fulton, sending him sprawling to the floor.

Near panicked, he fought to push the fetid thing off him. Hands appeared, pulling away the Vix and grabbing him by his combat harness.

"I'm okay," he blurted.

"Arms up," commanded Tate, as he examined Fulton for bites.

"I'm okay," said Fulton with a trembling voice.

"Not for long," said Rosse.

Everyone went still and listened. Somewhere, down one of the long hallways, they heard the grunts and hissing growls of Vix. They were coming.

"Let's go," said Tate.

Rosse grabbed Fulton and broke into a run.

They quickly reached the elevator and Fulton ran the card though the scanner.

Nothing happened.

"The mag-strip," said Wesson, looking up the hallway. "Turn the card over."

"Right, right," said Fulton, fumbling over the card.

A bellow of gasps and snarls erupted from the end of the hall as a mob of Vix appeared. They instantly broke into a sprint, charging the team.

Fulton's hand was shaking and he almost missed putting the card in the narrow slot.

The elevator chimed and the doors began to open.

"Rosse, Ota, get in," shouted Tate. "Monkhouse, Fulton, cover fire!"

As soon as there was room between the doors, Rosse dropped to the ground and started squeezing into the halfway elevator.

Tate, Monkhouse and Fulton shouldered their rifles and opened up on the Vix.

The leading edge of Vix staggered and fell as bullets ripped into them, tripping the ones close behind. Others jumped, clearing the tangle of bodies like athletes and kept coming.

"When did they start doing that?" blurted Tate.

"Next up!" shouted Rosse.

"Wesson, go," snapped Tate.

Without hesitation, she swiveled her gun behind her and dropped to the floor. Rosse and Ota grabbed her hands and yanked her into the elevator car as Tate slapped in a fresh magazine and switched to full auto.

The Vix were eating up the distance and only twenty feet away. Tate could smell cooking gun oil as his gun overheated. Gore flew off the Vix in chunks. Bodies dropped but more came.

Sparks flew from the swarm and they saw some of the Vix had prosthetic limbs.

"Where are they all coming from?" screamed Fulton.

Tate's gun went quiet as his magazine emptied. Out of reflex he dropped the empty magazine, reaching for a fresh one. They'd be on him before he ever pulled the trigger.

Hands grabbed his ankles and pulled. Tate barely shielded his face from crashing into the floor as he was yanked into the elevator.

Rosse and Monkhouse stepped over Tate and fired through the open doors.

Wesson grabbed the card out of Fulton's hand and swiped it, pressing the button for the next floor down.

"Get back," shouted Rosse.

He and Monkhouse pivoted away from the door as boney hands reached into the elevator, clawing at the air.

The doors closed but hit the arms and opened again.

Tate picked himself off the floor and reached back for his tomahawk.

"Make a hole," he barked, raising the axe.

Everyone squeezed back away as Tate hacked away. Putrid limbs fell at his feet, black blood splashed over his chest and arms, but he kept his grip on the tomahawk.

"Now," he shouted.

Ota reached out and hit the button for the next floor. A single arm grappled blindly as the doors began to close.

With a swift blow, Tate cleanly hacked through the arm and the doors closed.

With a shudder they felt the elevator begin to move.

Tate grabbed a rag from his pocket and wiped the disgusting muck off his face, but mostly just smeared it around, giving him a grotesque mask of war paint.

16

SEPARATED

"I don't like this," said Shy Girl, looking over Samuel's shoulder at the monitor.

Samuel stared at the elevator's security camera feed, running his fingers through his hair.

"These can't be cops," said Bottle Top.

"That guy," said Samuel, tapping the monitor. "The axe man. I think I know him."

Everyone looked closer at the screen. Samuel kept his finger under Tate's image.

"Nah," he said. "Maybe not. It's hard to tell with that crap on his face."

"You think they're after Roman's boy?" asked Shy Girl. "Maybe we should, you know, give him back."

"These guys look pretty harsh," said Bottle Top. "Most of ours are out in the city. We can't go toe to toe with them."

"Everybody just chill out," said Samuel. "We're good here. Spider's dogs will take care of them. Let's see how they do split up."

He moved his finger next to the elevator override switch.

"Weapons ready," snapped Tate.

The team acted as one. Everyone checked their weapons, put in fresh magazines, flicking safeties, fingers off triggers.

"If they didn't know we're here," said Wesson, "they know it now."

"No more screwing around," said Monkhouse, bringing up his rifle.

"Did it look like I was screwing around?" said Rosse.

"Short bursts," said Tate.

They waited for the elevator to reach the next floor. It felt like it would take an eternity. It bumped to a stop and chimed.

Hands tightened on their weapons as the doors began their slow open.

Nothing there.

The elevator opened into a large lobby that branched out to the left and right. Across the lobby was a security desk, behind it a large room concealed behind frosted glass walls. Cautiously, the team moved out of the elevator, their guns sweeping for any threats.

"No dogs," said Fulton, his tension coming down a notch.

"Which way?" asked Wesson.

"I'm not sure," said Tate.

"I think my radio's broken," said Fulton.

Rosse checked his. It wasn't working either.

"Figures," said Monkhouse. "Radio dampening."

"Huh?" grunted Rosse.

"No signal either," said Tate. "Another layer of security."

"That's just perfect," said Rosse. "If we split up, how're we gonna talk to each other?"

"Split up?" said Tate. "Next time you get in the elevator last."

"Where's the Vix?" said Wesson. "When the power came on, all the doors opened up."

Everyone's heads snapped up when a hazy shadow thumped against the frosted glass across the room. It moved listlessly, its face coming into gruesome focus as it pressed against the glass. It moved away from the glass and the shadow faded away.

. . .

Tate leaned around the corner of the lobby and looked down each hallway, left and right. "I don't see any open doors," he said.

"It doesn't make sense," said Monkhouse.

"Hang on," said Rosse. "They got big time security, like a prison. I'll bet ya anything they got a central security room. They can operate the doors remotely. Like upstairs when the power came on."

"There weren't any Vix in the halls until then," said Tate. "They opened all the doors and let the Vix loose."

"That didn't work, "said Monkhouse. Tate looked at him with his gore smeared face. "I mean, it almost did."

"They're trying a different tactic," said Tate. "They're waiting for us to head down one of these halls. Then they'll unlock the doors in front and behind us."

"We'd be the tasty center of a Vix sandwich," said Monkhouse.

Tate looked around the corner again. "There's cameras up and down the halls," he said. "Let's mess up their plans. Ota, can you take them out fast?"

Ota leaned around the corner, locating each of the cameras. He glanced back at Tate with a simple nod.

"Great," said Tate. "Do your thing."

Without a word, Ota stepped around the corner, drawing his pistol. The instant he brought it up, he fired so quickly, the three shots sounded like one. The cameras shattered in glass and sparks.

Ota pivoted, his pistol an organic extension of his hands. Before the echo of his shots had faded, his pistol was back in the holster and the cameras were ruined junk. It had taken him less than three seconds. His expression returned to calm indifference as the rest of the team gawked.

Rosse let out an impressed, low whistle.

"Glad you're on our side," said Monkhouse.

"They're not going to like that," grinned Fulton.

Across the lobby, the doors of the glass office buzzed and clicked open.

Blurry shadows, roused by the gunfire, jerked and twitched against the glass. One of them bumped against the door, cracking it open. Half its neck hung in ribbons over the collar of its shirt. Its black suit and tie smeared with stains.

"No, they aren't," said Tate.

"Forward or back in the elevator?" asked Wesson.

Dante could be anywhere on this floor, or one of the floors below. Finding him would be time consuming and risky.

"We do it the hard way," he said. "We clear every room on this floor before moving on."

The Vix stopped, partially through the door. Its sightless eyes looked right at the team. Everyone cautiously raised their gun in anticipation of the thing's wailing charge.

To their relief, it moved back into the office, the door closing behind it.

"We do this all the time," said Wesson, noticing the worried expression on Monkhouse.

"I'm never going to get used to those things," he said.

"We got another problem," whispered Rosse, peeking around the corner. "There's another one of them robots from Hell coming our way."

Sweat was beading up on Tate's face and he wiped his sleeve over his brow. He glanced between the frosted office and the direction of the robot.

"We shoot out the glass," he said.

"What?" said Monkhouse, balking at the idea. "All those Vix will come piling out."

"We go back to the elevator and let the dog take out the Vix," said Tate. "Then we shoot the bot."

"I like it," said Monkhouse, nodding. "Let's do that."

"Short bursts," said Tate. "Bust up the glass."

Everyone began shooting. Frosted glass shattered, raining down and spilling across the floor. The Vix, whipped into a frenzy, charged in every direction, colliding into furniture and each other.

"Back to the elevator," barked Tate.

Everyone turned, running to the elevator.

.   .   .

Samuel watched as the team sprinted to the elevator. His fingertip rested on the smooth surface of the override button.

Wesson ran in first, followed by Ota.

Samuel's lips curled into a smile as the mice entered his trap.

He watched Rosse, assault rifle up, back into the elevator. He waved Fulton towards him.

Samuel pressed the button, seeing the look of shock on their faces as the doors closed.

"What did you do?" shouted Wesson in alarm.

"I didn't do nothing," yelled Rosse, franticly pressing buttons to stop the doors.

"Stop it!" she said.

"I'm try'n!"

Rosse mashed the emergency stop button as Wesson and Ota struggled against the doors, but nothing was working.

"Tate!" she yelled.

Tate turned around, his face draining of color as he saw Wesson's terrified face disappear behind their only escape.

Tate's eyes darted around for another way out, but it only confirmed what he already knew. They were boxed in and the Vix were the lid.

The rotted mob snarled and churned as they piled out of the office.

"Everyone back," he said.

"Back where?" said Monkhouse, pale with fear.

The Vix came. Nobody had time to count. It didn't matter. They all knew it was too many.

As soon as one appeared in their gun sights, they'd shoot, and another would take its place; always closer than the one before.

Monkhouse was hyperventilating, on the verge of passing out. There was no time to think. Shoot, reload, shoot again.

Unconsciously, they were pushing their backs against the wall as the Vix clogged the narrow hall.

Fulton dropped an empty magazine from his rifle and reached for another. His hand caught on something and he looked down at the frag grenade in his vest.

Letting his rifle fall on its lanyard, he grabbed the grenade and pulled the pin.

"Frag out!" he shouted and tossed the Vix.

Tate's eyes flew open in alarm when he heard Fulton yell. The Vix were only 30 feet away.

He heard the pop of the grenade's safety fly off and watched in horror as it tumbled through the air.

"Down," screamed Tate.

Monkhouse and Fulton glanced at him, confused, but saw him drop into a fetal position and did the same.

The grenade hit one of the Vix in the head, bounced on another and fell to the floor. A sprawled Vix, flailing to get up, swatted the grenade, sending it skittering across the floor at the three hunched soldiers.

Tate heard the sound of clattering metal and watched in terror as the explosive rolled at them.

At any second the grenade would explode in a flash of needle-sized shards of steel. He lunged for it. His fingertips brushed against it, and it took a bounce, dodging out of the way.

Fulton saw Tate miss as the grenade changed course towards him. Yelping in fear, Fulton kicked at it, knocking it back at the Vix.

It exploded.

Jagged metal chips blew out, ripping through the Vix. Bone and meat sprayed across the walls, knocking them back and sending the remaining ones into a confused frenzy, running into walls and back towards the lobby.

The closed space magnified the shockwave, hammering the soldier's senseless. The world tilted and slewed back and forth. Blood leaked from their ruptured eardrums and noses.

Dull noise thrummed through Tate's ringing ears. He drunkenly looked around, trying to find where it was coming from. Monkhouse was groping for his rifle, his face and hands pocked with blood from the shrapnel wounds.

Fulton was rolling on the floor, clutching his smoldering boot. Blood oozed over his hands as he cried in pain.

Something in the back of his mind made Tate look down the hallway and it was only then he remembered the Vix. A pile of bodies lay heaped up just a few feet away. One Vix, pinned under the pile, gurgled as it feebly reached for Tate, its face and arm mangled by the explosion.

The ringing in his ears mingled with Fulton's screams. On hands and knees, Tate crawled over to the writhing private.

"I got you," he mumbled. "Hang on. I got you."

He fumbled in his combat vest and pulled out a small, metal tube. He broke the seal and bit off the cap, revealing several hair-thin needles. Tate stabbed it into Fulton's leg. The pressure trigger injected pain killers into his leg with a hiss.

Within seconds, relief washed across Fulton's face as the agony faded from his face. He laid back, catching his breath, tears streaming down his cheeks.

"Monkhouse," said Tate. "Can you move?"

"I'm numb," he said, his voice shaking. "I don't feel any pain. Is that normal?"

"You'll live," said Tate. "Wipe the blood out of your eyes. Can you see?"

Dragging his sleeve over his face, Monkhouse blinked the muck out of his eyes and smiled. The whiteness of his teeth contrasting with his blood smeared face gave him a macabre mask, but it hardly registered with Tate, who had seen worse.

"We need to move," said Tate, struggling to his feet. "Help Fulton up."

He braced himself against the wall and reached down for his gun. His hand was covered in blood and wiped it distractedly on his pants and gasped as blinding pain shot up his arm.

He brought his left hand closer to his face. Blood seeped thickly down his hand from the nub where his ring finger used to be. The top of his pinky finger was gone from the third knuckle.

CRACK, CRACK, CRACK

"The dog," said Monkhouse.

Tate looked beyond the pile of ruined Vix and saw the robot. The sound of its shots stirred the Vix who were running back and forth, knocking into it.

Tate brought up his rifle, gingerly avoiding touching his severed nub and took aim at the robot.

"Wait until the Vix are dead," he said, seeing Monkhouse lifting his gun to shoot. "Hit the camera."

A moment later, the last Vix was dead. The small panel on the top of the dog closed. Performing its strange prance, the dog rotated, looking for more targets.

Tate watched as it spotted them. The bot stumbled over the bodies that littered the floor as it approached the soldiers.

"Wait for it," he said.

Climbing to the top of the bodies, the bot stopped.

"Now," said Tate, the instant the dog's green light turned on.

Both rifles fired and the front of the dog shattered, sending it tumbling backwards, its legs flailing in the air. It clattered to the floor, twitching and sparking.

"Let's get the hell out of here," croaked Tate. "Fulton, can you walk?"

Propped against Monkhouse, Fulton tested his foot with an expectant grimace, but felt no pain.

"This stuff's great," he said, then noticed Tate's bloody hand and his face fell with regret. "Aw no, Top. I did that? I'm sorry. I didn't mean... what did I do?"

"Forget about that for now," said Tate, as his hand began to throb with punishing pain. "We're alive. I need both of you to get your heads straight. We're not out of this yet. Stay focused."

"I don't hear anything," said Wesson.

They listened in the motionless elevator for any hint of their friends. The sound of gunfire and an explosion had echoed down the elevator shaft, but everything had gone quiet.

"Do you think...?" began Rosse.

"Tate," she said into her radio. "Do you copy?"

They waited a moment, but all they got was static.

Rosse's face fell as he thought the worse. Wesson could see pain and sorrow in Ota's blue eyes.

"The radios aren't working, remember?" she said. "They could be fine. We don't know. Don't jump to conclusions."

Wesson fought to believe her own words and pushed away the dread squeezing her heart.

"We can't sit in this box," said Rosse.

"They would try to get to the next floor down," said Wesson, letting her gaze roam. "We should..." she stopped.

A shiver ran through Samuel as Wesson's eyes met his, or that's how it felt as she looked directly in the elevator's camera.

She stared at him with murder in her eyes. Doubt and fear trickled into his mind. He'd watched them wade through swarms of Vix and destroy his dogs. Maybe it would have been smarter to have given up his hostage, but that time was past. These soldiers were after blood now.

"Oh man," chuckled Bottle Top. "She looks pissed."

It troubled Samuel that his own people couldn't see what he did. He pried his eyes away from the monitor.

"Get Barrios," he said. "Bring him to the stairs. We're out of here."

"But we're kicking their butts," said Bottle Top. "Those guys are stuck in the elevator and the other ones are dead for sure."

Wesson aimed at the camera, pausing to let the image of the gun barrel sink in. A flash of light and the monitor turned to static.

That was the last camera. All of the monitors were electric snow. They were blind.

Maybe the other three were now shredded corpses, but Wesson's expression had burned into his mind. She was his death. He knew it.

"Do what I said!" he snapped.

"Yeah, okay," said Bottle Top, and took off.

Samuel reached across his console and hit the elevator button override. He'd send Wesson and her friends down to the power room, far below. That should buy him enough time to get away.

17

ABOVE AND BELOW

The elevator brakes released with a slight bump and it began moving down.

"Everyone out," ordered Wesson, pushing the escape panel open with the barrel of her rifle. "Rosse first. Quick."

Ota and Wesson locked their hands together, forming a stirrup. Rosse stepped into the hands and they hoisted him up.

He clambered through the hatch. Swiveling on his belly, he reached down to help the next up.

Ota grabbed Rosse's hand and was lifted off his feet.

"Get on the ladder, fast," said Wesson, reaching for Rosse's hand, hoping the rungs hadn't all been cut off.

She winced from Rosse's powerful grip and he pulled her out of the elevator in a single motion.

"Thanks," she said, coming up and planting her feet next to the hatch. "Go!"

Ota was nowhere to be seen as Rosse got to his feet. The ladder rungs were blurring passed them and Rosse grabbed one without hesitating.

"Crap," he grunted as his arm took his full weight.

Wesson launched herself at the ladder, landing on the rungs just behind Rosse.

The elevator disappeared, rumbling into the blackness below.

"Ota, come down," said Wesson. "Rosse, up. We should find the next floor somewhere in-between.

Tate pulled open another drawer at the security desk, finding only sign-in logs and pens and papers.

"Maybe the elevator's the only way," said Monkhouse.

"The only place I've ever seen without a fire escape is a missile silo," said Tate.

"What were you doing in a missile silo?" asked Monkhouse, dumbfounded.

The team had only recently learned of Tate's past as a Delta operator. They had no idea of the breadth and scope of his experiences, and like everyone else in the special forces community, it wasn't something he talked about.

Tate pulled open another drawer. He was looking for a map of the floor showing a way to the stairwell. He shuffled through the papers and folders.

Nothing.

Something else caught his eye. Under the papers was a button marked 'Emergency Only'.

This has to be it.

Tate pressed the button and was rewarded by the sound of an electric lock opening to his right.

"This way," he said, heading towards the sound.

Soon they found a narrow crack in the wall that ran from floor to ceiling; a hidden panel. Tate pulled at the edge and the panel opened to reveal a landing with stairs running up and down.

"Who hides a fire escape?" said Monkhouse.

Tate put a finger to his lips and stepped through the door. He gestured for Monkhouse and Fulton to follow. Once inside, he eased the door closed behind them.

Down below they could hear the sound of several people arguing.

. . .

"Tate, this is Wesson," said Wesson over her radio.

They'd found the next floor and had pried the doors open. It was her last chance to reach Tate before she entered another shielded floor.

"Do you copy?"

"Do you copy?" crackled Tate's earpiece.

Relief washed over the three of them as each heard her on their radio.

"Copy," he whispered. "We're in the stairway. Where are you?"

"Next floor down," said Wesson. "Everyone okay?"

"Banged up, but alive," said Tate. "We're in the fire escape stairwell and I think they're bugging out. I can hear someone below us."

"That explains it," she said. "We just found the door to the stairs. They left it open."

"Hold your position outside the door until I tell you," said Tate. "When you come in, fire off a couple of bursts, just for show. We don't want to hit Dante, or us."

"Copy," she said, trying to sound professional, but smiling with relief that everyone was okay.

Tate nodded to Fulton and Monkhouse who had been listening on the channel.

The voices below became more heated until someone shouted over them.

"Shut up!"

Tate knew that voice. It was Samuel. The voices quieted down to a murmur. Footsteps echoed up to him from the stairs below.

Peeking over the edge of the landing, Tate looked down, waiting until the gang members were about halfway up.

He estimated there were five of them, maybe six. It didn't matter. They were walking into Tate's trap.

He grinned. For the first time since they entered the building, he finally had the upper hand.

"Wesson, now," he said.

A moment later, bursts of gunfire shattered the quiet, echoing up and down the stairwell. The gang shouted in alarm and confusion; a couple of them fired blindly down the stairs.

"Our turn," said Tate, rising up and aiming over the railing.

Monkhouse and Fulton did the same and opened. The stairwell strobed with darts of fire as the cracks of their rifles rang off the walls.

Trapped above and below, the gang screamed in panic, yelling over each other for help.

"Cease fire," said Tate.

The blizzard of gunfire abruptly stopped, leaving only the cries of the desperate gang.

"Samuel," shouted Tate. "You're boxed in."

"Shut up," snapped Samuel, angrily staring down his people.

He waited until they had quieted down then leaned over the railing and shouted up to Tate. "I got your boy," he said.

He pointed at the blindfolded Dante.

Bottle Top roughly grabbed him by the shirt and shoved him to Samuel. Dante's ears were plugged with wadded cotton and he flinched when he felt Samuel's gun press against his neck.

"Let us go, or I cap him," said Samuel.

"Let me do the math for you, you moron," said Tate. "He dies, you die. You fight, you die. Drop your guns and I will let you go."

"Don't piss in my ear and tell me it's raining," said Samuel. "You're gonna smoke us, no matter what."

"I don't give a damn about you," said Tate. "I'm here for Dante."

Shy Girl looked at Samuel, desperate and hopeful. He put his finger to his lips and waved her back.

"Yeah, you're Roman's dog, right?" said Samuel. "Why would he let us go?"

"He wouldn't," said Tate, "but I will. Once I have Dante, I'm taking Roman out of action."

Samuel and his gang traded looks of confusion.

"What's he talking about?" said a gang member.

"You going to do what?" asked Samuel.

"As a matter of fact," said Tate, "I could use your help."

"Are you being real?" said Samuel, letting go of Dante. "You want us to join up with you?"

"You know he's going to keep sending people after you," said Tate. "Together, we can wipe him out. Problem solved."

"Who takes over his operation?"

"You can have it," said Tate.

Monkhouse and Fulton frowned at him, but he waved them off.

"You have to agree to my terms," he said.

"Man, this guy's trying to run you," said Bottle Top. The others murmured angrily in agreement.

"Screw that," said Samuel. "Nobody pushes us around."

"Yeah," said Tate, "that's very inspiring. So look, it's been a long day and you're standing between me and a cold beer. I'm going to roll a couple of grenades down there and we'll call it a day."

The gang's eyes went wide, expecting the metallic clattering of frags towards them at any second.

"Okay," said Samuel. "We're cool."

Tate grinned at Monkhouse and Fulton. "How about that?" he said. "All of you dump your guns over the rail."

The gang looked at Samuel, who lowered his pistol.

"Do it," he said.

"What if he's lying?" said Bottle Top.

"No," said Samuel. "He doesn't work like that."

He held his gun over the rail and let go. The gun clanged loudly as it smacked into the sides of the stairs, plummeting below, into the dark.

The rest of the gang grumbled in protest but followed his example.

"Send Dante up the stairs," said Tate.

Samuel untied the rag around Dante's head and pulled the stuffing out of his ears.

Dante blinked several times, adjusting to the light and rubbed his face where the blindfold had bit into him.

Without a word, he climbed the stairs.

Tate guardedly watched, making sure Dante was alone. His clothes were disheveled with streaks of dirt, but he looked unharmed. Dante smiled at Tate through red eyes and a stubbled face.

"Quite an adventure," said Dante. "Thank you for..."

His words faltered as he saw the bloody condition of the three soldiers.

"Are you okay?" asked Tate.

"A few bruises, but nothing more," said Dante.

"You look surprised to see us," said Tate, reading his frown.

"I thought Roman would send his own people," said Dante. He tilted his head thoughtfully. "On reflection, he isn't the kind of person to sacrifice his own people when he can use you."

"I'll bet this didn't work out the way you planned," said Tate.

Dante raised his eyebrows in mild confusion.

"You sabotaged the negotiations," said Tate.

"You saw that, did you?" said Dante.

"Not at first, but I worked it out," said Tate. "If you wanted out from under Roman, why not leave? It would have been a lot easier than blowing up the negotiations and kicking off that dumpster fire."

"I did come prepared," said Dante.

"The armored BMW?" said Tate. "How'd that work out?"

"I'm sorry I put you in danger," he said, looking gravely at Tate's hand. "I underestimated the intensity of the Brotherhood's reaction."

"That's a mild way to put it," chuckled Tate.

"Roman has a lot of power," said Dante, "but he couldn't fight an all-out war in the city. The outcry would bring the police, and probably the military down on his head. He'd have to piecemeal his battles with the Brotherhood. The odds would not be guaranteed in his favor. A prolonged war would weaken him and he'd become obsessed with it. Two factors I was going to take advantage of."

"You wouldn't need to go through all of that unless he's got something on you," said Tate. "Or something important to you."

"Close enough," said Dante, avoiding the specifics of his vulnerability. "As you have come to learn, once he's got his hooks in you, he doesn't let go. Now it looks like I'm back at square one. You hand me back to Roman and it all returns to normal. Well, *his* normal."

"I wouldn't unpack your bags just yet," said Tate. "Between us and the Brotherhood, we could do him a lot of damage. Maybe take out his operation."

"I don't mind sacrificing a gang, but I feel I should warn you," said Dante. "His operation is much larger than you may think."

"You can educate me after we get out of here," said Tate. "If he's the head of the snake, that's all I need to know."

"A single bullet would be all it took," said Dante.

"I've been a lot of things, but an assassin isn't one of them," said Tate.

"You're something of a boy scout," said Dante.

Tate chuckled. "I wouldn't say that but pulling the trigger on an unarmed man is harder than you think."

"Unarmed?" asked Dante. "By my count, he's threatened to kill you, your career and your people. That would not be my definition of harmless."

Tate frowned, considering the truth of Dante's words.

"And of course, he was responsible for the hanging of three of your solders," said Dante. "And those are just the ones you know about."

"There's more?" asked Tate, feeling his face flush with anger.

Dante nodded his head darkly.

"I had reservations about working for Roman from the beginning," he said. "Not that my previous employers were angels. He's a different breed."

"I think murderous psychotic is the expression you're looking for," smirked Tate. "But we have to shut him down first and I can't do that because I don't know where he is."

"I can help you there," said Dante. "Do you have a map?"

"Gosh," said Tate, patting the pockets of his vest. "I must have forgotten it when I was packing for an assault."

"Fair point," said Dante with a rueful smile. "Before I head back to Roman's, I'll show you on a map where his villa is. He's protected, but overconfident. If you want to cripple him, that's where to do it."

"Perfect," said Tate.

"And don't leave anything standing," said Dante, turning serious. "Nothing. Standing."

"I'll do what I can," said Tate, not sure what to make of his insistence. "Let's wrap this up. We can talk details later. Monkhouse, take

Dante and Fulton up to the ground level. Stay inside the stairway. Wait for me there."

"Got it," said Monkhouse.

He groaned under stiff muscles and tried to pull Fulton to his feet. Dante took the wounded private's other arm, and together they got him up.

"I'm okay," said Fulton with a sloppy grin. "I don't feel a thing. Really."

"Wish I could say the same," grunted Monkhouse, as they began up the stairs.

"Samuel," yelled Tate. "Send your people up. One at a time. Wesson," he said into the radio, "keep your end covered. If anyone comes down there, shoot them. I'll call you up in a few."

Several minutes later, Tate had checked all the gang members, making sure they were unarmed, then called up Wesson's group to join him.

"Holy crap!" said Rosse, seeing Tate's mangled hand.

He broke out his medkit and started working on the wound.

"Did they do this?" growled Rosse, flashing a menacing look at the gang members.

"Friendly fire," said Tate, wincing as Rosse put a dressing on his hand. "I'll tell you later."

Wesson stared at his hand, then saw he was looking at her.

"There was nothing you could have done," he said.

"I shouldn't have left," she said.

"Are you trying to make this all about you?" grinned Tate.

Wesson chuckled, shaking her head.

After Rosse had finished, Tate sat down next to Samuel, who'd been in quiet conversation with his gang. It worried him that the gang leader was already planning a double cross. Tate had to cement their truce if there was going to be any peace between them.

"Let's get this straight," he said to Samuel. "We don't have to like each other, but we don't stab each other in the back. Everyone gets though this alive if we trust each other."

Tate could see the wheels turning in Samuel's head, then he nodded in agreement.

"Yeah, okay," said Samuel, extending his hand. "The Brotherhood doesn't break a pact."

Tate shook it with his good hand. He wasn't convinced he trusted Samuel, but it was surprising how much significance even the most cutthroat lowlifes put on a handshake.

"Let's get out of here," said Tate, getting to his feet. "After you."

Samuel looked like he was about to object, but then shrugged his shoulders and motioned to his gang to start up the stairs.

"Where's your other people?" asked Tate as they climbed.

If Samuel was going to betray him, his first opportunity would be when they left the building. Half his team were wounded. They were low on ammo and they'd be exposed in that wide-open parking lot. It would be the perfect time for an ambush.

"I got a guy on the roof," said Samuel. "Shy Girl, tell Spider to call off his dogs and bring him down. Make sure he understands everything's cool."

Shy Girl glanced at Tate and his gun, then back to Samuel. He nodded, letting her know she could go and she started up the stairs.

"Monkhouse," radioed Tate. "One of Samuel's people is getting someone from the roof and bringing them down to you."

"Okay, Top," replied Monkhouse. "Got it."

"What about the others?" asked Tate.

"We stay spread out," said Samuel, tapping his temple. "Eyes and ears, you know what I mean? Takes a lot to run this city."

"That reminds me," said Tate. "There's a club called the Blue Orchid. I'd appreciate it if you left that one alone."

"I don't know that place," said Samuel, "but yeah, I'll tell my people."

"Thanks," said Tate.

It felt good to have a win under his belt. He thought about sending Teddy a note instead of telling him in person. He inwardly cringed, knowing he'd make an embarrassing fuss over him and Tate wasn't comfortable with the attention.

How many more stairs?

His legs were like lead. It had been a long day.

Was it still the same day? he wondered. Everything they'd been through jumbled together, making it hard to judge the time.

All of the Grave Diggers were exhausted and were sagging under the fatigue. They could feel the demand for sleep soaking into every move but knew this wasn't over until they were back home.

Wesson bit down on the inside of her mouth, using the pain to keep her alert. Rosse's cheek was red from slapping himself. Tate dug a packet of instant coffee out of his pocket. Wesson watched in disgust as he stuffed a pinch of granules under his tongue.

He tried to keep a poker-face but couldn't mask his watering eyes, making her laugh.

"We're coming up," he radioed to Monkhouse as they reached the last set of stairs to the ground level.

"Everything okay?" asked Monkhouse.

"Yeah," said Rosse, chiming in. "One big happy family."

They chugged up the final set of stairs and waited on the landing until Shy Girl Spider joined them. Spider eyed Tate and his group suspiciously, but Samuel brought him up to speed.

Spider shrugged and, reaching behind his back, pulled out a sawed-off shotgun from his waistband. He handed it to Samuel, who gave it to Tate.

Nobody had even thought to check Spider for weapons. Tate cursed himself for such a stupid oversight.

"Are there any security bots on the first floor?" he asked.

"No," said Spider. "It's cool."

Rosse reached for the door to the first floor but stopped as Monkhouse spoke.

"Just out of curiosity," he said, "did you ever have one of those bots wander off where they weren't supposed to go?"

"No, man," said Spider. "They got programming that keeps them on their own floor. I tried taking one to the roof for a pet..."

"You wanted that thing for a pet?" blurted Rosse.

"They're cool," shrugged Spider. "Yeah, as soon as we were off the floor the dog shut down. I tried all kinds of stuff, but it didn't wake up until I took it back."

"Thanks," said Monkhouse. "Good to know."

"Are there any traps on the first floor?" asked Tate.

"Man, relax," said Samuel, chuckling at Tate's caution. "I know my castle. Nothing up here to sweat about."

"Did my dogs do that?" grinned Spider, looking at Tate's hand.

"Hey," said Samuel, smacking Spider's head. "These people are friends."

Spider shrugged off the blow, hardly noticing, but kept looking at Tate's hand who didn't need reminding; the painful throbbing was almost all he could think about.

"We'll head outside with you," said Samuel to Tate. "Just in case any of my people are coming back and see you. I'll make sure everyone knows we're working together."

Tate nodded and motioned for Monkhouse to lead the way onto the first floor.

He was craving the smell of fresh air and the feel of it on his face. Actually, he was craving feeling anything besides his painful hand.

Sunlight was tinged with yellow-orange as the afternoon was turning to early evening. Tate felt confident they'd be able to return to the base unseen and before anyone might come looking for them.

They filed out the glass doors and into the broad, open parking lot.

"We got our rides hidden in the trees outside the fence," said Samuel. "Low profile, you know?"

Tate nodded, but said nothing. He was tired and didn't feel like talking. All he could think about was how good it would feel to lay down in his bed.

"Hey, man," said Samuel, "I'd love to see the look on Roman's face when he finds out we're teaming up."

"He can't find out about us," said Tate, flushing with worry. If Roman caught wind that they had formed an alliance, he wouldn't stop until all of them were dead.

"Just thinking it," said Samuel. "He's not gonna hear it from us."

He held out his fist to bump with Tate, who released his rifle to use his good hand.

The smile on Samuel's face changed to confusion as a puff of dust bloomed off his chest.

"Down!" yelled Tate, grabbing Dante and yanking him to the ground.

There was no confusion in his mind. He knew exactly what just happened. The rest of the Grave Diggers dropped on command, leaving Samuel and his people looking bewildered.

Then Tate heard it. Several muffled coughs from the tree line.

Samuel and his people staggered as a hail of bullets punched into them.

Tate pivoted on his belly, facing the direction of the silenced gun fire. He fired without any real target, hoping at best to suppress the shooters. He and his team were sitting ducks, without any conceal-ment in the parking lot.

His rifle bucked and the bolt locked open. He rolled onto his side, patting his vest for a magazine. There were none.

"Need a mag!" he shouted.

The gang members toppled over all around them as he heard the guns of his team fall silent.

"I'm empty," shouted Wesson.

"Same," hollered Rosse.

"Drop your weapons," bellowed a synthetic female voice from the tree line.

18

THIS IS GOING TO HURT

Whoever had ambushed them had singled out the gang members. Tate recognized that if the shooters had wanted, he and his team would already be dead.

"Cease fire," he ordered.

"Show me your hands," shouted the voice.

"Do what she says," yelled Tate.

He and the team struggled to their knees and put their hands in the air.

After a moment, several black-clad figures emerged from the trees. Their faces were covered with balaclavas and they were clad in black assault armor. The figures quick walked across the parking lot with automatic rifles up and ready.

Tate eyed his attackers, not knowing what would happen next. Once they were close enough, he saw each of them had a badge stenciled on the chest plate of their armor.

"You guys are cops?" blurted Rosse in disbelief.

"What are you doing here?" asked Tate, as one of them kicked his rifle away.

They were well outside the city and jurisdiction. It made no sense.

The police ignored him as they rolled over the bodies of the gang members and photographed their faces.

Tate recognized the practice; proof of death. He'd done it many times to confirm an assigned target had been hit.

"Who are you working for?' he asked.

They continued as if he hadn't spoken. The police checked every face of the living against their data pad until they stopped with Dante.

"Got him," said the female cop. "Mr Barrios, you're to come with us."

"Who is 'us'?" he asked.

"Nesto San Roman sent us to retrieve you," said the cop.

"Crooked cops," scoffed Rosse. "You don't deserve to wear a badge."

"What the hell is this?" growled Tate. "I told Roman we'd get him out."

"And you did," said the cop flatly. "We're handling it from here."

They helped Dante to his feet as Tate boiled with anger. Roman had used him. Worse still, he was helpless to stop them from taking the one person who could show him Roman's base.

"Just a moment," said Dante to the police. He walked over and crouched to eye level with the kneeling Tate. "I appreciate what you and your people did for me. Unfortunately, we'll have to cancel our eleven-twenty-nine dinner."

Tate frowned in confusion and Dante's expression told him nothing else.

"Let's go," said the female cop.

Two of the cops escorted Dante, guiding him by the arms, while the rest of them backed away, weapons trained on Tate and his team.

"You people stay here for the next ten minutes," said the cop.

It was an order. Tate wanted to retaliate but had nothing to back it up with. Most of them were out of ammo and going against a fresh, fully equipped enemy would be a short and one-sided fight.

Rosse cursed under his breath as he sat back on his heels.

"I feel like we was robbed," he said.

"We were," said Tate, clenching his good hand in anger.

"They're all dead," said Monkhouse, glancing at the bodies around them.

Tate felt someone looking over at him. His gaze landed on the pale face of Shy Girl; her lifeless eyes fixed on him. He had walked her into a death trap. It didn't matter that he didn't know what would happen. Guilt was nimble that way. It didn't care about facts and logic.

"What do we do now?" asked Wesson.

"We go home," said Tate, tearing his eyes away from Shy Girl. "Fulton needs a doctor."

"Don't anyone worry about me," said Monkhouse, raising his hand. Rivulets of dried blood streaked his face from the shrapnel wounds. "But thanks for asking."

He felt everyone staring at him and squirmed uncomfortably. "Don't judge," he said. "I laugh through my pain."

With Rosse and Ota supporting Fulton, the ragged team headed back to their car and home.

Out of habit, Tate did a head count as the last of his team climbed out of the tunnel and back into the shed.

"Wesson," he said, "rouse the doctor and tell him we'll be waiting at the hospital."

"He's not going to like this," she said.

"You're tough," grinned Tate. Doctor Biscot had a well-earned reputation for his abrasive bedside manner. Being woken up in the middle of the night was going to hone that attitude to a whole new edge. "You can handle him."

Wesson pursed her lips, un-amused, and left.

What was originally a basic field hospital had struggled to keep up with the growth of Fort Hickok. The Army was reluctant to divert its better equipment to their bastard child, the AVEF, but someone had twisted the right arm and now they had a decent medical facility.

They could hear Biscot swearing in the distance before they could see him. Everyone quickly got out of the way as he walked past the battered team, unlocked the door and went inside as if they weren't there.

Lights snapped on as a worried corporal ran to the door. "He's already here?"

"Afraid so," said Rosse.

"Where's my Charlie?" shouted the doctor.

The corporal dashed inside. "Here doctor."

The Army's occupational code for a nurse was 68-C, or Charlie. The doctor didn't bother with learning names, instead naming his staff Charlie One, Charlie Two, etc. His charming nature guaranteed no one stayed around long enough that he reached Charlie Three.

"Do I have a patient, or am I supposed to give myself a prostate exam?" growled Biscot.

Rosse and Ota helped Fulton through the door and the nurse guided them into an examination room. He helped ease Fulton onto the bed as the doctor washed his hands, grumbling.

"Middle of the damn night," said Biscot. "I'm not running an all-night diner."

Another nurse came through the door and quickly began assisting with Fulton under the glare of the doctor.

He shrugged into his white coat, scowling at the filthy soldiers messing up his emergency room. "You," he barked at Monkhouse. "Wait for me in the other room. I don't need to smell more than one at a time."

Ota took Monkhouse behind a curtain.

"I appreciate the inconvenience," said Tate, trying to smooth things over.

"Yeah," said Biscot. "Me too. So, what's your problem?"

Tate held up his bandaged hand. The material was caked with dried blood and dirt.

"You call yourself a medic?" asked the doctor, frowning at Rosse.

"It looked better when I first put it on," he explained. "I tried to immobilize it, but he..."

"Whatever," said the doctor, as he began to remove it.

"Watch it!" snapped Tate, at the less than gentle treatment of the doctor.

"This has to come off," said the doctor. "You couldn't figure it's going to hurt?"

"You could try being..."

"Where the hell's your fingers?" asked the doctor, holding Tate's gruesome hand inches from his nose. "I can't do anything with this. Clean it, stick it in some ice for the pain."

"Hang on, doc," said Rosse, searching his pockets. He pulled out a bundle of gauze and unwrapped it, revealing an icepack containing Tate's finger.

"Good for you," said the doctor, picking up the finger.

"How'd you get that?" asked Tate.

"I'm trying to concentrate," said Biscot. "Chat later."

He sniffed the finger then examined it under the stark light of a surgical lamp.

"Looks like a clean amputation," he said, nodding with approval. "If you're going to lose a finger, this is the way to do it."

"You can put it back on?" asked Tate, hopeful.

"Depending on how picky you are," said Biscot. "I could put a duck's head there if you want."

Tate began to seriously weigh how much he was willing to go through with Biscot before walking out, minus a finger. He took a deep breath and gave it one last try.

"I mean, can you reattach it and will my finger work?"

"Do you play piano?" asked the doctor.

"Uh, no."

"Good," said the doctor. "Cause if you didn't before, you aren't now. Otherwise, I think I can work with this.

Charlie Two," he said.

The two nurses working to cut off Fulton's boots stopped, looking at the doctor with apprehension.

"Hanson?" said the nurse, pointing to himself.

"Sure," said the doctor. "Clean this man's wound and this finger. Give him a local pain killer. Prep him for micro-surgery. Mix up bonding agent to fuse the bone."

"Yes, sir," said Hanson, taking the finger.

"And don't get fancy," said the doctor. "Just give me surfaces that will heal."

"Yes, sir," said Hanson.

"Not like he won't find another excuse to blow it off his hand again."

Hanson left with Tate's finger, looking for the needed supplies.

Biscot walked over to examine Fulton.

"Thanks, Rosse," said Tate. "That was quick thinking."

"Thanks, Top," smiled Rosse.

"How'd you even find it?"

"Monkhouse," said Rosse. "He gave it to me. It was inside his shirt."

Tate made a mental note to thank Monkhouse. The idea of losing a finger had lost all meaning while he was fighting killer robots and swarms of Vix. Now that he had time to think about it, having all his fingers was important to him.

"I know this man," said the doctor, looking down on Fulton's face.

Fulton looked up at the doctor with a crooked smile.

"You brought him in with trauma to the chest and arm?" asked the doctor.

Tate flashed back to the first mission of the newly-formed Grave Diggers. They had barely survived.

"Yes," he said. "You helped him before."

"Since when do Vix shoot back?" asked Biscot.

"That, uh," stumbled Tate, "that was a training accident."

"The shrapnel in his foot?"

"Training accident," said Tate.

"And that?" said Biscot, frowning at Tate's hand.

"Training accident," they said in unison.

The doctor looked at Tate with open skepticism. The nurse had removed Fulton's boot and sock and was just finishing up swabbing off the blood.

"You morons keep this up," said the doctor, bending over Fulton's foot, "you'll all be dead before you go into the field."

"Occupational hazard," smirked Tate.

The doctor glared at Tate.

"Sorry," said Tate, dropping the smile. "How bad is it?" he asked, changing the subject.

"See that blood?" said the doctor, pointing to the bloody rags on the floor. "Anytime you see that stuff on the outside of the body, it's bad."

"It's been a rough day, doctor," sighed Tate. "Can you be just a little less difficult?"

"Sure," said the doctor. "All I've got is a crappy x-ray machine, living in the damn stone ages. Hey kid," he said to Fulton, who was watching him with distracted interest. "Wiggle your toes."

Tate watched as the toes on Fulton's foot wobbled, feeling relief spread through him.

"Mostly tissue damage," said the doctor. "Likely some tendon damage too. He's lucky the boot slowed down the shrapnel, otherwise there wouldn't be a foot to look at."

Hanson came back in holding a steel dish with Tate's finger floating in a bed of ice.

The doctor looked at him, exasperated.

"What am I supposed to attach that to?" he said. "You got a whole soldier that hasn't been prepped."

"I'm ready for you to clean my hand," said Tate.

"Come with me, sir," said Hanson, leading Tate away.

"He's not a sir," hollered Biscot. "I'm a sir. Moron."

It was well after midnight and Tate was dead on his feet. Monkhouse had been released after seventeen pieces of shrapnel had been taken out of his face. He was lucky that he shielded his eyes before the grenade had gone off, or he'd be blind.

Fulton would stay overnight. The doctor wanted the swelling in his foot to go down before he would attempt to remove the shards of metal.

Tate didn't expect Fulton to be released soon, and once he was it would be a couple of months of rehab before he could return to active duty.

The doctor had reattached his finger, which even amazed him. Tate had thought it would require hours of surgery. He examined the lightweight but hard cast fitted around his hand.

"Pay attention," said the doctor. "If you don't want that finger to rot off your hand, you'll do what I say."

"Sorry," said Tate, refocusing his attention.

"I fused the bone between the first and second knuckle," continued the doctor. "I had to bridge the missing tendons, but once it's healed up they shouldn't come apart. I used some synth-tissue to replace the missing pad. Your finger shouldn't reject it, but we won't know until it does, or doesn't."

"I can't tell you how much I appreciate you saving my finger," said Tate.

"You could if you tried hard enough," said Biscot.

Tate opened his mouth to apologize, but the doctor waved him off.

"Doesn't matter," he said. "You seem like the kind of guy who can't be trusted to follow orders, so I used poly-carbon for the cast. It's strong enough to protect against some shock damage, but it's not indestructible. Short version, don't be stupid."

Tate briefly looked at the cast. It was supposed to be flesh colored, but looked like a life sized, plastic doll hand. His thumb and fore-finger were free to use, which he was grateful for.

"See me in a month," said the doctor.

"Thanks," said Tate, opting to play it safe and not give the doctor any verbal ammo to beat him up with.

"Get some rest," said the doctor. "If the base commander pulls another assembly, you can tell him I gave you permission to miss it."

Tate almost missed the doctor's choice of words.

"Another?" he asked.

Biscot looked at Tate with a wry smile.

"The base commander called a general assembly yesterday," he said. "Had everyone roll out for inspection."

"The entire base?" marveled Tate. "Why?"

"Because he's a dick," said Biscot. "How should I know? Any questions about your hand? No? Good. I got an empty bed waiting for me."

Tate puzzled over the missed assembly as he headed to his quarters. When Wade discovered Tate and his team weren't present, he had to have sent his MPs to find them. They would have reported back they were nowhere on the base.

Why they hadn't been arrested as soon as they set foot back on the base?

The front door of his quarters came into view. There was no MP standing watch, ready to take him in.

What is Wade up to?

As he walked through the door and saw his own bed, everything else lost their priority.

Tate dumped his gear on the floor; never mind how neat Fulton kept his place.

———

"It's like someone grafted a creepy doll hand onto your wrist," said Kaiden, gazing at his cast.

"Can you try to concentrate?" said Tate.

"Yeah, of course," she said. "Sorry. What were you saying?"

"Roman owns the city police," he said. "They jumped us and..."

"The entire force?" said Kaiden.

"No," he said. "But it's clear he's got enough on the payroll to..."

"Does it itch?"

"What?"

"What do you do if your hand itches?" asked Kaiden.

"Here," said Tate, exasperated.

He put his hand out for Kaiden to look at. He'd never known her to have a macabre side, but she seemed fascinated by the cast.

"Is it strong?" she asked.

"I don't know," said Tate. "I'm not going to test it."

Satisfied, Kaiden seemed to have lost interest in his cast and leaned back into her chair, prompting Tate to continue.

"They grabbed Dante right out of my hands," he said.

"Hand," she said, holding up her hand, mimicking the shape of his cast.

"I could have lost my finger," said Tate.

"I'm just trying to take your mind of the fact that you lost part of your pinky," she said. "They grabbed Dante, go ahead."

"He was going to show me Roman's location," he said.

"He was lying," she said, after thinking it over.

"What do you mean?" said Tate.

"If he really wanted you to attack Roman," she said, "he would have told you how to find him."

"I don't think so," he said. "It's why he sabotaged the negotiations with the Brotherhood."

"Did he say anything significant?" asked Kaiden.

"We were ducking bullets," he said, rubbing his jaw. "There wasn't much chitchat. Wait... He did say something about missing dinner, but I thought he was trying to be clever."

"This guy made a living working under pressure," she said. "Does he strike you as the kind of person who makes lame jokes at a time like that?"

Tate paused, mulling over her question. He and Dante had had their car set on fire, riddled with bullets and rammed by a truck. He'd been taken hostage and beaten. Through it all, Dante had been nothing but self-possessed.

"He was trying to tell me something," he said.

"Not trying," said Kaiden. "He did tell you something. You just haven't figured it out. What did he say?"

"When the cops were helping him up, he said he was sorry we would miss dinner," said Tate.

"Miss dinner?" she asked. "Those were his words?"

"No," he said. "Our dinner appointment." He snapped his fingers as the memory came back to him. "He said we'd have to cancel our eleven-twenty-nine dinner."

"Does that number mean anything to you?" asked Kaiden.

"No," he said, delving into the possible meanings. "Eleven. Maybe he meant one, one?"

"It's too short to be coordinates," said Kaiden. "An address?"

"Roman's villa is in the jungle," said Tate, shaking his head.

"Let's come at this from a different angle," she said. "How did the cops know where to find Dante?"

"Same way we did," he said. "Dante's got a tracker." His face lit up as realization dawned on him. "That's what he was talking about. It's the frequency of Dante's tracker."

"Would Roman tell him his own frequency?" she asked. "Seems like the kind of thing you don't tell someone you want to keep under your thumb."

"He wouldn't," he said. "Not intentionally. Dante is smart. He probably started working out what the frequency was the day Roman tagged him. We need something that can read that frequency."

"We wouldn't be able to pick up on that tracker from this distance," said Kaiden.

"Roman did," said Tate.

"True," she said.

"You have resources," he said. "Can you find him?"

Kaiden looked at him with a pained smile.

"I don't have a secret decoder ring with answers to every problem," she said. "What about Nathan?"

"I might have already used up my favors for a while," said Tate. "He wasn't happy about it."

"I might be able to persuade him," she said. "He likes me."

"I think you have a very different definition of 'like' than other people," he said.

"You're running out of options," said Kaiden.

"I don't even know if I'm right about the frequency," he said, wondering if his guess was taking him in the wrong direction.

"The tracker would be too small to transmit over a far distance," she said. "I think you're right. It's not a frequency."

"That's it," said Tate. "The number is how he's located. The search transmission does all the heavy lifting. It has the reach to cover a long distance and pings that specific number and the tracker responds."

"Like locating an emergency beacon," said Kaiden.

"Exactly like a beacon," he said, getting to his feet. "The helicopter. It's equipped to locate emergency beacons. I know the sergeant that does the maintenance on the Blackhawk."

"Will he help?" she asked.

"It depends on how much beer I'm carrying," said Tate.

19
———

NIGHT RUN

S ergeant Franks was the chief mechanic on the base. He could fix
or rebuild anything. "Except my last four marriages," he'd say.

Replacement parts were hard to come by; sometimes impossible
and that was where he shined. He could use cannibalized toaster
parts to fix a helicopter. If there wasn't something to cannibalize, he'd
disappear into his workshop with a piece of scrap metal and fabricate
a part.

Someone once joked that if a professionally trained engineer ever
saw Franks' jigsaw mashup of parts and workarounds, they'd run in
terror. Since then, anything the mechanic touched was dubbed a
Franks-enstine machine.

Walking into the maintenance building, Tate spotted Franks
lecturing a handful of new trainees furiously taking notes, hoping to
learn the ways of the master and harness his magic touch for
themselves.

"Take a break," said Franks, spotting Tate who was causally
tapping his leg with a small packet.

The trainees moved off a short distance and Tate told him he was
putting together a training exercise for his team.

Franks glanced between Tate's lopsided grin and the packet. He knew Tate was full of bull but weighed which he was more willing to sacrifice. His suspension of disbelief or what was inside the envelope.

"Yeah, I can help," said Franks.

Together they walked to the helipad. Tate always felt a thrill when he saw a Blackhawk. Nearly every operation he'd ever been in had begun by climbing into one. They were tough, agile and could take a beating.

Franks climbed into the pilot's seat and Tate sat next to him in the co-pilot's position.

Sitting in the chair, he marveled at the packed flight deck of switches, buttons and controls in front and above him. There was almost nowhere you could put your hand without touching something.

Franks settled into his seat with familiar ease, looking at Tate with expectation.

Tate handed it over.

Franks glanced out the window, even though he knew nobody was there, then opened the packet. He let out a low whistle as he took out an aged CD case. A gate-drive would have made it easier for Tate. All he had to do was download a digital version, but Franks had lovingly rebuilt a vintage CD player and Tate knew it was CDs or nothing at all.

"Airwolf, season two, episode five?" said Franks. His eyes roved over the case like it was treasure.

"The Hunted," smiled Tate.

Franks had once confessed his secret addiction to the cheesy 80s TV show over several beers. Tate wasn't one to judge and saw an opportunity to get on the mechanic's good side. Finding the old recordings had been more luck than skill, but the first time he handed one of the rare CDs to Franks, he had a friend for life.

Clearing his throat, Franks tore his eyes away from the CD and stashed it in his jacket.

"Okay," he said. "Let's see what we can do about your training exercise."

Reaching to the overhead panel, he switched on a bank of batteries. The flight deck lit up in a confusing array of screens, gauges and pilot interface.

"What's the number?"

Tate read it and Franks switched the function of the center screen to tracking. He punched in the number on the keypad and Tate watched with anticipation for a small blip to appear.

The seconds dragged by. Nothing happened.

"Looks like your number's no good," said Franks. "Or there's too much clutter to pick it up at ground level."

Tate leaned forward and looked up at the sky.

"I know what you're thinking," said Franks. "I can't take a helo out for a joy ride anytime I want."

Tate stared at the pocket where Franks had put the Airwolf CD. The look wasn't lost on the mechanic.

"All right, all right," he said, and fired up the Blackhawk's engines.

They put on their headsets as the turbines began their familiar whine. Franks' hand moved over buttons and switches as rotors picked up speed until they were ready to fly.

"Don't touch anything," he grumbled, as he grasped the collective.

"What if you have a heart attack and we're way up there?" chuckled Tate.

"Well," said Franks, pulling up on the collective and lifting the Blackhawk into the air, "I guess it sucks to be you."

As they rose higher, Tate watched the ground fall away, taking in the sweeping vista of the jungle. Flying above everything, he felt a strange mixture of being very small in the grand scheme of things, but free from earthly cares.

His wandering thoughts were interrupted as the tracking screen began chiming.

"There ya go," said Franks happily. "The old girl works like the day she rolled off the assembly line."

Tate scribbled down the longitude and latitude and stuffed the note in his pocket.

"That's a long way to go just for training," said Franks.

"The reward is in the journey."

Franks took the hint.

"That's all I needed," said Tate. "I really appreciate it."

"If I'm going to be honest," said Franks, as the helicopter descended, "I'm happy for any excuse to fly. But that doesn't mean you stop bringing me more Airwolfs," he added quickly, seeing Tate's grin.

The Blackhawk gently rocked as its skids touched down on the helicopter pad and Franks shut it down.

Tate spent a few friendly minutes shooting the breeze with the mechanic, but inside he was chomping at the bit to rush back to his quarters and finalize the mission plan to attack Roman. After all this time, he finally had the location of the crazy psycho's villa. Tate's new purpose in life was to burn it all to the ground. With any luck, the scum would be in when it happened.

Tate had reviewed the operational plan with Wesson who had studied his plan over the past few days. Her questions and observations about the plan were insightful. Together they hammered out the bugs and turned it over to the rest of the team to study.

Everyone was assembled in their makeshift briefing room. Kaiden distractedly leafed through the mission folder as Tate answered a few of the team's questions before getting down to the final recap.

"Roman's villa has an excellent vantage point from the top of this hill," he said, pointing to the blurry image he was able to get from the old satellite archives.

"Hey, Top," said Rosse. "I'm not crazy about all this guesswork. We don't know what's out there. What happens if we run into something we can't handle?"

"We adapt," said Tate. "We work the problem."

"We don't even know what kind of security forces he's got there," said Monkhouse, worried.

"We're not always going to have the luxury of drones or satellite recon," said Tate. "And they don't always tell the whole story. The moment we put boots on the ground things can change quickly. Your ability to rapidly adjust to a changing situation is one of the best skills you can have. Monkhouse, did you study the mission briefing?"

"Yes," he said.

"What do you think?" asked Tate.

Monkhouse opened his folder and flipped through the pages.

"Not as many crossword puzzles as I like," he said. "A little dry in places."

Chuckles rippled around the room, except Rosse who rolled his eyes with a groan.

"I would have," smiled Tate, "but we don't have three weeks for you to figure it out."

Everyone laughed, Rosse the loudest, and Monkhouse took the good-natured jab with a grin.

"Okay, back on topic," said Tate. "Based on the briefing, what kind of security force is at the villa?"

Monkhouse looked thoughtful as he collected his thoughts. "Okay. The villa is secluded and secret. Roman's been running his business out of there for a few years and nobody's attacked him, so he must be pretty confident it's a safe location. I'd guess he'll have ten, maybe fifteen guards, tops."

"Very good," said Tate. "Ota, describe the most likely features about the villa we'll have to deal with."

"The villa was built by his former boss," he started, without hesitation. "There'll be a central compound surrounded by a high wall patrolled by his security. The boss was a central figure in the drug cartel. That made him a high value target of the national police. He'd be prepared in case his villa was raided. There's probably a safe room and an escape tunnel that leads out of the villa and under the wall."

"What do you think, Kaiden? Did we miss anything?"

She closed the folder and leaned back, clasping her hands behind her head.

"You left out infrared cameras," she said. "There could be motion sensors outside the wall. He might have defensive measures like antipersonnel mines, or maybe simple booby traps. Trip wires, spikes..."

Tate could see the everyone's faces turning pale.

"Snipers on the walls," continued Kaiden.

"Thanks," he said, cutting in.

"I wasn't done," she said.

"You're done," he said.

"How the heck are we supposed to get through all that?" asked Rosse.

"He didn't read the brief," said Kaiden.

Rosse shot her a heated look. She cocked her head and smiled back at him.

"We're not," said Tate. "We're going under it."

"The escape tunnel," said Monkhouse.

Tate knew this was an issue with Wesson and the look of dread washing over her face confirmed it.

"This isn't like Cuba," he said. "There won't be Vix waiting to surprise us."

"But how do we find that?" asked Rosse. "It's camouflaged, right?"

"This is a simple but important lesson in critical thinking," said Tate. "Think this through. You're in the middle of the jungle. There can be any number of Vix around at any time. That tunnel serves one purpose."

"Escape," said Rosse.

"What do you do next?" asked Wesson. "You've got a force attacking your villa. Once they know you're not there they'll come searching for you."

"There's miles of jungle in every direction," added Tate.

"No way he'd try to make it out of there on foot," said Rosse. "He's gotta have a car, or chopper close by."

"That's right," smiled Tate, pleased to see them putting the pieces together.

"As soon as he leaves the tunnel, he's exposed," said Wesson.

"It's a car," said Ota.

Chairs creaked as everyone turned to look at him, amazed to hear him speak up.

"Why is it a car?" asked Tate, wanting to keep the momentum going.

"The noise of a helicopter would draw everyone's attention," he said.

"And gunfire," said Monkhouse.

"If he's driving outta there," said Rosse, "he'd need a serious set of wheels, and a lot of fuel. Maybe a mounted machine gun for defense. That's what I'd have."

"Chances are very good that he would want to exit the area quickly," said Kaiden. "The car isn't fast enough, but it would get him to a plane or helicopter that's far enough away it could take off with minimum risk of being shot down."

"This scenario is about eighty percent of what I've seen when I've gone after guys like this," said Tate. "Confidence in how well you're hidden from your enemies plays a large part in how much they'll invest in other security measures."

"The higher the confidence," said Kaiden, "the less secure their compound."

"Like Bin Laden," said Wesson.

"Who?" asked Monkhouse.

"Just like," said Tate, pointing at Wesson. "Monkhouse, less crosswords and more reading."

Monkhouse shrugged with a pained grin. "I thought there were no dumb questions?"

"Dumb and ignorance aren't the same thing," smiled Tate. "Back to Bin Laden. He was hiding out deep in friendly territory, and even his neighbors didn't know he was right next door. His only security was a handful of armed followers, a couple of dogs and a steel door."

"Great," said Rosse, rubbing his hands together. "We fake an attack on the villa to flush out the scum. He sticks his head out the tunnel and we toast him. Easy peasy. Back home in time for dinner."

"Roman isn't our target," said Tate. "We want to wipe out his cache of intel and get Dante. Any other questions?"

"How're we getting there?" asked Rosse. "We can't touch the chopper without the base commander's say-so, and he ain't' saying so. Specially not us."

Tate had wondered about that too, but the solution had already revealed itself, thanks to Roman.

"Monkhouse," he smiled, "you know how to fly a helicopter."

"Yes," said Monkhouse, looking puzzled.

"Can you fly a plane?"

"It's been a while," he said, "but sure."

"Where are we gonna get a plane?" asked Rosse.

"Roman's going to deliver one for us," said Tate. "He just doesn't know it yet."

The Beechcraft Charger struggled through the night sky, high over the dense canopy below. The cool white of the new moon frosted the edges of the aircraft, but from the ground, the plane was nearly invisible. The hazard and navigation lights had been disabled long ago. The pilot didn't want to be seen.

Except for the pilot's seat, all of the others had been removed to make space. The interior of the Charger was loaded with packages of cocaine.

The pilot had been keeping a close eye on his flight time and knew he should've been able to see the makeshift landing lights meant only for him.

"Worthless," he swore, as he picked up the radio from the co-pilot's seat.

He was very tempted to break radio silence and yell at the idiots for slacking off, but knew he'd get chewed out for it.

The radio was only to be used when he got close to his return base. Someone on the ground would say a phrase and he'd give the counter phrase. If they matched, everyone was happy and they didn't shoot him out of the sky.

Pushing down his frustration, the pilot put the radio back. If the lights didn't appear soon, he'd overfly the landing strip in the next couple of minutes. According to his instructions, he could circle just one time. If the lights didn't come on, he was supposed to head back.

He smiled at the thought of returning with a full load, explaining the ground crew had dropped the ball. At the very least, they'd be beaten and sent to work in the fields. More likely they'd all be shot. That was okay with the pilot. He didn't like them anyway.

The wing dipped as he started to bank into a turn and the lights winked on below him.

With a curse he quickly corrected his direction and lined up on the lights. The Beechcraft gently nosed down as the pilot kept his eye on the altitude. The altimeter was off by several feet and had been broken for weeks. Nobody cared, except him and complaining didn't help.

The pilot braced as he committed to the landing, anticipating the jolt of the wheels hitting hard earth at any moment.

"Almost there," he said. "You can do this."

The landing gear smacked down, slamming the pilot into the thinly padded seat. The airframe squeaked and groaned from the impact but quickly recovered as the plane rolled down the earthen landing strip.

Another successful landing, as far as the pilot was concerned. He throttled back the engines and brought the aircraft to a stop.

"You jerks are lucky I..." he began, throwing open his door.

A flashlight beam caught him in the face, dazzling him.

"Are you stupid?" he said.

Something hard and small bumped into the side of his head. Something that felt a lot like the barrel of a gun.

"Okay, okay," he said. "So you were late on the landing lights. No big deal. I won't tell anyone"

"What's your name?" asked a voice behind the blaze of the flashlight.

"My na...?" stammered the pilot, confused. "Who are you? The cops? It's cool. I work for Roman, too."

"Name?" persisted the voice. The gun pressed more firmly against his head for added emphasis.

"Peter," said the pilot. "Look, if you want the drugs, they're yours. I didn't see any faces. Heck, I'll even unload the plane for you."

"Thanks, Peter, but we're going to need everything," said the voice. "Get out."

"Sure, sure," he said, "but we're cool, right?"

He fumbled getting out, giving him the brief second to grab his radio and push it under his shirt.

As the stepped out of the plane, Wesson put a black sack over his head then bound his hands behind his back with a pair of flex cuffs.

"Put him in the car," she said, handing the pilot over to Rosse.

"Come on, flyboy," he said, and led him by the arm to the car.

Tate opened the door to the Beechcraft and looked at the tightly wrapped packages of drugs.

"Let's get this unpacked," he said.

"Do we burn it?" asked Monkhouse.

"Burn it?" said Kaiden, shaking her head. "Your people have a lot to learn."

Tate sighed when Wesson stopped and stared at Kaiden.

"What's that supposed to mean?" asked Wesson.

"Don't get yourself worked up," smiled Kaiden. "I'm not saying we should sell it ourselves."

"We're taking that stuff out of circulation," said Tate.

"That's several pounds of opportunity," said Kaiden. "It might come in handy."

"It could also make our lives very complicated," he said.

"You're so glass half empty," she said. "Do you really want to throw an option like that away?"

He only smiled.

"What?" she asked.

"Oh," said Tate, "I can't help enjoying the irony of using Roman's own plane against him."

The first time Tate had used the smuggler's tunnel, he had spotted the landing strip. He tucked that piece of information away for a rainy day. A delivery plane was the last piece of the puzzle behind how Roman moved his drugs through Fort Hickok.

He had kept an eye on Cruz and his crew, suspecting they'd all meet at the old shed ahead of the arrival a new drug shipment.

The look on their faces was almost comical when Tate and his fully equipped team came through the door. In the face of over-whelming firepower the smuggler's tenuous loyalty to Roman crumbled. Cruz quickly pieced together something bad was coming Roman's way.

"Don't forget about my family," said Cruz, between a plea and a threat.

"I won't," said Tate.

20

TRACERS

Kaiden shrugged and helped unload the plane, but Tate knew her. She didn't give up that easily.

"Monkhouse, find someplace to stash that cargo," he said.

Wesson fixed him with heated disapproval but said nothing.

Rosse returned, giving Tate a thumbs up.

"The pilots locked up in the car," he said. "He's not going anywhere."

"You sure?" asked Tate.

"You're asking an ex-prison guard if I know how to secure someone?" grinned Rosse.

"Right," said Tate. "Good work."

"What are we going to do with him?" asked Rosse.

"We'll let him go when we get back," said Tate.

A few minutes later, Monkhouse and Ota appeared out of the darkness and confirmed where they'd hidden the drugs.

Tate called everyone together and explained the next phase of the operation. This wasn't news to anyone; they'd covered this days before, but experience had taught him the importance of keeping everyone on the same page, no matter how simple an operation was.

"Everybody climb in," he said.

"You're kidding, right?" said Rosse, looking at the confined space inside the plane.

"Wesson and Kaiden in the back," directed Tate.

"Just like two peas in a pod," smiled Kaiden.

Wesson didn't like or trust Kaiden when they had first met, but over time she grudgingly accepted the outsider. Kaiden still rubbed her the wrong way, and sometimes it seemed like she purposely got on her nerves. Now Tate was packing them together like sardines for the next couple of hours. Wesson was not happy.

"Ota and Rosse next. Deal with it, Rosse," said Tate, as the big medic made a show of how little room there was for him.

Ota tied his hair into a ponytail, making him look like a Viking, then climbed in.

"Monkhouse," said Tate. "You're up."

Monkhouse climbed into the pilot's seat and Tate took the co-pilot's seat.

"Right, let's see what we have here," said Monkhouse, turning his flashlight on the instrument panel for the first time.

His jaw fell open. All of the original instruments were mechanical. Some of them were rusted and broken, others were missing entirely. Someone had bolted a plywood square onto the panel and mounted a digital avionics display screen to it.

"This is...," he began.

"Unique," finished Tate, nodding to the others behind him.

"That's the word I was looking for," said Monkhouse, taking the hint.

He began to say something, but Tate cut him off.

"I get it," said Tate quietly, "but it's this, or we go on foot."

"Here we go," said Monkhouse, and began the startup procedure.

He pressed the ignition for the left engine which instantly growled to life.

He looked at Tate with a surprised smile.

"That's a promising sign," he said.

He pressed the ignition for the right engine. Tate looked out his window and watched the engine start up.

Both of them frowned as Monkhouse tapped the lifeless flight control screen on the console. With all the other instruments broken or useless, the digital display was the only way to know their speed, altitude and direction.

"Maybe it's got an on switch," said Tate.

"Nobody put's an on switch on their only flight control," said Monkhouse. "It's supposed to turn on when the plane turns on. Without this there's no way to know where we're going, or if we're going up or down. We could fly into a mountain. This is a bust. I can't..."

Tate smacked the display with the side of his hand. The display sprang to life.

"That's a sensitive instrument," said Monkhouse. "You can't just whack it around."

"I took a shot," said Tate. "Sue me."

"Don't do that again," said Monkhouse.

"You're the boss," smiled Tate, and settled back in his seat.

Monkhouse experimented with the column of buttons next to the screen until a map appeared filled with confusing symbols.

"Now we're getting somewhere," he said.

"Could we get somewhere faster?" grumbled Rosse. "My legs are cramping up back here."

"This is the flight chart the pilot was using," said Monkhouse, ignoring the noise behind him. He pointed at a bold line that stretched across the map. "This is the course he's been following between here and where they load the drugs."

"How do I put in Dante's coordinates?" asked Tate, as he fished the paper with the numbers out of his pocket.

"Use that keypad to your left," said Monkhouse.

Tate tapped the numbers into the system. A moment later, a new icon appeared on the display.

"That's Roman's villa," he said. "We'll be landing about three miles from our target," he said over the team's radio.

"Hope my legs still work when we get there," said Rosse.

"Time to go," said Tate.

Monkhouse nodded and added power to the engines. The plane started to roll and he used the peddles to move the rudder on the tail, turning the plane around to face the airstrip.

"I can't see where the landing strip ends and the trees begin," he said.

"Pull up as quickly as you can. The other pilot did this all the time. It'll be fine," said Tate, not sure if he was trying to convince himself more than Monkhouse.

"He did it with an empty plane," said Monkhouse.

"If it makes you feel better," said Tate, "you can say, 'I told you so' after we crash."

"Right," said Monkhouse.

He pushed the throttles up. The twin three hundred horsepower engines growled to a roar and the plane began moving. The airframe squeaked and rattled as the plane picked up speed, absorbing the shocks of the rough landing strip.

They could see nothing ahead and darkness filled the windshield. Tate suppressed the urge to tell Monkhouse to pull up. He imagined an unyielding barrier of trees racing at them. And with every second, the growing certainty they were about to slam into them squeezed his heart.

Tate's eyes were locked on Monkhouse's hands, willing them to pull back on the yoke. Monkhouse's gaze jumped between the windshield and their speed. Anxiety creased his face as he tightly gripped the yoke.

"Come on. Come on," he said.

Tate watched the airspeed, not knowing what magic number Monkhouse was waiting for.

"Monkhouse?" he said.

"Now," said Monkhouse, pulling back on the yoke.

Their stomachs sank as the plane leapt into a steep climb. Every fraction of a second was a lifetime of expectation between life and death.

There was no terrible crunch or sheering metal. They were flying.

Relief washed through Tate and he could see the tension drain from Monkhouse in the soft light of the flight display.

"Good job," he said, patting Monkhouse on the shoulder.

"Thanks," said Monkhouse. "Can we never do that again?"

"Every day's an adventure," said Tate.

Monkhouse eased the throttles back, bringing the engines to a steady drone.

"Okay, guys," he said over his shoulder. "Next stop, psycho drug lord."

The Beechcraft flew smoothly along their course, riding the gusts of turbulence with little complaint. Monkhouse kept the plane at a steady altitude and after a while, Tate slumped down in his seat and pulled his boonie hat over his eyes.

It was going to be a busy night and he needed any sleep he could grab.

Mateo flinched awake as a hungry mosquito lanced his arm. He slapped, cursing the spawn of hell, crushing the insect.

"Serves you right," he mumbled, scraping the corpse off his skin.

The clock showed 3:40 AM, sending him into another string of swearing. He still had five hours left before he could go home. He was already feeling the nagging itch of the mosquito bite. His plan to sleep through his shift were looking less likely by the minute.

There was little to nothing to see outside except stars above and shadows below. In the daylight, it was a wonderful view from high up above the jungle canopy.

Rough planking made up the floor and walls of Mateo's treehouse. From here he watched for the planes that smuggled Roman's drugs and instructed them to which ever landing strip had a new shipment prepared to load.

It was quieter at night. Only of couple of experienced pilots could fly when it was dark. The inexperienced ones that tried never lasted more than one trip and ended up as a smoking crater, lost somewhere in the open jungle.

There was only one pilot out tonight; Peter. Mateo liked him. He knew the ropes and even told Mateo he was fine if the makeshift air traffic controller wanted to use the time to catch up on his sleep. Mateo didn't need any more permission than that.

But now he was awake and bored. He picked up his radio, wondering if Peter would be close enough to get the signal.

"Hey, buddy," said Mateo. "You hear me yet?"

He listened to the hiss of static for a moment but got no reply. He turned the radio off, saving the battery and considered flipping through his small stack of comic books. He knew all of them front to back, even the ads for superhero posters, action figures, body building supplements and magic tricks.

He dismissed the idea as soon as he thought of it. Mateo believed he was moving up in Roman's organization when they took him out of the coco fields and promoted him to man the watch tower. The boss who ran the fields scowled at him when they called Mateo off the line.

"See that?" he smiled. "They know I'm made for better things, but you're gonna still be here, eating dust."

The truth was *they* didn't know he was made for better things and they didn't care. The novelty of his new job and expectation for further advancement had died a miserable death over a year ago.

In many ways he wished he was back in the fields. At least he had something to keep him busy there. All he did here was watch the jungle grow.

He leaned out the window, listening to the chorus of sounds. Animals and insects competing over each other in an almost endless stream of noise. But there were those times the jungle would go very quiet. The silence made his blood run cold. Somewhere in the black pools of night was a Vix.

He could imagine it below him. Shuffling around the base of his tree, looking for a way to reach him.

He knew they couldn't climb, but that never stopped him from double checking the latch on the trapdoor, leading to the ladder.

Maybe some of them could climb. No one would ever know. The ones who thought they were safe found out, but now they're dead, or one of those things.

Mateo shook his head to break free of his personal nightmare when his ears pricked up to a new sound. In the distance he heard a low, steady drone. A smile creased his face as he recognized the sound of Peter's plane. He didn't remember the type it was, even though Peter never stopped talking about it.

The pilot was proud of all the fixes and upgrades he'd made to it.

Mateo didn't understand half the things he talked about, but it sounded really impressive.

He'd asked Peter if he would teach him how to work on planes and was excited when he agreed. Mateo saw his next big chance to get ahead. He shook Peter's hand a dozen times when they'd met at the hanger. In reality, the Beechcraft was a piece of junk, but to Mateo it was a sleek, exotic machine and he was about to learn all its secrets.

When Peter opened the engine cowling, Mateo's heart fell. In front of him was a baffling jumble of wires, hoses, cylinders and things all strapped to a metal shell. His mind reeled at what complex magic of gears and pistons lived inside that. Overwhelmed, he decided being a mechanic was not in the cards.

Reading his expression, Peter closed the cowling and changed the subject and gave Mateo a cold beer. The pilot never teased him or brought it up again.

Mateo switched on the radio, eager to talk to his friend. "How did your flight go?"

He knew the answer. It was always the same, but he only had a handful of greetings. There was no reply, only static. He frowned at the radio, slightly confused.

The drone of the engines was louder and Mateo knew the radios were within easy range.

"Can you hear me?" said Mateo.

Nothing.

A broken radio wasn't common; the boss put a lot of priority on security, but they had back up procedures just in case.

"Hey, you're getting close," said Mateo. "The rules are you have to say something."

If the pilot couldn't communicate, they were supposed to turn on their hazard lights and wiggle their wings. Even if their lights failed, the final signal was to rev the engines a couple of times.

None of that was happening. Mateo began to feel his heart

pumping faster as doubt creeped into his mind that maybe the person flying that plane wasn't Peter.

Clipping the radio to his waistband, Mateo crossed the room to a ladder that disappeared through an opening in the roof and climbed up.

The ladder stopped at a wood-framed platform braced to the few remaining limbs near the very top of the tree. Bolted to the platform was a tarp-covered heavy machine gun.

It was still dark and Mateo had to grope for the tarp before pulling it off the gun. He squinted into the starry night sky, searching for the plane.

"Oh man," he said as he pulled back on the gun's charging handle. "I hope that's not you."

The gun's bolt slammed a large round into the chamber and Mateo grabbed the weapon's dual grips.

The sound of the plane was very loud now and he knew it had to be close. He swiveled the gun as he aimed by sound. His heart was thudding in his chest. Not from excitement, but dread. If he got this wrong, if he shot down one of the boss's planes and killed one of his pilots, they'd stake him out in the jungle and watch the Vix come for him.

It was a horrific punishment, but Mateo was sure they'd do something even worse if he let intruders get passed him.

He still couldn't see the plane, but his gun had a lot of bullets and he could afford to guess its location.

What is it called? Spray and pray?

Mateo centered his sights on a dark patch of sky and pressed the trigger.

Monkhouse didn't need any help staying awake. His eyes were constantly checking the plane's position, making sure they were on course, flying level and checking the status of the engines.

Something streaked through the sky, leaving a momentary trail. His first thought was he'd seen a falling star, but frowned because that star was going up, not down.

He saw another out of the corner of his eye, then another and they seemed to be getting closer.

He looked down out of the window and saw a strobing flash of yellow, illuminating the trees below.

"Holy crap," he said, and turned the yoke hard right.

Tate fell against Monkhouse's shoulder and sprang awake.

"What's happening?"

Bullets sprayed into the sky around them and the plane shuddered as several punched into the wing.

"Someone's shooting us," blurted Monkhouse.

The machine gunner must have seen sparks when the bullets hit because the stream of bullets were focused around them.

The right engine erupted in a ball of flame and smoke. Everyone shouted in alarm as the plane jolted and pitched over. Monkhouse turned the yoke to the left, trying to level out as warning lights lit up the panel buzzers yelled for attention.

"What's wrong?" yelled Rosse.

"Everything!" said Monkhouse, as he battled to steady the plane.

"Can you reach the airfield?" asked Tate.

Monkhouse spared a glance at the flight chart, calculating the distance.

"Maybe," he said. "I don't know."

Tate looked at the chart then out the window. In the distance he saw pale light winking off a body of water.

"If you're not sure," he said, "I want you to ditch the plane in that water."

"I'm not sure," said Monkhouse.

"Turn left," said Tate. "I think that's a lake over there."

The right wing of the plane dipped down and they turned away from the water.

"I said left," Tate shouted over the noise.

"Tell that to the plane," said Monkhouse.

Tate grabbed the co-pilot yoke and muscled it to the left. The right wing rose and the plane banked back towards the water.

Tracer fire from the machine gun flew into the sky around them, but nobody had time to think about it. They had graver concerns.

"There," said Tate, pointing to the water.

"I see it. I see it," snapped Monkhouse.

Outside, they heard a terrible screech of metal and the left propeller stopped spinning.

"We lost oil pressure," said Monkhouse. "The engine seized."

"How do you know?" yelled Rosse, looking for something to hang on to.

"Because the big spinning thing just stopped," said Monkhouse.

Machine gun tracers arced up far behind them as the gunner's bullets probed the dark sky.

Monkhouse flipped a couple of switches and the warning buzzers turned off. The quiet was as terrible as the noise. Wind moaned over the plane as they glided towards the small patch of winking light in a sea of blackness.

"Everyone brace," said Tate over his shoulder.

"There ain't anything to brace against," said Rosse, his voice a mix of anger and fear. He looked at Ota who was sitting with his eyes closed and chin resting on his chest, seemingly unruffled by the chaos.

"Long, slow breaths," said Ota, somehow aware of Rosse's gaze.

Rosse began chugging like a freight train and Ota put a hand on his arm.

"Slow," he said.

"Yeah, okay," said Rosse, and slowed his breathing.

In the back, Kaiden felt Wesson clutching her knee. She looked at her, but Wesson's eyes were fixed dead ahead. Kaiden wasn't sure if Wesson was even aware she was holding on to her.

Kaiden had been in so many close calls she'd begun to think life had made a game of teasing her with death. She dried her sweaty palms on her pants as her heart thudded in her chest.

Wesson's fingers dug into her leg and Kaiden put her hand on Wesson's, gently squeezing back.

Tate looked out the window and could see the twinkle off the water's surface stretching out around them. They were mere feet above the water.

21

ABORT

"I'm going to try and drag the tail in the water," said Monkhouse. "That'll slow us down a little and maybe we won't all snap our necks when we crash."

They seemed to glide for an impossible time as he tried to slowly bring them down.

The Beechcraft suddenly shook with a roar as the tail hit and skipped over the water before everything happened at once.

The last thing Tate saw before wrapping his head in his arms was Monkhouse letting go of the yoke and bracing.

The tail bit into the water and everyone was thrown forward. An instant later the plane went from forty miles an hour to zero as the nose pitched forward and buried itself into the water. The windscreen shattered and blew into the cockpit as the plane's momentum vaulted it over, flipping it on to its back and saving everyone from being crushed against each other.

Cold water splashed over the tangled heap of the stunned team.

Tate didn't know which way was up and felt like he'd been hit by a truck. He tried to focus for any stabbing pain of a broken bone, but the plane was filling with water and he had to move. He blinked his eyes in the darkness, too confused to know if his eyes were really open.

"Get offa me," barked Rosse.

His voice brought Tate out of his haze and grounded him into action. He groped his chest and found the flashlight still clipped to his vest.

The light snapped on and he could see he was on his back with one leg sticking out of the shattered windscreen.

"Everyone out!" he said. "Check the people next to you. Make sure they follow."

Shock hit him as he saw Monkhouse face down in the rising water. He grabbed him and pulled him up.

Monkhouse's head lolled against his chest and his eyes remained closed.

Tate was able to push open his door and backed out, keeping a grip on Monkhouse. He felt the wing under his knees and used it to brace himself as he pulled Monkhouse out of the door.

He swept his flashlight along the plane and saw Rosse and Ota nearby, but that was all.

"Where's Wesson and Kaiden?" he called, feeling panic grip his chest.

"We're here," said Kaiden. "We're on the other side of the plane."

"Are you okay?" he asked.

"We're fine," said Wesson after a short pause.

Monkhouse began coughing and opened his eyes, flailing in alarm.

"I got you," said Tate. "You're okay."

Monkhouse quieted down and looked around.

"Everyone's all right," said Tate. "You got us down safely."

"I did?" said Monkhouse.

"Wesson and Kaiden, join up on me," said Tate. "You just relax," he said to Monkhouse. "I'll tow you in."

"Can we ever land like normal people?" asked Monkhouse.

Tate waited until the team was together before heading to the shore.

It wasn't long before they felt the lakebed under their feet and dragged themselves out of the water.

Tate had them sit down and check themselves for injuries. All of them were sore and battered, and he guessed there were a few concussions in the group, but they were alive and able to walk.

"Oh hell," he blurted, with the realization they'd left their weapons on the plane. "We have to go back and get our guns."

"Relax," said Rosse. "I grabbed 'em on the way out."

"You're amazing," said Tate, impressed the big man didn't sink with the extra weight dragging him down.

"Yeah," said Rosse. "I know."

Each did a weapons check, doing their best to clear them of mud and water.

"Look," said Ota.

Nobody could see what he was pointing at, but it wasn't hard to see what he was talking about as distant lights began stabbing though the jungle.

Tate swore under his breath as he took out his map, shielding his flashlight as he estimated their position.

Everyone backed into the deeper shadows of the wall reeds and waited in silence until he clicked off the light and put the map away.

"Roman's men?" said Rosse.

"It's not a rescue party," said Kaiden. "They'll start closer to the villa and work their way out. We have time."

"Time for what?" asked Wesson.

"To get out of here," said Tate. "We're aborting the mission."

"Aborting?" said Wesson.

"The plan depended on stealth," said Tate.

"Where are we supposed to go?" said Rosse. "We're five hundred miles..."

"Five hundred and eighty-three," said Monkhouse.

"Five hundred and eight three miles from home," said Rosse. "Are we gonna walk all the way back?"

"There's a set of foothills just north east of here," said Tate, ignoring him. "Roman's villa is a couple of miles the other way. By the time his patrols get here, we'll be on the other side of those hills. The map shows a road about ten miles after that. It's not perfect, but it's the best plan we have. Like Kaiden said, they'll be looking for us closer to the villa before spreading out. Let's go."

They collected their gear and prepared to head out.

"Down," hissed Wesson.

Everyone dropped to the ground as a searchlight panned across the tops of the tall grass.

"Follow me," said Tate, and headed along the shore, staying low.

The searchlight landed on the white carcass of the Beechcraft and several voices shouted with excitement.

Tate and the team kept along the shore, making good time as the sound of a truck came smashing through the brush.

They traveled a good hundred yards before they turned into the tall grass. Tate and the team disappeared as the patrol came to a stop and several men jumped out of the truck and headed to the shore.

They moved at a crouch through the wide field of tall grass, their back and knees aching for relief. They reached the cover of the jungle, leaving behind the swarming patrols, and headed for the foothills.

The night sky had slightly paled and the texture of the jungle around them revealed itself in shades of grey.

Sore and wet, they stopped a short distance from the opening to the pass which lead through the foothills.

They quietly gathered around Tate and he explained their next move.

"The jungle breaks just beyond those trees," he whispered, pointing to a stand of thick woods in the distance. "Wesson will scout ahead. The rest of us will follow, single file. Move quietly."

Wesson was an exceptional tracker, and Tate never hesitated to put her skills to work when they were in unfamiliar territory.

She eased her way towards the stand of trees.

The rest of the team followed her example; stopping when she stopped, listening and looking.

Reaching the trees, she paused, motioning for everyone to wait. She placed her steps carefully, like a stalking predator, avoiding anything that would make noise. She paused again, only a thin vale of foliage between her and the mouth of the pass.

She became very still and narrowed her focus to the terrain in front of her.

She wasn't looking, or listening for any specific thing. That was the trick. If you formed a preconception of what you're looking for, your mind filtered out everything that didn't match your expectations.

Wesson had no expectations. Her senses were open to anything out of harmony to their surroundings and she found it.

At first all she saw was the bent stem of a fern, but the sight sent a tingle up her spine. Like a photograph slowly developing, all of the signs that things were not right began to show themselves to her.

Brush had been moved to create camouflage. Areas of sparse grass had been trampled then covered with loose dirt. She closed her eyes and listened. The jungle was alive, behind her, but there was an unnatural quiet at the mouth of the pass.

Ahead of her, someone softly grunted as they eased a cramped limb.

Carefully, she eased away from the stand of trees, moving silently until she reached her waiting team.

"It's an ambush," she said. "They're hiding, waiting for us."

"How did they know we'd come this way?" asked Monkhouse.

"They didn't," said Tate. "They're here to cover all the bases."

He took out his map. It was light enough now that he could see it clearly.

"Is there another way out?" asked Wesson.

"Yes," he said, pointing to the map. "Here and here."

"I say we head for the one that's farthest away," said Rosse. "They set up a welcoming committee for us here because they think we'll take the shortest way out. We go the long way around instead."

"The problem isn't the distance," said Tate. "It's the number of men. If Roman has men to spare from his patrols, he's got enough to cover the other ways out of here."

"If they're spread out all over the place," said Monkhouse, looking worried, "we can't go anywhere without running into them. We're caught inside a net."

"They're scattered around trying to find us," said Kaiden. "But if they knew where we were, they'd all come running."

"A diversion," said Wesson.

"Exactly," said Tate.

"Even if we sucker them into all come running," said Rosse, "as soon as they figure out they've been tricked they can beat us back to either pass long before we get there."

"We're not going back to the other passes," said Tate.

"I like where your head's at," said Kaiden, knowing what he was planning.

"We draw them off, creating a gap in the patrols," said Tate. "We go right through it and hit the villa."

"The vil..." stammered Rosse. "How bad did that crash knock your head?"

"I didn't crash," said Monkhouse. "I ditched."

"You," said Rosse. "Don't start with me. Top, you said the villa was a no-go."

"Was is the operative word," said Tate. "Roman's men switched priorities when nobody attacked the villa. They're covering the passes because they think whoever was in the plane is trying to get away. They're not looking for us at the villa."

"We attack the one place they're not expecting," said Kaiden.

"I don't want to be the guy that keeps poking holes in your plans," said Rosse.

"And yet you are," said Kaiden.

Rosse glared at her, flushing red.

"Go ahead," said Tate, trying to head off further friction. "I can't think of everything. I depend on the entire team's input."

"I was say'n," said Rosse, "we can't trigger their trap and get away. We'd have to keep 'em busy long enough, an hit 'em hard enough that they call in reinforcements. Those guys'll be closing in like a noose. By the time we, what ya call it, break contact, we'll be surrounded."

"That's always a risk," said Tate.

"I have something that should keep them busy," grinned Monkhouse, taking off his pack.

"What have you got?" smiled Tate.

Monkhouse was a good choice for the teams' engineer. Creative, adaptive and good with his hands, he brought an original mix of problem-solving skills. Like the others on his team, Monkhouse kept his past to himself. But some of his more uncommon talents made Tate suspect he had a shady past.

"This is pretty cool," said Monkhouse, reaching into his pack. "Just don't freak out."

"What have you got?" asked Tate, suddenly feeling he should be very worried.

"Remember our last mission?" said Monkhouse.

"What did you do?" asked Tate, already fearing he knew the answer.

Juan's knees were numb and soggy. He'd been crouched behind a pile of ferns, waiting to ambush whoever had crashed the plane into the lake. He glanced at the others in his party. Some were sleeping while others just looked off into space.

When the alert came in that someone had tried to sneak into Roman's territory, Juan felt a rush of excitement as he and the other soldiers were ordered to assemble. Seeing all the other guards armed and eager made him feel like he was part of something powerful and to be feared.

He was going to get to shoot someone. He never got to use his gun guarding the peons working in the coco fields. They never tried to escape or fight back when he kicked them. They were like herding cattle.

Sometimes they'd find a small group that had survived the Vix and they'd be hauled in as extra labor. If they got out of line, or tried to give him attitude, he could beat them up, but not so bad they couldn't work.

His enthusiasm for the hunt quickly faded after an hour of point-less waiting. He wasn't even allowed to smoke. The guard in charge of

Juan's group was a fool and stupid. Anyone could see this ambush was a waste of time. If the intruders were coming this way, they would have been here by now.

Juan was eager for action.

A foreign sound interrupted his grumbling and he perked up his ears, carefully listening.

He wondered if it was his imagination, then he heard it again. A strange, high-pitched buzzing, and it was getting louder. It wasn't footsteps, but he heard rustling.

The sound wasn't natural, and his mind raced through the possible answers. Was it a drone? Were they looking at him at this very moment? He could be a sitting duck and wouldn't know it until it was too late.

He gripped his assault rifle, his finger hovering over the trigger as doubt and panic ate at his confidence.

The buzzing was very close and then stopped. Nothing else happened. The seconds ticked by in silence. What was happening out there?

Juan couldn't wait any longer. He stood up, aiming over the top of the ferns. There was nothing there but jungle. His eyebrows knitted together in confusion. Something made that noise. He knew he heard it.

One by one, the rest of his group stood up.

A green light panned across Juan, making him flinch. He swiveled his gun left and right, looking for a threat, then heard the odd sound again.

Juan pushed the ferns aside and saw a strange, four-legged thing standing motionless on the ground. It had a sleek, angular, black body, but no head, and reminded him of a dog.

"You are not authorized," said the dog in a slurred, artificial voice.

A panel flipped up on the top of the dog, peaking Juan's curiosity.

The dog made a soft popping nose and three holes appeared in Juan's head.

The other guards gaped in surprise as Juan stood there for a few seconds, before he went down like a felled tree.

"What are you doing?' shouted the leader. "Fire!"

The soldiers began spraying bullets at the dog, kicking up fountains of dirt all around it in panicked shooting.

The dog went into defensive mode, targeting and killing the terrified soldiers.

The leader ducked behind a large rock and grabbed his radio.

"This is Angel at the east pass," he screamed. "They're here. We're getting wiped out. Bring everyone."

"How many are there?" came the reply over the radio.

"I don't know," said Angel. "Thirty."

"Thirty?" said the voice in alarm.

"Maybe more."

One of his solders fell at his feet, part of his head missing. His remaining eye stared blankly at the sky.

"They're killing us!" said Angel, edging on hysteria. "Everyone's dead."

"We're coming," said the radio. "Hold them there."

Angel looked at the radio like it had just turned into a fish. Did the idiot on the other end of the radio not hear a word he'd just said?

His men were getting slaughtered. He wasn't going to stick around to be one of them.

Angel dropped the radio, his breath coming in rapid fire gulps. He glanced around to see what was left of his remaining men. Some were cowering behind cover, and others spraying wildly.

The man next to him screamed; his lifeless body splashed into the mud.

Angel's last fiber of will snapped. With a garbled cry of panic, he scrambled over the corpse of his soldier and fled into the pass.

The growl of engines grew around them and Wesson rapidly signaled everyone to hide. Two jeeps and a truck packed with soldiers burst into the open at break-neck speed. The team dove into cover and the jeeps raced by.

The sound of engines faded and the team breathed easy.

"That makes the third one," said Wesson.

"They're sending everything they got," smiled Tate. "They must think they're up against a small army. Nice work, Monkhouse."

Monkhouse grinned, shrugging awkwardly at the complement.

"Well," he said, "it's what I do."

"This doesn't give you cart blanch to drag every killing machine back to base," said Tate firmly.

"Understood, Top," said Monkhouse, feigning shame.

The pale, cream-colored walls of Roman's villa were visible from their hiding spot at the base of the hill. Large fields of yellow-green coca plants surrounded most of the hill.

"I don't see anyone working the fields," said Wesson.

Tate nodded absentmindedly, noting the detail, but focused on their goal.

"Ota," he said, "check the walls for guards."

With a nod, Ota unslung his sniper rifle and blew strands of his long, blond hair out of his face before bringing the scope to his eye. His favorite rifle, the Dragunov, was under lock and key at the base. Tate had managed to get him a modified Remington 700 from the black-market gun dealer.

The model was only a few years old and came with advanced optics and built in ambient sensors.

Ota chose to turn off the scope's computer and do the shooting himself. Tate knew he was a remarkable marksman and suspected the computer only got in the way of his skills.

Tate exercised his patience, choosing to wait until Ota was satisfied that he'd scanned the area thoroughly.

"I only see two guards on the wall," he said. "They're making a circuit of the walls."

"That's better than I was hoping for," said Tate.

"Did you notice the dirt road?" asked Ota. "It was near the bottom of the hill, opposite us."

"Do you think that's connected to the escape tunnel?" asked Wesson.

"Let's check it out and see," said Tate.

The group didn't encounter any of Roman's guards as they clung to the cover of the jungle, surrounding the base of the hill.

As they neared where Ota had seen the road, Monkhouse called Tate over the radio.

Everyone stopped, crouching down.

Tate went back, finding Monkhouse looking out between the heavy brush towards a corner of the fields.

"What is it?" asked Tate, fearing another patrol had shown up.

"I found the laborers," said Monkhouse, pointing towards the fields.

Following his direction, Tate saw four large, crudely-made pens. They were surrounded by a mob of Vix, franticly trying to claw their way in. Inside, laborers huddled together, crying for help.

"Looks like they lock them up when they're not working," said Tate.

"They left them there?" said Monkhouse, feeling his anger rise.

"Maybe Roman's men use the Vix instead of guards," said Tate. "Come on. We need to stay on mission."

"Wait a minute," said Monkhouse, stunned. "What about them?"

"They're safe," said Tate. "If the Vix could get through, they'd have done it by now."

"We can't leave them there," said Monkhouse. "It's wrong."

"There's a lot of wrong in this world," said Tate. "We don't have the luxury to right every one of them. This is one of those times."

"It's not just the Vix," said Monkhouse. "Those people are being kept as slaves."

Tate couldn't be angry with Monkhouse. There had been too many times he had to choose between two evils, letting the lesser evils live on. It was a brutal reality and one that he struggled to come to terms with.

"Let's say we go out there and set them loose," said Tate. "Then what? Where do they go? Are you going to be like Moses and lead them out of captivity?"

Monkhouse considered Tate's words. He saw their harsh reality but didn't like it.

"I don't know what they'd do if we freed them," he said, "but if we leave them locked up, we're making the decision for them. Maybe they'd choose to stay, as crazy as that sounds, but they'd be deciding their own lives."

Tate looked across the field to the terrified laborers. Their screams of fear carried easily on the air.

"Rosse, Kaiden," he said into his radio. "Come here. Ota and Wesson, keep an eye out and let me know if you see any soldiers coming our way."

Monkhouse smiled at him.

"Don't say it," said Tate, holding up a finger to silence him.

"What?" said Monkhouse.

"That I won't regret this," said Tate, his expression grim.

Before Monkhouse could reply, Kaiden and Rosse showed up.

Tate explained what they were about to do. Rosse was on board with it, but Kaiden was not.

"It's a mistake," she said. "How many times have we seen these things go sideways on us?"

"I know," said Tate.

"Okay, boy scout," she said, smiling. "But if one of those laborers even looks like they'll sound the alarm on us..."

"I get it," said Tate.

"I don't get it," said Monkhouse. "What does she mean?"

"She means don't stand between her and them, hero," said Rosse.

They spread out, hiding behind the foliage, each of them settling their gunsights on a different Vix.

"Now," said Tate.

22

STORM ON THE SEA

To the astonishment of the laborers, four of the Vix dropped. The people looked around in confusion but saw nothing.

Over the snarls of the Vix they heard muffled cracks and four more Vix dropped.

"I don't have a target," said Kaiden.

"Me neither," said Rosse.

The remaining Vix were on the other side of the pens with the laborers blocked their shots.

"Let's say hello," said Tate, and stepped into the open with the others following.

It didn't take long for one of the Vix to see them. Its growling howl caused the others to look and seeing the team, they charged.

Aiming, the four team members held their fire, waiting for the Vix to move away from the pens.

"I don't like standing in the open like this," said Monkhouse.

"This was your idea," said Kaiden.

The Vix wheeled around the corner of the pens, making a mad dash for the exposed team.

One by one, they fired, taking careful aim. The Vix moved with insane speed, but making no attempt to dodge, the team cut them down before they were in reach.

Satisfied the Vix were eliminated, Tate and the others quickly ran to the pens. Each of the doors were secured with a simple lock. Tate rightly guessed the armed guards were the real deterrent.

The laborers were quick to understand what was happening as the four Grave Diggers broke the locks and opened the doors.

"Who are you?" they asked.

"Doesn't matter," said Tate. "Most of Roman's men are far from here."

"You're free to go," said Monkhouse.

"Go where?" said one of the men. "They'll find us again and beat us. No, I'm not leaving."

"Did they beat the man out of you?" sneered a woman, fire igniting in her eyes. "They worked my son to death. *He* killed my son." She pointed at the villa on the hill. "You," said the woman, pointing at the Grave Diggers, "didn't come here to free us, did you? If you are here to kill the devil who lives up there, go home. You can't get in."

Several of the people murmured in agreement.

"My son was forced to work on those walls," she said. "Make them stronger and build traps."

"Did he work on anything else?" asked Kaiden. "Maybe a tunnel?"

"No," said the woman, turning away. But her fire had died away and was replaced by a hint of fear.

"We will never repeat what you tell us," said Kaiden. "If you want Roman dead, then help us."

The woman stared at her, clear brown eyes bored into her, searching for any deception. Making up her mind, she stepped closer to Kaiden.

"Yes!" said the woman. "He never told me where. If they learned that I knew they would kill me."

"Franco," said someone in the crowd.

"Yes, Franco," she said. "Where are you? Come here."

Several hands pushed a reluctant man into the open.

"You worked the tunnel," said the woman. "You tell them where it is."

"What if they find out?" said Franco, looking around nervously. "What if one of you turn me in for more food?"

"Don't be a fool," hissed the woman, slapping him with her leathery hand. "These are your people. Tell them where the tunnel is before I beat you myself."

Franco withered under her glare. "There's a dirt road," he said.

"Yes, we saw that," said Tate.

"It is a trap," said Franco. "The road is bait for anyone looking for the tunnel. There are many explosives all around there."

The Grave Diggers traded looks of alarm.

"The tunnel is on the other side of the hill," said Franco, pointing in the direction where Tate and the team had already been.

"We just came from there," said Rosse. "We didn't see nothing."

"It's hidden," said Franco. "There are two rocks, used as markers. That is where the entrance to the tunnel is."

"Are there any traps?" asked Tate.

Franco shook his head and shrugged doubtfully.

Tate's static crackled as Wesson radioed him. "Top, I don't know what you're doing, but the clock's ticking."

"We're on our way," he said. "Meet us back where we first came to the base of the hill."

"Copy," said Wesson.

"They have many guns inside that place," said the woman. "Open the gates and we will take them. We will make these monsters pay for what they've done to us."

Scattered among the laborers were looks of fear and doubt, but the greater part of them were set with angry determination.

"We'll open them as soon as we can," said Tate. "We have to go."

Tate left the peasants and jogged back the way he came with the rest of the team behind.

They soon met up with Wesson and Ota. Tate explained what had happened and how they'd missed the tunnel entrance.

It didn't take long to find the two rocks marking the entrance. Now that he knew what he was looking for, the rocks did seem oddly out of place.

They probed the grass around the rocks and found something hard, just under the dirt.

Clearing away the grass revealed a large, steel hatch. Testing it, they found it wasn't locked.

"I guess when you're run'n for your life, you don't want to worry about where you left your keys," said Rosse.

"Monkhouse," said Tate. "Check for wires."

Monkhouse got down on his knees and crawled around the hatch, gently checking around the seams, while the others stood a safe distance away.

He sat back on his haunches and gave a thumbs up.

With the others covering him, Tate opened the hatch leading into the tunnel.

The tunnel was made for easy and fast movement. The high walls and ceiling allowed someone to stand fully upright. The hard packed, dirt floor was smooth, eliminating the chance of tripping over.

Lights were embedded in the ceiling every few feet, making it easy to see ahead and behind.

"Wesson," said Tate. "You first. Watch for tripwires, sensors, anything that can trigger a trap or alarm. Everyone behind me. Rosse, you bring up the rear."

"I'm on it," said Wesson, her voice firm, but brittle.

It was almost a cruel joke the way she had been thrown into situations that forced her to travel through tunnels. Tate admired how she was tackling her fears.

"I'm right here with you, okay?" he said.

Wesson's shoulders relaxed a little as some of the tension fell away.

"Thanks," she said, smiling.

She headed into the tunnel with Tate and the others following behind.

The tunnel began sloping up, and soon the incline became much steeper.

They had gone a good distance when Wesson stopped.

"There's a door," she said over the radio.

Tate leaned to the side and looked over her shoulder. He saw a smooth, flat door.

"Check it," he said.

The tunnel was too narrow for Monkhouse to squeeze by. This one was up to Wesson.

She didn't rush, carefully examining for any dangers. Tate weighed what options would be left if they couldn't get past the door. Being honest with himself, there weren't any.

"It's clear," said Wesson, flushing Tate with relief.

She cracked the door open enough to look inside.

"It's a ladder," she reported.

The steel ladder was made of welded rebar with strong bolts holding it solidly to the side of a tall shaft going up.

Shining her light up the shaft, she could dimly see something blocking the top.

"It goes about thirty feet up and stops," she said.

"Lead on," said Tate.

Wesson began climbing with the team behind her.

The ladder ended with a hatch over her head. It was smooth metal with only a welded handle. Very carefully, she took hold of the handle and pushed up.

The cover lifted easily, without noise, and she cracked it open just enough to peek out. She listened for movement or sounds of alarm, but everything was quiet. Looking through the crack, her eye was level with the floor of a room.

The floor and walls were brushed steel. A metal desk ran the length of the distant wall. Above it was a series of security monitors. Looking to the right she saw a thick door with reinforced latches.

"I think we found a safe room," said Wesson. "I'm going in."

Leading with her gun, she eased the hatch all the way open and climbed into the room.

"It's empty," she said.

The others quickly followed, spreading out as they reached the top.

Tate checked the security monitors. Roman had cameras set up to monitor several of the rooms and hallways in the villa.

Next to the monitors was a simple map of the villa. It was a U-shaped structure with the safe room located in the middle were the left and right wings met. Small icons appeared on the map, designating which cameras were active.

"Escape tunnels," said Monkhouse. "Safe rooms. Not exactly the luxurious life of the drug kingpins I see in the movies."

"I guess this means you're rethinking your career goals," chuckled Rosse.

"He doesn't even have a swimming pool," said Monkhouse.

"We need to find where Roman would keep things of value," said Tate. "Records…"

"Things he'd use for blackmail," smiled Kaiden.

"Especially that," he said. He glanced at the security monitors out of habit but saw no signs of people. "Looks like everyone's out looking for us so we have the place to ourselves. We'll split up in groups of two. Rosse and Ota, you two check this room for anything that could be useful. Wesson and Monkhouse, take the left wing of the villa. Kaiden and I will take the right. Questions?"

Everyone shook their heads and the teams split up, leaving Rosse and Ota in the safe room.

"Guess I'll start with these," said Rosse, walking up to a set of filing cabinets.

Ota started on the other side.

Tate and Kaiden moved down the hall to the first set of doors. They were thick wood, carved with a floral motif.

Kaiden moved to cover Tate as he tested the doorknob. He nodded, indicating it was unlocked. He pushed the door open and Kaiden braced her assault rifle against her shoulder, ready to fire.

A quick sweep of the room told them it was empty. They moved in and began searching.

Down the other end of the hall, Wesson and Monkhouse were doing the same.

All of the doors were the same, heavy wood with carved motifs.

.   .   .

.

Rosse looked up and saw Monkhouse and Wesson come into frame on a security monitor as they entered a room.

"Wesson," he said into his radio, "I see you on the camera."

"Can you figure out how to switch the camera?" she said. "And check a room before we go in?"

"Yeah," said Rosse. "Lemme see what I can do."

He scanned the control board, seeing the controls were all labeled. He looked at the map of the floor plan and switched one of the cameras.

"I think I got the next room on camera," he said. "You'll have to go in before I know I got the hang of this thing."

Wesson and Monkhouse finished checking for hidden safes or cubby holes and went into the hall to the next door.

As they entered the next room, Rosse saw them on camera.

"Yeah, I see you," he said. "Looks like we got a system now."

"Thanks," said Wesson. "I'll let you know when we're ready for the next room."

"Got it," he said and went back to searching the room.

Tate and Kaiden were on the third room and hadn't found what they were looking for.

"He'd want something valuable nearby," she said.

"Like his office or bedroom," said Tate.

"I don't get the impression he's much of an office kind of person," said Kaiden.

"Bedroom it is," he said. "Rosse, this is Tate. Can you flip through the camera feeds and tell me if you see something that looks like a master bedroom?"

"Okay, Top," said Rosse, and headed back to the control panel.

He turned the dial for one of the cameras and saw a small camera icon appear on the map of the villa.

"Anything yet?" asked Tate.

"No, not yet," said Rosse, and continued switching the camera feed.

"We're ready for the next room," said Wesson.

"Right, okay," said Rosse. He'd lost track of where Wesson and Monkhouse had gone and quickly switched the camera he'd been using for them.

The feed changed and Rosse uttered a short curse as he grabbed at his radio.

"Stop!"

In the hallway, Wesson and Monkhouse froze outside the door.

"There's people in there," said Rosse looking closer at the black and white image.

"Someone's in a chair and there's another guy with a gun," he said.

"What about the one in the chair?" asked Wesson, carefully putting her back to the wall next to the door. "Does he have a gun?"

"I don't see one," said Rosse, "but I don't think he wants to be there. He's gotta a sack over his head. I'm gonna say he's a prisoner."

"What's the guard doing?" asked Monkhouse, following Wesson's example and moving to the other side of the door.

"Nuth'n," said Rosse. "Just pacing around the room."

Wesson reached out and carefully closed her hand on the doorknob.

"Not locked," she whispered. "Monkhouse, when I open the door, I'll go in and sweep left, drawing the guard's attention. You take him out. Be careful you don't hit the prisoner."

"Can we wait a second?" said Monkhouse nervously.

"What is it?" she said.

"This all sounds really dangerous," he said. "Rushing an armed guard."

Wesson's eyebrows rose in disbelief.

"Are you serious?" she said.

"Hang on," he said, reaching into his combat vest. He took out a small notepad. "Unlatch the door, but don't open it."

He knelt down in front of the door.

"Monkhouse," she growled. "Get up."

"Just go with me on this," he said. "Rosse, tell me when the guard bends down."

"Do what Wesson's telling ya," said Rosse.

Monkhouse slipped the notepad under the door just as the guard was walking by.

The guard stopped in surprise and looked curiously between the notepad and the door. After a moment of puzzling over it, he bent down to pick it up.

"He's picking it up," said Rosse.

Monkhouse threw himself against the door.

The heavy door flew open, slamming into the guard's head and sending him toppling backwards onto the floor.

Wesson and Monkhouse held their guns on him, but the guard was out cold.

"See?" said Monkhouse. "Wasn't that safer?"

"We're having a serious heart to heart when we get back," she said.

It only took a moment to recognize that the person in the chair was bound and no threat to them.

Wesson pulled the cloth sack off, revealing the bruised and battered face of Dante Barrios.

"A pleasure to see you again, Sergeant," he said through swollen lips.

"Dante?" she asked.

Tate and Kaiden were just finishing up in Roman's private gym when Wesson called him over the radio.

"Top, this is Wesson. I just found Dante."

"Great job," said Tate. "Put him on the radio."

Monkhouse took out his knife and cut the rope around Dante's hands and ankles. Dante flexed his hands and rubbed the circulation back into his wrists before taking the mic from Wesson.

"Sergeant Major," said Dante. "What an unexpected but welcomed surprise."

"I was in the neighborhood," said Tate, "and thought sneaking into Roman's villa would be a fun way to break up the boredom. Speaking of which, where does he keep his important files?"

"If you mean the information he's blackmailing you with," said Dante, "that would be in his office."

"So he's got an office," said Tate, smirking at Kaiden who shrugged in response.

"Where are you now?" asked Dante.

"In the gym," said Tate.

"Turn right as you enter the hall,' said Dante. "It will be the third door."

"Copy," said Tate. "Wesson, take Dante back to the safe room and wait for us there."

Tate and Kaiden headed out of the gym and began counting doors.

Rosse had been monitoring the conversation and switched the cameras to follow Tate and Kaiden in the hallway.

Wesson reached out to help Dante stand up, but he waved her off.

"I'm fine," he said, "but thank you. Your knife looks very sharp," he said to Monkhouse. "May I borrow it?" He put his hand out to Monkhouse.

The request caught Monkhouse off guard, who looked at Wesson for direction.

After a moment's pause, she nodded and Monkhouse handed him the knife.

To their shock, Dante pulled back his sleeve and cut into his forearm. His face creased in pain, but his hand never wavered.

"What are you doing?" blurted Monkhouse.

Dante didn't answer. Instead he pushed the tip of the blade into the wound and pried out a small metallic capsule.

"I wouldn't get very far with this in my arm," he said, displaying the bloody device. "It's a tracker."

"That's how we found you," said Wesson.

"So I gathered," he said, "and it's how Roman's been keeping me on a very short leash."

Dante stepped over to the guard and began unbuttoning his own shirt.

"You didn't shoot him, did you?" he asked.

"No," said Monkhouse.

"Excellent," said Dante. "Digging around for a bullet would take more time than we have."

He rolled the guard onto his back and straddled his chest. He pinched the guard's nose closed and put his other hand over his mouth.

Wesson and Monkhouse traded looks of shock, not sure what was going on, or if they should do something about it.

The unconscious guard hardly struggled, then went still.

"Would you mind stripping him?" Dante asked Monkhouse.

"Uh," he stammered. "What's going on?"

"I'm sure he's beyond caring," said Dante, as he took off his own pants.

Wesson was too stunned by everything that had just happened to feel embarrassed as Dante undressed in front of her.

Tate and Kaiden came to the third door and found it unlocked.

"You don't need to lock doors when your employees are terrified of you," he said.

"Never underestimate torture as an effective management tool," she said as they looked around the room.

The office was tastefully appointed with floor to ceiling windows that looked out onto a personal garden surrounded by a low wall. Outside, lush ferns and grass served as a frame for a koi pond. A small waterfall splashed into the edge of the pond, creating sparkling ripples and a soothing sound of running water. Beyond the garden was the villa's courtyard. On the other side of that they could see the large gates, barring them from the outside world.

The office walls were paneled in rich wood and adorned with colorful paintings, highlighted by recessed lighting.

"Cultured tastes for a psycho," said Kaiden.

"I wouldn't give him too much credit," said Tate. "Before Roman killed him, this place used to belong to his boss." He switched to his radio. "Dante, we're in the office. Where's the files?"

Rosse switched to another camera and found Tate and Kaiden. He saw the camera icon appear on the map of the villa. A second later, a curious square, green icon appeared.

Rosse's eyebrows knitted together as he tried to make sense of it. It had to be there for a reason, but what?

"Hey, Top?" he said. "A weird symbol just showed up on the map of your room."

"Weird how?" asked Tate.

"I dunno what it means," said Rosse, feeling vague unease. "I don't like it."

"You don't like it because you don't know what it means?" asked Tate. "Or you don't like it because..."

"I just don't like it, okay?" said Rosse.

"Relax," said Tate. "I'm only trying to understand why you're feeling nervous."

Rosse looked around, rolling his eyes. "I'm in a steel box, in the belly of a psycho's mansion, surrounded by an army and hoping I don't accidently hit a button that says, 'Hey, a bunch of numb nuts are strolling around your house. Why don't ya go there and shoot them all?'."

Tate and Kaiden smirked at each other before he worked the grin out of his voice.

"Let me know if anything changes," he said, deciding there was nothing he could do about it. "Dante?"

"I'm here," said Dante. "The safe is behind the Rembrandt."

Tate and Kaiden scanned the paintings on the wall, not sure which was which.

"You got to give me more than that," he said. He noticed the sharpness in his voice. They had already been there too long.

By now, the soldiers would have searched the area and knew they'd missed the intruder. They'd be headed back to the villa.

"The Storm on the Sea," said Dante. "The painting of the boat."

"Got it," said Tate, seeing the only painting with a boat. "I thought spies were supposed to know about art," he said to Kaiden.

"I don't do art," she said.

Kaiden got there first and pulled the painting. It swung away on sturdy hinges, revealing a locked safe.

"Do you have the combination?" she asked.

"Don't need it," said Tate, pulling out a plastic box from his vest. "I had Monkhouse make me a batch of thermite gum."

"Aren't you the clever one," she said.

Tate applied the sticky gum to the face of the safe door and waved Kaiden back. She shielded her eyes as he ignited it. The thermite roared to life in a blinding pillar of flame and heat.

Tate and Kaiden moved further back from the searing heat as molten metal dripped down the wall and puddled on the floor.

In the safe room, alarms bellowed off the walls, jolting Rosse and Ota.

The green icon on the map began throbbing red as the security panel came to life with warning lights.

"Top!" yelled Rosse over the blaring sound. "Get outta there."

In the security monitor, Rosse could see that Tate and Kaiden weren't reacting to the alarm and rightly guessed the sound was only in the safe room.

"No!" yelled Ota, who suddenly charged across the room.

Rosse looked up and his stomach balled into a cold knot as the thick metal door of the safe room swung closed.

Ota threw his body against it, but it didn't budge. Rosse ran to the door and they heaved on it, but it had locked closed.

23

TRIGGERED

O ver the sound of the burning thermite, Tate and Kaiden heard something crash by the door. They grabbed their guns and spun towards it. Thick metal bars now barred their way out. They instantly understood what was happening and turned towards the windows.

Large bars quickly slide from the walls, slamming together in front of the windows.

"Top," yelled Rosse over the radio. "We just got locked in the safe room. We can't open it."

Everything was happening at once and it was all bad.

"We have a problem here, too," said Tate. "There's security bars locking us in."

"We're on our way to you, Top" said Wesson.

"Good," he said, feeling like this was just the beginning of their problems. "Rosse, see if you can find a way to override these bars."

"You got it," he said.

The thermite sputtered and flamed. Red, glowing metal ringed a large hole in the front of the safe. Tate unsheathed his tomahawk and caught the edge of the melted hole. He pulled and the door easily swung open.

. . .

In the safe room, Rosse and Ota desperately scanned the various controls and panels, looking for anything that would open the doors or retract the bars.

"This is very bad," said Ota from behind Rosse.

"It's all bad," said Rosse. "What now?"

Rosse joined Ota who stood across the room, looking down at another monitor.

The cold knot in Rosse's gut squeezed tight, and he felt like he was going to vomit.

The monitor displayed a map of the villa. Pulsing red icons appeared littered throughout the building.

Below the map, in large, bold text, the word Detonation flashed next to a timer. The numbers were running down. Whatever they were going to do, they had seven minutes left to do it.

"The entire villa is wired to blow up," said Ota.

"You guys!" yelled Rosse, as panic froze the air in his lungs. "The whole place is a bomb."

"What did you say?" asked Wesson as she, Monkhouse and Dante ran down the hall.

"The villa is going to blow up in six and a half minutes," said Rosse.

Tate froze in the middle of stuffing the contents of the safe into a bag as Rosse's voice crackled over his radio. He looked at the bars, then at Kaiden. Her face reflected the same cold dread spreading down his spine.

"We're screwed," she said.

"Top," called Wesson from the hallway, peering at them through the bars.

"Help me lift these," he said.

None of them believed it would be that easy, but they had to try something.

All of them gripped the bars and pulled, grunting and strained to lift them. The bars didn't even budge.

"Tell me you have extra thermite," said Kaiden.

Tate patted his vest, already knowing the answer. "No."

"Five minutes," barked Rosse, his voice cracking with fear. "I can't find an override. I can't find nothing. Damn it, wadda I do?"

Tate and Wesson looked at each other in silent resignation. He passed the bag containing the contents of the safe through the bars.

"Rosse," he said. "You and Ota take the tunnel..."

"What? Like hell!" said Rosse. "We ain't leaving you."

"How much time is left?" asked Tate.

"Four and a half minutes!"

"You don't have a choice," said Tate, as he set the timer on his watch. "Go. Now."

Rosse's face fell in despair and he turned to Ota.

"I got nothing," he said. "You?"

Ota shook his head and Rosse's heart sank. Sadness filled the room as Ota bent down and opened the hatch to the ladder below.

"Not unless you want to die," he said.

Ota bent down as he got his footing on the rungs of the ladder. "This is all we have left. There's no shame in choosing to live. Or die."

His head disappeared beneath the floor, leaving Rosse looking at the black hole, feeling the grief filling his chest. He glanced around the room, hoping by some miracle an override switch would suddenly appear. It didn't.

Like a man walking to the gallows, he stepped onto the ladder and closed the hatch behind him.

"Take this and get out of here," said Tate, shoving the bag into Wesson's hands. "Meet up with the others at the bottom of the hill."

There was no time to argue. The suddenness and finality of the moment didn't care what anyone felt or wanted. It was happening.

Wesson's mouth opened and closed, but her words were too feeble to match her emotions.

Monkhouse put his hand on her shoulder and gave her a gentle squeeze. "He's right."

Tate checked his watch.

THREE MINUTES

"There's no point in dying with us," said Kaiden. "Go."

Wesson's eyes shimmered with tears as she turned away and they headed down the hall.

"Well, this sucks," said Kaiden, falling into a plush chair.

Tate started laughing and she looked at him, puzzled.

"I was just thinking how much I'd love to see that on your headstone."

"Yours should be, 'No good deed goes unpunished'."

Heavy with regret, but committed to their decision, Wesson, Monkhouse and Dante broke into a run.

"This way," said Dante, pointing to their left.

They turned into a short entryway and broke through the double doors into the courtyard.

"We'll take that," he said, pointing to a shiny, new SUV parked in the corner of the courtyard.

"Monkhouse," said Wesson, "open the courtyard doors."

He split off for the big doors while Wesson and Dante ran for the SUV.

"I'll drive!" she said, running around the front of the SUV. Dante pulled open the passenger door, but Wesson had stopped in her tracks.

Bolted to the sturdy bumper of the SUV was a spool of steel cable and a winch. Her eyes flew across the courtyard where she spotted the low wall of the private garden. Just beyond she could see the glint of the bars blocking the windows.

"You drive!" she yelled.

"Top," she shouted with a jolt of renewed excitement. "We're coming for you."

Wesson looked at her watch.

TWO MINUTES.

"Damn it, Wesson," snapped Tate in her ear, "I'm giving you a direct..."

"Shut up and meet me at the window," she said, almost laughing.

Monkhouse stopped tugging on the door, wondering what was going on.

Wesson grabbed the reinforced hook at the end of the steel cable and released the catch, allowing the spool to unwind.

Tate and Kaiden went to the window and saw Wesson running to them, pulling the cable behind her.

"This one's a keeper," smiled Kaiden.

"Stand back," said Tate, backing away from the window.

Kaiden moved to a safe distance and he fired at the bottom of the window.

Fractures spiderwebbed across the glass and the windows shattered into a waterfall of glinting shards.

Her heart thudding in her chest, Wesson vaulted the garden wall. She was violently jerked back in midflight and landed hard on her back.

She knew what happened before she hit the ground. She ran out of cable.

"Bring the car closer!" she yelled.

Dante was already in the driver's seat, frantically looking for the keys, but they weren't there. The driver's door opened and Monkhouse pulled Dante out by the shirt.

"Sorry," he said.

ONE MINUTE.

Monkhouse grabbed his assault rifle and hammered the butt into the steering column. The plastic housing shattered, exposing a confusing rope of wires.

"Push it!" screamed Wesson, pulling furiously on the cable.

"Release the break," said Dante, as he ran behind the SUV. The sunbaked skin of the SUV seared Dante's hands and he yelled behind clenched teeth but kept pushing.

The car wasn't moving. Monkhouse hadn't released the brake.

"The break!" yelled Dante, his voice brittle with anger and pain.

"Hang on!" snapped Monkhouse, as he cut through the wires with his knife.

FORTY SECONDS.

Wesson's face was streaked with dust, sweat and tears. Her hands were bleeding as the rough edges of the hook dug into her.

"Never mind," said Tate, through the bars. "Get out of here."

"Shut up!" she yelled.

Tate brought his rifle to his shoulder and fired. Spouts of dirt flew up along the edge of the wall next to Wesson.

"The next one goes in your arm," he growled.

"The hell with..." she began.

Her words were cut short as the SUV roared to life. Rooster tails of dirt flew up as the tires dug in and Monkhouse charged toward Wesson.

She jumped over the garden wall, pulling the cable and passed it though the bars.

FIFTEEN SECONDS.

Tate grabbed the hook and threaded it through several bars then back to Wesson.

TEN SECONDS.

"Now," she yelled, as she clipped the hook over the cable.

Monkhouse threw the SUV into reverse and stomped on the gas.

There was no time to get out of the way and Wesson dropped to the ground and covered her head.

The cable twanged as the slack instantly ran out.

Monkhouse gripped the wheel with sweat-soaked hands, fearing the next thing he'd see was the front bumper ripping off the SUV.

With a rending crash, the bars ripped out of the wall. The jagged bars brushed above Wesson's back and clattered across the dirt.

Tate and Kaiden jumped through the window, yanking Wesson to her feet and scrambled to the SUV.

ZERO SECONDS.

The ground under their feet heaved as a pressure wave punched the ground, kicking up dirt and pebbles.

Windows shattered in a brilliant flash of heat as gouts of flame shot through the openings.

Tate, Kaiden and Wesson jumped into the SUV in a confused heap as the walls of the villa blew out. Chunks of concrete, steel and brick rocketed across the courtyard, punching into the car and shattering the windshield.

Monkhouse jammed the SUV into reverse and hammered down on the gas.

"Get down," he yelled, as he craned his neck to look out of the rear window.

The SUV's engine howled as it reversed toward the gates. Monkhouse fought the wheel as the car madly twitched left and right. The gates filled the rear window.

A massive eruption lifted the villa in the air then disappeared in a concussive shock wave and hurled the SUV backwards.

"Hang on!" said Monkhouse.

The SUV slammed into the gates with a horrendous screech of twisting metal.

The back of it caved, spraying shattered glass over the occupants. The driver's seat punched Monkhouse in the back, knocking the scream out of his lungs. Something cracked as he was thrown against the steering wheel and a sharp pain stabbed him in the chest.

The gate's hinges were ripped out of the concrete walls as the SUV blew through like a cannon ball, sending one of the gates spinning to the ground.

Rocketing past the large walls, the SUV swerved out of control as it raced towards the edge of the hill.

Gasping for air, Monkhouse put his foot on the brakes, but the SUV never slowed down.

He tried to give a warning, but all that came out was a painful wheeze.

The top of the hill dropped away and the SUV launched backwards into the air, leaving a trail of dust like a comet. Everyone gasped in the moment of terrifying weightlessness.

The car slammed down with punishing force. Monkhouse instinctively tried to wrestle the car straight as it slewed down the hill. The steering wheel suddenly spun, snapping his wrist.

Dante threw himself at the wheel, righting the SUV before it could turn sideways and flip.

Rosse and Ota came out of the tunnel and dove out of the way as a cloud of heat and smoke jetted out of the tunnel entrance.

They looked up the hill in time to see the twisted carcass of an SUV plow backwards into a thick clump of brush and trees.

Dust and steam billowed around the wreck as Rosse and Ota risked falling debris and ran to the crash.

Inside was a groaning tangle of bodies. Rosse grabbed the passenger door and it fell off in his hand. Ota ran around to the driver's side where Monkhouse looked at him through a dirt-caked and bloody face.

The two men gingerly eased their teammates out of the SUV and carefully laid them on the ground.

Rosse went into triage mode, directing Ota as his assistant. A throng of freed laborers appeared, gapping between the mangled wreck and the survivors on the ground. Rosse quickly put them to work, tending to the wounded.

After his initial exam, Rosse was deeply relieved to find nobody was seriously injured but there were plenty of torn muscles, sprains and concussions to go around. He administered pain killers to everyone harshly warning them not to mistake the lack of pain for lack of injury.

Tate was sitting up, under the shade of a tree, sipping water he'd been given by one of the laborers.

"We're not out of the woods yet," he said. "If the alarm didn't give us away, that explosion was a giant signal to every soldier in this valley. They'll be coming back here in a hurry."

"We can help," said the woman they'd spoken to before.

Tate assumed she must be the group's leader.

"I can't ask you to fight for us," he said.

"Look at you," she chuckled. "You're in no shape to fight for yourselves. We will help you escape."

"How?"

"All of you," she said to her people, "help them up."

Calloused hands lifted the team members to their feet among hisses of pain.

"Where are you taking us?" asked Tate, as the laborers helped walk them into the jungle.

"To the helicopter," said the woman with a grin.

"What about you?" he said. "You have to get your people out of here before the soldiers get here."

The woman dismissed him with a wave of her hand and kept walking.

They hadn't gone far when they came to a high screen of tangled trees and vines. She led the group through a concealed opening and the foliage opened up to a large, flat pad of concrete. Sitting in the middle of it was a helicopter, but not the top of the line, luxury air limousine he was expecting. This was pure San Roman.

There was nothing sleek about this aircraft. Stubby wings extended from the fuselage. Mounted underneath were pods loaded with air to surface rockets.

The angular cockpit looked like a viper's head. Under the nose of the cockpit was a ball turret with a minigun.

Tate's grime-streaked face cracked into a broad smile. "Merry Christmas."

"You take care of the soldiers for us," directed the woman.

"Oh," he said, sporting his own smile, "I think we can definitely do that."

"Monkhouse ain't gonna be flying anything today," said Rosse.

Tate knew the only other person on the team who could fly was Fulton.

"Dante?" he said. "Do you know how to fly?"

"I do," said Dante through his split lip.

"Would you mind helping these nice people kick some ass?" said Tate.

"It would be my absolute pleasure."

"You'll need both eyes," said Tate, pointing to the rivulet of muddy blood snaking down Dante's head and over one eye. "Rosse, can you clean up our pilot?"

Rosse got to work on Dante, who winced as his battered wound was dabbed clean.

"It ain't perfect," he said, "but it'll keep the blood out of his face. You're good ta go," he said, giving Dante a pat on the shoulder.

Dante walked around to the pilot's door and began the chopper's start up sequence.

They loaded the wounded, strapping them into the center seats. Ota and Rosse took the outside seats next to the sliding doors.

Tate climbed in the co-pilot's seat and looked over his shoulder at Kaiden with concern.

"What?" she said. A nasty gash ran across her forehead. Caked blood covered half her face, but her eyes twinkled with malice. "Under all this I still look better than you."

Tate chuckled as the laborers moved back. The helicopter's rotors picked up speed. The twin turbines rose to a pitched roar and Dante lifted the chopper into the air.

The ground fell away with stomach clenching speed, making Tate grip the overhead handle. He looked at Dante with doubt.

"She's a little touchier than I was expecting," explained Dante. "I'll get the feel of it."

Tate looked out the window to see they were already high up with an amazing vista of the surrounding territory.

"Over there," said Rosse, pointing to a long column of dust rising out of the green blanket of jungle.

Tate settled the helicopter's headset over his ears and adjusted the boom-mic closer to his mouth. "Looks like the entire force is heading back."

"Nothing like blowing off the entire top of a hill to attract attention," grinned Dante. He dipped the nose of the helicopter and flew towards the column.

"Do a fly-by first," said Tate. "Rosse and Ota, identify any heavy, mounted guns as our primary targets. One of those hits us and this'll be a very short flight."

"Copy," said Ota.

"Got ya," said Rosse.

The jungle opened up to reveal a column of jeeps and pickup

trucks pounding down a well-worn dirt road towards the remains of the villa.

"Roman wasn't in the villa," said Tate. "Do you think he's down there?"

"I don't know," said Dante. "We're not exactly on speaking terms these days. If he's not away on business, he'll be down there. He's not the armchair general sort. He'll be in the lead car giving orders."

Tate looked out his side window as they flew over the column. The lead car was a full size SUV. The windows were blackened, making it impossible to see inside. Even covered in dust, the sunlight glinted off the polished paint and Tate thought he saw chrome rims on the tires.

"Looks like the fates are smiling down on us," he said.

The radio came alive and an excited voice crackled in Spanish. Tate looked at Dante for explanation.

"They want us to follow them to the villa," said Dante. "They think we're with them."

"Hey, Top," said Rosse. "I see a couple of mounted guns in the back of the column and four in the middle."

"What about you, Ota?" asked Tate.

"The same," said Ota.

"Make one more pass," said Tate to Dante. "Then turn around and we'll come up from the back of the column. Once we hit them, they're going to bail out. Rosse and Ota, that's where you come in. Target anyone shooting back. Secondary targets are the runners."

Rosse and Ota acknowledged and readied their weapons.

The radio crackled with an angry voice, barking at them in Spanish as the helicopter flew down the length of the column.

Tate flipped up the safety covers, exposing the master switches for the helicopters rockets and gun. Panel lights changed from green to red as he armed the weapons. The heads-up-display appeared on the windscreen showing weapons status and targeting.

"Apparently he's not pleased that we aren't following orders," said Dante.

They passed the last of the vehicles and he banked the helicopter, turning around.

Dante lined up on the column and Tate grasped the weapon's controls. His finger hovered over the trigger.

"If he's mad now, "said Tate, "wait till he sees what happens next." He toggled from the mini gun to the rockets.

"Weapons free," he said, and pulled the trigger.

24

PARTING WAYS

Rockets sizzled out of the helicopter's pods, leaving trails of smoke as they raced towards the column.

The rear vehicle exploded in flame and smoke as Tate walked the rockets up the column, giving priority to the cars with mounted guns. Plumes of orange fire billowed up through the line of vehicles.

The lead cars reacted more quickly than the others and swerved off the road. Rockets slammed into empty dirt, narrowly missing them.

Behind him, Tate could hear the chatter of guns as Rosse and Ota opened up. Below them, soldiers were piling out and running into the jungle.

Tate quickly toggled to the nose mounted gun and slewed the targeting recital to the lead SUV as Dante banked sharply for another run.

The SUV was just beyond the turning radius of the nose gun and Tate ground his teeth with impatience, having to wait until the helicopter turned enough to free up the gun.

The doors of the SUV flew open just as the targeting reticle reached it. Tate squeezed the trigger.

The cockpit vibrated from the angry buzz of the mini gun. The SUV rocked and sparked from the relentless hammering of bullets.

Tate peered through the smoke and trees, looking for Roman, but it was impossible to guess.

He jumped his aim from one running figure to another, firing bursts at each one before the helicopter had moved too far away.

Toggling back to rockets, he watched for tracers flying up from the jungle canopy. In reply, he sent rockets lancing into the rich, green foliage. The ground fire stopped amid geysers of smoke and debris.

"Get us back over that lead car," growled Tate.

Dante leaned the stick over and the helicopter banked sharply into a tight turn.

Tate lined up the remaining rockets on the area surrounding the SUV and fired.

The rockets had hardly left the pods when he toggled to the nose gun.

"Put everything you've got in a hundred-foot perimeter around that SUV," he snarled.

His pent-up anger at Roman had been unleashed and now he was hungry to destroy the man and everything he symbolized. He willed his hate to guide every bullet and rocket at the man.

The nose gun buzzed, hot metal chewed up the jungle, sending chunks of wood and leaves flying in all directions, exposing the ground below.

The sound of guns and rockets died out, leaving only the whine of the turbo engines over their heads.

"I'm empty," reported Rosse.

"Same," said Ota.

The mini gun was dry, but Tate's white finger stubbornly strangled the trigger. The red faded from his vision and he force his finger to release the trigger.

Below, what was left of the column was a wreckage of steel and flesh. Flames and smoke ran the entire length as loose ammo cooked off in the heat.

Tate turned to their next steps.

"Do you think we have time to top off the tanks?" he asked.

Dante looked down at the destruction scattered below them.

"I'd venture to say more than enough," he grinned.

"Hey, Top," said Rosse. "The folks we freed, are they gonna be okay? I mean, we might'a knocked out Roman's thugs, but some of them are gonna turn into Vix."

"I think they'll be fine," said Tate. "All this noise and flame will attract any wandering Vix and give the people time to get back to their village."

"That's good," said Rosse. "Yeah, that's good."

The evening sky was washed with vibrant oranges and purples as the helicopter's skids touched down amid billowing dust.

Tate was glad to be back at base and felt the tension drain away.

Dante powered down the engines and the rotors slowed above them.

"Nice flying," said Tate.

Dante only dipped his head in acknowledgement, keeping his attention on shutting down the helicopter.

Tate unbuckled and got out. His stiff legs complained as he walked to the side door and checked on his team.

"How do they look?" he asked Rosse.

"Monkhouse got the worst of it," said Rosse. Fatigue creased his face and dark bags made his eyes look sunken in the fading light. "His wrist is busted and so are a couple of his ribs. Wesson's probably got a concussion."

"I'm fine," she said.

"She should take it easy for a few days and get checked out," continued Rosse, ignoring her.

He squinted, looking closer at Tate.

"You took some pretty good licks," he said.

"I'll see the doctor in the morning," said Tate. "I know how he likes repeat visits. What about Kaiden?"

"Nothing critical," said Rosse. "Like everyone else, banged up some and a gash across her jaw." He sighed and glanced at the weary people beside him. "Let's just play it safe and say everyone needs to see the doctor."

"Okay," said Tate. "Wesson, start getting everyone through the tunnel. I'll finish up here and meet you in the shed."

"Copy," she said, trying to sound alert and sharp, but the droop of her shoulders and her husky voice betrayed her exhaustion.

Tate met Dante at the nose of the helicopter and they shared a smile.

"Heck of a day," said Tate, blowing out a long breath.

"It's been an adventure," said Dante.

"Where do you go from here?" asked Tate.

Dante looked into the sky as he pondered his future. The light had faded and the chorus of insects filled the air. Brilliant points of light began to litter the evening sky and a gentle breeze brought the earthy smell of damp wood and soil.

"It's been a long time since I've traveled," he said. "I imagine some of my past employers would welcome me back. If they're still alive."

"Sounds like a good plan," said Tate amiably. "Do you need a ride to town, maybe something to eat?"

"Army food?" chuckled Dante. "Haven't I suffered enough? But thank you. If you wouldn't mind, I'd like to borrow your car."

He nodded towards the SUV.

"Sure, not a problem," said Tate.

"Since you're going my way," said Kaiden, "I'll tag along."

"You're not one for long goodbyes," said Tate.

"I almost got blown up with you," she smiled. "I think our relationship has moved past long goodbyes. Do you mind?" she asked Dante.

"Not at all," he nodded. "I'd enjoy the company."

"Speaking of company," said Tate. "Can you do me a favor and drop someone off for me?"

"Of course," said Dante. "Who?"

"He's already in the car," grinned Tate. "I'll introduce you."

Now it was Dante's turn to look surprised as Tate lead him to the car.

"Just drop him anywhere," he said, opening the door.

The pilot woke up with a start then began swearing as he saw Tate's face lit by the dome light.

"My friend's going to drop you off in town," he said. "I wouldn't try to get back to Roman. If he's still alive, he won't be in a good mood."

The pilot frowned as he processed the new situation, then nodded in understanding.

"And don't give my friend a hard time," said Tate, turning serious. "I'll hear about it and you don't want to see me again, do you?"

The pilot shook his head and his temper drained from his face.

"Good," said Tate, patting the pilot on the knee. "Everyone's friends now."

Dante winced as he eased himself into the driver's seat. "You wouldn't happen to know anywhere I could find a place I could unwind and freshen up."

"Go to the Blue Orchid," said Tate. "Tell Teddy Moon I sent you. He'll look after you."

"I appreciate it," said Dante, starting up the car.

Tate realized this was the last time they would cross paths. He didn't know Dante very well, and certainly wouldn't call him a friend. That word was reserved for a very select few who had earned it, but he like Dante and felt a pang of regret that he was going.

"If circumstances allow," said Dante, reading Tate's thoughts, "I'll keep in touch."

"Yeah," said Tate. "I'd like to know you landed on your feet."

"Thank you," said Dante. "Thank you for rescuing me."

Tate began to wave off the gratitude, but Dante persisted.

"I understand you didn't come to save me," he said, "but a lesser man would have left me there."

Tate could only nod in silence, feeling uncomfortable under the complement.

"Take care," said Dante.

"You, too," said Tate. "And I don't want to ever see you again," he said, frowning at the pilot.

The pilot nodded his head in complete agreement.

"Heal up," said Kaiden, climbing into the car. "I'm going to be away for a few weeks, so stay out of trouble."

"I make no promises," said Tate.

He stepped back as Dante pulled away. He took a moment to appreciate the quiet then turned towards the tunnel entrance, already fantasying about crawling into bed.

He flinched as he grabbed the first rung of the ladder and looked down at his hand. The cast protecting his severed finger had cracked sometime during all the action of the day. He'd forgotten all about it until now.

He sighed heavily, imagining the chewing out and rough treatment he was going to get from the doctor.

The rest of the team were gone, waiting for him in the shed. It was the first time he'd been alone in the tunnel and something about the long, narrow corridor made him feel isolated and alone, especially after having spent the past day surrounded by his team.

He soon reached the other end of the tunnel and climbed up, being sure not to aggravate his already painful hand.

As his head cleared the floor, he saw the rest of the team, oddly bunched together at the other end of the shed.

Something was wrong, but his mind and reflexes were too dull to react before rough hands grabbed him by the shoulders and pulled him out of the tunnel.

His hand instinctively reached for his Colt but stopped when he felt the barrel of a gun jab the back of his head.

"Stand down, Sergeant Major," said a familiar voice.

Tate lifted his hand away from his holster and turned.

His gut clenched when he saw Colonel Wade sitting at the table surrounded by his MPs.

Besides Lewis holding the gun to his head, Tate counted three more. Out of habit he sized them up, looking for an advantage. Swanson, Parks and...

Tate stopped, bewildered. The last MP was Cruz.

Is that how Wade knew they'd be coming out of the tunnel? Did Cruz sell us out?

Lewis nudged Tate's head with his gun as a warning before taking his Colt and tomahawk.

"I'll want those back," said Tate.

"We all want something," said Wade. "At the moment what I want is for you to sit down and explain what you've been doing."

Lewis pulled out the chair across the table from Wade and shoved Tate into it.

"Hey!" barked Rosse.

"Take these deserters to the stockade," said Wade.

"How can we be deserters?" slurred Monkhouse through his pain killers. "We're here, aren't we?"

"Shut up," snapped Lewis, and punched Monkhouse in the stomach.

He dropped to his knees, painfully gasping for air.

"Try that with me, ya punk," growled Rosse, balling his meaty fists into sledgehammers.

"Happy to," sneered Lewis. The other big MPs tensed for a fight.

"That's enough," said Wade.

Lewis glared at Wade who stared him down. The MP grunted and backed away from Rosse.

Wesson and Ota helped Monkhouse to his feet as he coughed up red spittle.

"He's got serious internal injuries," said Rosse. "He needs a doctor right now."

Wade stared at the group like they were insects. "Sergeant Swanson, take that man to the infirmary," he said. "*After* you've locked up the others."

"I said now," snapped Rosse, causing Lewis to threateningly step closer.

"His injuries will be looked after the sooner you begin to cooperate," said Wade. "Report back to me once you're done."

"Yes, sir," said Swanson, saluting.

Tate watched with mounting fury and despair as the MP herded his team out the door. This was a bad situation, and he knew Wade was just getting started.

"Now then," said Wade as he casually examined the pile of Tate's weapons. "Where do we start?"

"You tell me," said Tate, knowing he was so deep in a hole, playing nice at this point wouldn't make the slightest difference.

"Desertion," said Wade. "Disobeying a direct order. Insubordination."

He ran his finger on Tate's gun and eyed the gunpowder residue.

He pushed Tate's gear to the side and rested his elbows on the table.

"Murder of non-combatants. Endangering those under your command. Abuse of authority. Violating rules of engagement, and I'm just warming up."

"Sounds like you have everything you need to court martial me," said Tate. "Why am I sitting here?"

"Do you see that?" asked Wade to his MPs. "This is a man who's able to think under pressure. Typical for you trigger pullers. When I joined, I decided the courtroom would be my battlefield. The law was my weapon. I was in the JAG. A judge. I lost count of how many soldiers like you I sent to prison."

"How'd you end up in an arm pit like this?" said Tate. "Your *gun* blow up in your face?"

"That's a funny story," said Wade, failing to hide his irritation. "Bu, back to your first question. You're sitting here because I want to know what you've been doing."

Tate stared at Wade for a long moment. The colonel folded his hands and smiled back with the confidence of someone who held all the cards.

"Consider this, um, discussion off the record," he said. "Who knows, you might even say something that could help your team out."

Tate couldn't miss the blatant hint. Tell Wade everything or the team will pay the full price of the law.

"After those three soldiers were hung outside the camp," said Tate, "I discovered some of the personnel were being employed to smuggle drugs."

Tate briefly glanced at Cruz, who visibly stiffened.

"I tracked down the supplier," said Tate, turning his attention back to
Wade.

"A supplier?" asked Wade, sitting up in his chair.

"A major manufacturer," said Tate. "He was running a direct line from his operation, though this camp. My guess was he was breaking the shipments into smaller pieces and using different forms of distribution to reach into cities further north."

"Do you have the name of this person?" asked Wade.

"Nesto San Roman," said Tate.

"I'm impressed," said Wade. "For someone with seemingly limited resources, you have a considerable amount of intel."

"If you say so," said Tate, trying to avoid explaining his own close involvement with Roman.

"What were you and your team doing at Roman's base of operations?" asked Wade.

Tate was about to answer but stopped as he realized he hadn't said anything about what they'd done today.

"Don't be a narcissist," scoffed Wade. "You're not the only one able to connect the dots. After discovering the person behind the hangings was also using your precious camp as a drug pipeline you decided to go cowboy, again. What happened at Roman's villa?"

Tate paused a long moment. It occurred to him that Wade's interest was focused on today's attack more than all the rules they'd broken. Something wasn't right here. He sensed the pieces were right in front of him, but he couldn't see them.

"Well?" asked Wade.

"It's been a long day," said Tate. "I really need water." He needed a moment for his exhausted mind to think clearly.

"Yes, fine," said Wade impatiently. "Give him some water."

Cruz grabbed a bottle of water from a nearby shelf and tossed it to Tate.

What was Cruz doing here? Did he sell me out? Is that how Wade knows about the tunnel? Why's he so interested in Roman?

"You said you found Roman's operation," said Wade. "What did you do?"

"We discovered a large group of local peasants being held against their will and used for slave labor. We set them free," said Tate, glancing at Cruz. The smuggler showed no reaction.

"I see," said Wade. His brow furrowed and if Tate didn't know better, it looked like Wade was disappointed. "Did you encounter any resistance?"

"Roman's soldiers? Yes."

"And?"

"We wiped most of them out," said Tate. "The survivors took off."

"I'm impressed," said Wade, cheering up. "What about Roman's operation. The crops and so on?"

"The villa was leveled," said Tate.

"Leveled?" asked Wade. "Completely?"

"Roman wired it to self-destruct," said Tate. "Why are you so interested in this?"

"What happened to Roman?" pressed Wade. "Did you kill him?"

Tate threw a quick glance at Cruz and hoped his answer wouldn't get him shot. "I can't say for certain. Probably."

Cruz didn't react. If he felt anything, he was keeping it hidden deep inside.

"Did you destroy the cocaine fields?"

"What's going on?" asked Tate.

Wade slammed his palm on the table, knocking over the bottle of water. "Answer the damn question!"

"No," said Tate.

Wade sat back and considered him for a long time. There was a dark cleverness in Wade's eyes. Tate was restless and his instincts were buzzing that he was caught up in something bigger than he realized, but he resisted shifting around in his chair.

"Sergeant Major," chuckled Wade, "you have been of incalculable help."

Tate stared at Wade's smug face with bored indifference, happy to let the awkward silence drag out.

"You're having a moment here, I get it," said Tate, "but it's been a long day and I think we both agree I could use a shower."

Lewis scowled and raised his hand to punch Tate, but Wade stopped him with a wave of his hand.

"You think you're smart" said Wade, "But did you ever once ask yourself why an officer of my rank and skills would come to this festering hell hole by choice?" he said.

"My first guess would be judicial misconduct," said Tate.

He knew he had hit a nerve; Wade's smile fell off his face like a sheet of broken glass. For only an instant, he glanced at the Colt on the table, and Tate wondered if he was about to get shot with his own gun.

The moment passed and Wade relaxed, taking a deep breath.

"You'll be surprised to learn that Roman and I were acquainted some time ago. I was a judge at the time and two officers were brought into my courtroom. They were accused of smuggling narcotics. Roman's narcotics. I didn't know who he was until I came home to find him holding a gun to my son's head. You can put the pieces together from there. The next day I acquitted the officers. Roman rewarded my ruling with impressive generosity. After that, he sent me regular payments. Sizable payments. In return, I made sure that his employees got released and any charges dropped."

"That sounds like you had a good system going," said Tate. "But Roman has a habit of moving the goal posts."

"Ah, well," said Wade. "Change is inevitable. Roman's expectations became unrealistic, but he was... insistent. My rulings began drawing attention and I warned him that I was risking an investigation of misconduct. He didn't care."

"He doesn't strike me as the sympathetic type," said Tate.

"It was inevitable," said Wade. "I was disbarred and I thought my usefulness to Roman had come to an end. I was free. But he had other plans for me and my life only got worse from there. I did terrible things. I didn't recognize who I had become and what I was capable of."

"Everyone has their limit" said Tate. "You reached yours."

"I did," said Wade, looking thoughtful.

"But you paid the price for it."

Wade took a shuddering breath. He exhaled, his eyes fixed on his hands splayed out on the table.

"No. My son did."

25

NO WIN

"I'm sorry," said Tate. He knew the misery of losing a child. As much as he hated Wade, there was a deep, human element within him that sympathized with him.

Wade looked at Tate curiously before clearing his throat and going on.

"It was a galvanizing turn in my life. I decided that if Roman could take everything from me, I would do the same to him. I found out he was operating from somewhere south of this base and got myself transferred. It only made sense that he'd use the base as a pipeline for smuggling."

"It's easier to find something when you know what you're looking for," said Tate.

"He hung those three soldiers as a message," said Wade. "Roman wanted me to know he was watching everything I did. If he wanted to scare me, it would take more than a few bodies in a tree."

"But he didn't suspect why you were here," said Tate.

"If he had, I would have been the one swinging from a rope," chuckled Wade. "Just like you, I uncovered who his people were," he said, nodding to Cruz. "It took a little arm twisting from my MPs, but I persuaded them to work for me. The only thing left was to find out where Roman was hiding. Once I had that, he was as good as mine and he would suffer. I'd keep him alive so he could watch me take everything he had."

"You weren't going to destroy it?" asked Tate.

"What?" said Wade. "No! I'm going to take over the entire operation. You already cut off the head of the snake. Everything's there, well except for the villa, but the fields are untouched. I'll move in with a small detachment of soldiers from here and announce I'm seizing the illegal property. Over time I'll round up locals to act as a militia and transfer the soldiers back here."

As crazy as it sounded, Tate couldn't deny it was a textbook copy of how competing drug lords amassed power.

"You didn't stop the flow of drugs," said Wade, "but you were instrumental in a change of management."

"Where does this leave me and my people?" asked Tate.

He suspected he already knew the answer and it wasn't good. But he took a shot and asked. After all, the day had been filled with so many twists and turns that maybe the colonel was crazy enough to let them go.

"You and your people are a dangerous loose end," said Wade. "All of you are under arrest. Tomorrow you'll be processed and transported to the Willhelm military prison."

Tate's face paled, instantly recognizing the name. Willhelm had a reputation rivaling the most hellish prisons on earth, but not because of the inmates. The warden aggressively enforced a strict code of military discipline. The inmate who broke the rules was at the mercy of the guards, and they had none.

The darkest rumor about the prison was that convicted soldiers went in, but nobody had ever met one who had served their time and was released.

The prison was established after the Vix outbreak on a small island, three miles off the southern edge of Rhode Island. In the beginning it was like any other well-run, orderly military correctional facility. But once the current warden took over, the prison slowly transformed into a hell hole.

Any inmate wanting to escape was invited to try. The walls were guarded and ringed with razor wire. Outside the walls, the island was crawling with Vix. Tate once talked to a guy who claimed he used to make supply drops there. He saw guards routinely dumpineg scraps of food over the walls to attract the Vix.

The conditions of the prison weren't a secret. From time to time, an officer wanting to make a name for themselves would apply enough pressure that an investigative committee would be sent to the prison. Following protocol, the committee would give advance notice to the warden of their arrival.

The inspections were documented and even reported in the military news. Each time the prison passed with flying colors. It was widely agreed, Tate included, that it was all smoke and mirrors and the committee did little more than a cursory glance before enjoying a generous meal by the warden.

If the truth were exposed, it would be a huge embarrassment to the Army, not to mention the ensuing criminal hearings and finger pointing. No, it was better that what happened at Willhelm was swept under the carpet.

Wade could easily read Tate's expression and smiled, knowing he'd hit a nerve with the rugged, combat-seasoned sergeant major.

"I know the warden and several of his guards," said Wade. "I'll call ahead and let him know that you and your people should be treated fairly."

Tate could read his thinly-veiled meaning. He and his people weren't going to prison. They were walking into a death camp. None of them would live to see the outside world again.

Tate had to act, now. His mind was suddenly racing, trying to think of a way out. Kaiden immediately came to mind, but they were being shipped out in the morning. There was no way to reach her. If not, it could be weeks before she returned to camp and discovered they were gone.

He glanced at the Colt .45. It looked so close, but dangerously far. Wade's face cracked into a smile.

"Don't let desperation cloud your judgement," said Wade. "These men would kill you before you reached it."

"There's another option you haven't considered," said Tate.

"A plea deal," smiled Wade. "This should be interesting."

"We work for you," said Tate.

Wade blinked in surprise then studied Tate's eyes for any sign of deception.

"You're good," he said. "That would have never crossed my mind."

"You'll need to rebuild your security forces," said Tate. "We can train them. We can recon your competitors defenses and provide valuable intel."

Wade sat back, tapping his finger on the table as he thought about Tate's offer.

"You make a compelling argument," he said, sitting up. "Okay, I'll give this some serious thought and tell you in the morning. In the meantime, my sergeant will escort you to the stockade. We'll talk more tomorrow."

Tate didn't know if Wade was playing him or not, but maybe, just maybe he had bought his people some time.

"That's all for now," said Wade, standing up.

To Tate's utter surprise, Wade extended his hand. Just a moment ago the same man had told Tate that he and his people were going to be murdered.

The reach for Wade's hand would put him within inches of his Colt. Three MPs, including Cruz, still remained. Tate could taste how quickly he could pick up the gun and shoot all three of them before they could react, but then what? Hold a US Army colonel hostage? Force him to release his team and go on the run? Murder him and hope a military investigation would believe his story?

He saw Cruz's eyes watching him closely.

Tate's hand hesitated for a fraction of a second before he took Wade's hand and they shook.

Is he really thinking of taking the deal?

Parks pulled out a pair of flex-cuffs.

"That's not necessary," said Wade. "The sergeant major wouldn't do anything to endanger his team."

Parks nodded and pushed Tate towards the door.

Tate didn't have any ideas and it was premature to try anything now. He didn't resist and walked out to the waiting Humvee.

They crunched over the gravel, walking to the Humvee as one

thought after another piled on top of each other as Tate's mind raced through his options. Every minute brought them closer to the morning. Nothing was coming to him.

He choked back a bellow of frustration, refusing to face the reality. Wade had him in a no-win situation.

Colonel Wade took out Tate's Colt and eyed it with interest.

"This belonged to a brave but stupid man," he said to his MPs. "I think I'll keep this. A reminder of Jack Tate who killed Roman and handed me that scumbag's empire. I hope Roman suffered."

Wade frowned, seeing the smear of oil and grit the gun left on his hand.

"Clean this up," he said, handing the gun to Lewis.

"What about the prisoners?" he asked, taking the gun.

"Kill them tonight," said Wade matter of factly. "Take the bodies out through the tunnel and bury them in the jungle."

"Yes, sir."

"Good work, Cruz," said Wade. "I think you'll go far in my new organization."

Cruz only nodded.

"Have a helicopter ready for me after breakfast," said Wade. "I want to see what's left of Roman's... my villa. We'll have to round up those damn laborers."

"They might resist," grinned Lewis.

"Shoot them," said Wade.

A deafening crack and flash of light shattered the air. Wade jumped to his feet, mouth gaping as blood spouted out of Lewis' broad chest. The big MP staggered backwards, his mouth wordlessly opening and closing.

Another shot hammered Wade's eardrums and the back of Lewis' head blew out, splattering the wall behind him.

Wade wheeled around, his eyes wide in surprise and panic. He saw Cruz staring at him; a tendril of smoke curled up from the barrel of his gun.

Wade pointed at him. "Before you..."

Cruz fired twice. Wade's chest heaved as the bullets punched into him, smashing bone and flesh. Wade held out his hands, trying to ward off further shots as blood began to dribble out of his mouth.

He backed into the wall; his terrified eyes locked on Cruz as he slumped to the floor.

The spark of life faded from Wade's eyes, but still held the terror of his own death.

Cruz ignored the carnage as if they weren't there and crossed the room, opening the trapdoor to the tunnel.

He grabbed Wade by his boots and dragged him to the tunnel entrance.

26

CIGARS AND WHISKEY

T ate closed his eyes as he took a long draw on his cigar. The smoke mingled with the aftertaste of his whisky and a satis-fying blend of textures.

He paused, letting the flavor linger before finally releasing the smoke with a sigh of contentment.

Undisturbed from his revelry, he grew aware of the low murmurs of conversation and clink of glasses.

Tate looked at the wide mirror across the bar from him, reflecting the entirety of the Blue Orchid behind him.

Teddy moved among the tables, decked out in an immaculate, white double-breasted coat and press slacks. He greeted his customers, sharing witty anecdotes or warm handshakes.

Teddy Moon was practically sparkling and his mood was conta-gious as each table he left was infused with smiles and laughter.

Reaching for his whiskey, Tate heard something clink and glanced down to be reminded of the new and absurdly re-enforced cast Doctor Biscot had forced on him.

This new version looked like it could shrug off a bullet better than any body armor he'd ever worn. It was needlessly bulky but Tate wasn't going to let it get between him and his drink. He tipped back the glass, once more losing himself in the warmth of the whisky.

This was Tate's Zen and the Blue Orchid was his sanctuary.

He was at peace. Mostly.

"This place is awesome!" grinned Fulton, bumping Tate with his elbow. "Have you seen the women here?"

Tate's shoulders sagged and he caught himself before sighing loudly. After Fulton's recovery, he wanted to do something special for the young private. He had been climbing the walls, stuck inside, as he endured the slow recovery of his foot.

He still hobbled slightly, but Biscot assured Tate that it would fade in time and Fulton would be as good as he ever was.

"If you want my medical advice," Biscot had told him, "teach the nitwit how to throw a grenade."

For once, Tate completely agreed.

"There's some pretty ones here," he said. "How's your drink?"

The glass in front of Fulton was nearly empty; a condition it had experienced three times so far.

Let him have a good time. He'll pay for it in the morning though.

"It's great," said Fulton, and downed the last of his glass. "It's all great. This place is great. You're great."

"Don't get carried away," chuckled Tate.

"I'm going to come here all the time," said Fulton.

Tate's smile faltered but came right back. Fulton's enthusiasm for the Blue Orchid may be tarnished after his hangover.

"Hey, Top," said Fulton, "Monkhouse said you guys all got arrested, but then we weren't. He wouldn't say what happened and nobody'll talk to me, like it's a big secret."

"Monkhouse has a big mouth," said Tate. He tensed, remembering that night and struggled against the dread of what would happen to them when morning came.

"What happened?" asked Fulton.

"I don't know," said Tate.

Fulton frowned at him.

"Honestly," he said. "That night Wade put us in the stockade. By morning, he was gone. The morning shift was just as surprised as we were. No files were ever charged, so they let us out."

"But..." started Fulton, "that guy hated you, right?"

"Wade hated all of us," said Tate, "and he had us dead to rights." He shrugged, trying to fit together the puzzle without all the pieces.

"He packed up in the middle of the night and just left?" scoffed Fulton. "No goodbye or nothing." He mulled that over for a few bleary moments. "What a jerk."

Tate smirked, but he was just as mystified as everyone else. When they opened the cell door and said he could leave, he thought Wade was toying with him. As the reality of his newfound freedom sunk in, he was filled with questions.

Nobody had seen Wade or his men leave. Tate checked the colonel's quarters and office. It was as if the man had never been there. They were spotless and empty. His personal vehicle was gone.

None of it made sense.

When he returned to his own quarters and found his Colt and tomahawk laying on the bed, it only reignited his questions.

He searched the base for Cruz, but he was missing too.

"Jaaaaaack!" said Teddy, approaching with a broad smile. "I can't thank you enough for getting those Brotherhood bums out of my hair."

Teddy's signature cologne pleasantly mingled with Tate's aromatic cigar. The man had a knack for charisma.

"You're welcome," said Tate.

The memory of Shy Girl's dead eyes reached out from the back of his mind and a wave of melancholy rolled through him. He hadn't told Teddy the details. Only that he wouldn't have to worry about the Brotherhood anymore.

Teddy glanced at their glasses, making sure his guests were being looked after.

Tate had laid out several dollars for the drinks and Teddy brushed them aside.

"Your money's no good here," he said, tapping the bar, getting the bartender's attention. "Mac, anything these two want is on the house."

"Yes, sir," said Mac with a nod. "Let me freshen those drinks for you, gentlemen."

Tate didn't argue. He had learned a long time ago the futility of debating with Teddy Moon. He smiled graciously and thanked Teddy.

"You're one of the good ones, Jack," said Teddy.

Tate caught site of Rocko as he came in; he was hard not to notice as he nearly ducked coming through the door. Tate didn't think it was possible for anyone to be drunk enough to face off with the big guy.

Rocko looked around the room until he spotted Teddy, who saw him at the same time. The bouncer nodded and tried to stand discreetly by the door.

"Excuse me," said Teddy, patting Tate and Fulton on the shoulders.

"Did he say we could have anything we wanted?" slurred Fulton.

"I think you've had enough to drink," said Tate good naturedly.

"I was thinking of trying one of those cigars," said Fulton.

Tate chuckled, imagining Fulton turning green and spending the rest of the night kneeling over the toilet.

"That's going to be a hard pass tonight," said Tate. "But, if you still feel like one after tomorrow, you can have one on me."

"Deal," said Fulton.

Something plucked at Tate's instincts, drawing his eyes to the large mirror across the bar. He saw Teddy and Rocko talking. Focusing his attention on them, he noticed an indistinct tension in their body language. Rocko handed something to Teddy and they both looked in Tate's direction. Something was coming his way and a growing suspicion told him he wasn't going to like it.

Teddy said something to Rocko, who nodded and went back outside.

"Hey, hey, hey," said Fulton. "I think that girl just smiled at me."

"Hang on just a minute," said Tate.

He turned around, watching Teddy walk over to him.

"Do you have something for me?" he asked.

"Yes," said Teddy. "I don't run a delivery service, but the man who gave this to Rocko said you would want to see it."

He put a simple envelope on the bar next to Tate.

He looked at it for a moment, toying with the idea of not opening it.

"Are you in some kind of trouble?" asked Teddy.

"Looks like I'm about to find out," said Tate. He tore open the envelope and tipped out a folded paper. He read the short note written inside and the heady effects of the whisky evaporated, swept away by a chilling wave of dread.

Tate dropped the note on the bar where Fulton slid it closer, dropping his head down so his nose almost touched the paper.

"You missed," read Fulton. "What's that other part say?" he asked, pointing to a scrawled word on the note.

"Roman," said Tate flatly.

"I don't get it," said Fulton.

Tate took a long drink of his whisky but tasted nothing.

"It means I'm going to be looking over my shoulder for a long time."

The End

Thank you for reading No Good Deed.
Your reviews help keep this series growing.

ENJOY THIS FREE BOOK

Add this free prequel to your library!

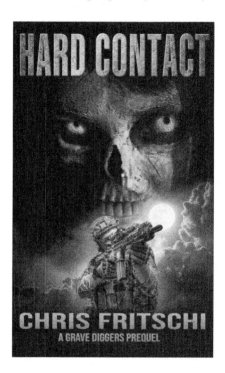

A simple mission turns into terrifying fight for survival.

This special forces team is about to walk into something more horrifying and relentless than they could ever imagine.

BOOKS IN THE SERIES

Is your Grave Diggers library complete?

ABOUT THE AUTHOR

Chris grew up on George Romero, Rambo, Star Wars and Tom Clancy, a formula for a creating a seriously good range of science fiction, action, paranormal, and adventure novels.

———

Chris is currently working on The Grave Digger series, an action packed thrill ride that will have you hooked right up to the last page. It's Tom Clancy meets Dawn of the Dead and X-Files, and it's guaranteed to keep you on the edge of your seat. Jack Tate, ex-Delta operator, has assembled a rag-tag team of rookies and motley group of wannabes is all he has to go up against a secret cabal who are plotting a takeover of the United States. Can they do it before time runs out?

———

website: chrisfritschi.com

Printed in Great Britain
by Amazon

59395561R00173